A Self-Portrait in the Year of the High Commission on Love

A Novel

David Biespiel

STEPHEN F. AUSTIN STATE UNIVERSITY PRESS

For more information:
Stephen F. Austin State University Press
P.O. Box 13007 SFA Station
Nacogdoches, Texas 75962
sfapress@sfasu.edu
www.sfasu.edu/sfapress

Managing Editor: Kimberly Verhines
Book Design: Meredith Janning
Cover Art: *Self-Portrait* by Karin Luts (1904-1993)
Distributed by Texas A&M Consortium
www.tamupress.com

ISBN: 978-1-62288-244-1

Also by David Biespiel

POEMS
Republic Café
Charming Gardeners
The Book of Men and Women
Wild Civility
Pilgrims & Beggars
Shattering Air

MEMOIR
A Place of Exodus: Home, Memory, and Texas
The Education of a Young Poet

ESSAYS
A Long High Whistle: Selected Columns on Poetry
Every Writer Has a Thousand Faces

EDITIONS
Poems of the American South
Long Journey: Contemporary Northwest Poets

RECORDINGS
Citizen Dave: Selected Poems, 1996-2010

For J.E.B.
(1907-2004)

Whoever you are, come forth!
~ Walt Whitman

Contents

SALAZAR

LATE AT NIGHT, FORTY YEARS AGO, when I was eighteen, I was smoking a spliff in Manolo Salazar's truck on the Gulf Freeway on our way to Galveston when a turkey vulture appeared suddenly from out of the darkness.

At first I thought it had grazed the hood of a pickup ahead, then fell to the pavement with a sharp pain. But the bird managed to fly up again, swerved and collided with another car, shattering the passenger side window in a burst of broken glass.

Nearby cars slowed, but didn't stop.

The turkey vulture stumbled along the asphalt, and I wondered if the red head was cut, or if the cuts were bleeding, when it turned and briefly gazed at our pickup as we passed by.

Neither the bird, nor the long winds coming gently, stirred the traffic. The hot cars crossed and recrossed the lanes. The gray clouds of late September drifted under the last of the sky in low puffs. The sun flared down on the roads that threaded past strip malls into the neighborhood of brick one-stories out toward Hobby Airport. Planes coming and going overhead. Lane upon lane of exhaust stink. Green headstones of street signs. Each solar plexus of each person in the cars like a simple cross.

Salazar twitched eagerly, delicately, at the steering wheel. He had a thin, unremarkable mustache. His dark eyebrows were also thin, his eyes brown and close together. We were almost the identical age, born seven days apart, in February of 1964. We got made under the same sky, one of us would say when people learned about it. The very same, said the other.

With the windows down, I looked at the dark clouds to see how little had changed overhead since we drove out of Gulfgate. The lanes grew blacker to hide themselves, and they lengthened under the evening spray of headlights. The surface of the asphalt softened, and as the sky became night, so the windows of apartment complexes brightened in reds and flickering blues. Instead of watching the freeway, I closed my eyes and guided my thoughts down the ramp toward Alameda Mall into the passing neighborhood of lanky strip malls, past pawn shops and drive-thru beer shops, Spec's Liquor, Popeye's, past Whataburger, a Western Inn, and a Jack in the Box, up through a series of intersections with furniture outlets and the Fiesta, where we liked to go late at night to score beer.

We had been drinking and smoking weed since early morning.

I stared at the dirty floor of the red pickup and inhaled the musk of cigarettes in the dashboard ashtray, while humming along with George Jones on the tape deck. A half-empty, Big Red long neck was between Salazar's legs, resting up against the seam of his jeans. The inside of the pickup was plain: bare floorboards, saddle blankets for the bench seat, a worn dash, a stack of paperbacks upended between us. Squeezed above the crooked visors were scraps of receipts, postcards, notebook paper with hand-scrawled directions, shopping lists, a plastic lighter, pencils, rolling papers.

Beyond the dashboard and the clean windshield, I could see the cloud-cut skies, with the humidity dusted down on top of us. The sounds of tires on the asphalt bumped over the ground. The cars and trucks lifted the dust into the air. A pickup stalled on one of the feeder roads sank in the dust, high as the hood. The big clouds moved up over our heads. Heavy clouds, ready to rain.

"Look at those cars," Salazar said.

"Like tombs."

"That's something."

"You could power all our bodies forever with this traffic," I said.

He slapped the steering wheel. "You're wasted, man."

"Not much of me left, mi hijo."

We both laughed.

"Don't count on it, Duke."

"Come again? What's that?"

"You're the kind of guy that hangs on," he said.

I inhaled the purity and simplicity of our talk, all our concentration on a few words, and I looked around and thought: this is how I want to live.

In Salazar I saw, and he saw in me, something both of us wanted but couldn't get, not as the sons we were. Him, the oldest son of a broadcast evangelist. Me, the only son of the Grand Rabbi of Houston. We told ourselves: we wanted to be rid of our lives, and we believed that. We were conscious of wanting freedom. In all our classes, in Honor Society, in student government—for him, it was effortless, while I had to work hard at it—we assured ourselves: this is preparation for something else. We'd cooked up this escape on Chimney Rock Road, back on the first day of school, while driving to the Stop-N-Go in Braeswood Square to buy a Hostess cherry pie and a Dr. Pepper from the soda fountain. We sloped into the Stop-N-Go and sloped out. Sitting shotgun, I fished out a silver flask of Jim Beam from my knapsack and poured a shot into each of our cups. I wasn't afraid to get caught, but kept an eye out the half-open window. Salazar and I were rushing to get back to class with Mildred Donne, a favorite English teacher we'd had both junior and senior years, who taught the International Baccalaureate courses that seemed to cover the entirety of English literature: Beowulf to Richard Wright, in that era. The workload was grueling. Students had to read one or two books a week—*As I Lay Dying, Dubliners, The Great Gatsby, Heart of Darkness, 1984, Huckleberry Finn, Catcher in the Rye, Night, Native*

Son, Main Street, Brave New World, Catch-22, The Diary of a Young Girl, The House of the Seven Gables, The Raisin in the Sun, Pride and Prejudice, One Flew Over the Cuckoo's Nest—lots of Romantics, lots of Walt Whitman, Emily Dickinson, epic poems, *The Aeneid*, and *The Divine Comedy*.

The day we decided to light out for the territory, as we called it, after Huck Finn, was a hot afternoon when we came walking slowly back up the hallways to class. Easily, as I lagged behind, I could feel the bourbon warming my cheeks. I walked slower, all the students roving from one class to the next, and let myself get carried along the bustle of hundreds. Faces gradually clarified in front of me. Each student carried the same hairstyle, smile, angles of their faces.

Our plan was to slip past the barriers at Porretto Beach, then drive toward Freeport, then farther, to Corpus Christi, on down the coast. Then, we didn't know where. Somewhere, out there.

In the pickup, I realized that I couldn't keep up my old existence much longer, and yet, out on the highway, I was afraid, aware that something had to give, and I sensed that a turning point, long imagined but until now indistinct, was imminent. By tomorrow, it'd be clearer.

Over the highway, the heat and dust advanced, restless, luminous, and, underneath it, the facts of the previous days were long gone. The traffic cruised toward the causeway. Three road signs appeared.

BRIDGE MAY ICE IN COLD WEATHER
VILLAGE OF TIKI ISLAND
CLINICS, HOSPITALS

"Better grab a jacket," Salazar said. "It could be chilly."

"How many did you bring?"

"Three," he said. "Plus, Mamá's serape."

"Three?" I twisted to reach behind the bench seat where we'd stored our duffle bags, and sat up to see a pair of black-masked seagulls slip in and out of the wind over the bridge.

"I told Mamá we might not be back for a night or two, you know, till Monday. I told her, not to worry, that we'd drive in from the beach to school, and she made me bring jackets. In case a couple got wet. She doesn't know we're not coming back."

"You gave her the 'there's no first period on Mondays anyway' treatment?"

"You know it."

Salazar crossed his hand to the knobs on the radio and flipped the cassette. George Jones growled: *Nothing ever hurt me half as bad as losing you.* I waved a small, black-bound notebook at the windshield then started to shove it into my pocket.

"All I brought was my license to kill," I said.

"What you got in there?"

I read from a random page: *"Door knobs. Flowerpots. Sour mash and chocolate milk and cold, cold water from a well that's icy all the time, all year, all the time, colder than any other water."*

"That ain't Texas, man," he said. "That's some made up shit."

We bobbed our heads to the music.

Needless to say there wasn't much of Salazar's life I didn't already know. He had been raised in Hispanic Gulfgate by doting, divorced parents who were neither rich nor poor. He had a brother two years younger that the entire family babied. At school he was stellar. National Honor Society. Student Council. Latino Medal of Honor. He said he wanted to join the Army and spoke about being a drill sergeant at Fort Bliss. Liked to say, I'm going to El Paso. I'm going to be the most subversive air defense jefe they ever seen. I'm going to scare the blood right out of them killers. They ain't going to want to pull the trigger once I'm done with them. Going to fill them with my socialist convictions.

He lived in an untidy bedroom in his mother's ranch house, where his mother called him, mi hijo. Mi hijo! Come here now. Mi hijo! Help me with these dishes. The red desk in his bedroom, which is where he wrote imitations of Pablo Neruda and stories modeled after Gabriel Garcia Márquez, he called Monk's Island. Monk's Island was entirely covered with piles and piles of notebooks and paperbacks, assorted blue pens and yellow pencils, tattered erasers, paper clips, empty glass bottles of Coca Cola, sheets of paper with Salazar's large scrawl on them, full of arrows and crossings out and doodles of boats and stickmen and crucifixes, Spanish books stacked opened on top of each other, mirrored sunglasses and another pair of wire-rimmed John Lennon-type, a pile of albums askew among their jackets and sleeves, a one-hit pipe made of wood, and, appearing lost amid all that, a scattering of marijuana seeds and stems. Get in here, Duke, get in here, he'd say, when I'd arrive after the evening prayer service at my father's synagogue, to get high and talk books or do homework, nine, ten, eleven bong hits late into the night, then we'd watch a rerun of *Star Trek* on the small black-and-white TV shoved to the corner of Monk's Island. Other times, smoothing the thin mustache above his lip, he'd say, Get in here, Duke, get in here, take a look at what I just wrote, and he'd read the first sentence of a new story: *In those days, Haruki and Patrick, who had become close friends after Pedro's accident, hated all believers.*

I had popped open the mini cooler under the dashboard. The traffic was thick.

"You thirsty?" he asked

"Why not?"

"I mean after what you just did."

"I don't want to talk about that," I said, and bent forward to crack open Lone Star beers for each of us. Each silver can crinkled inside brown paper sacks. We both drank and watched the traffic slow. Drivers slumped in their seats like they could smell the aroma of their own mortality, their eyes full of interrupted dreams, awaiting the time, whenever it came, that they'd be laid under the ground by shovelfuls of dirt, headstones decorated with pebbles or faded flowers or draped with a humidity-softened Texas flag. Some of the drivers seemed on their way, their heads drooping like gladiolus. I nodded at a bald white man with his elbow out the window. "I wonder what that one is?"

"Baptist. Can tell by his skin," said Salazar.

"Not Jewish."

"Not Catholic."

"Could be Catholic," I said. "Looks beatific."

"Beatific, shit. Look at him. He drinks all the time. Vomits first thing in the morning. If he was Catholic, the tequila would put him to sleep. When he's had enough, just passes out. Puts his head down and curls up like a lousy cat."

"Yeah, right," I said. "All fetal. Dribs of drool."

"Dribs of drool," he cackled. "Ladies and gentlemen, give it up for Dribs of Drool! After a little nap he'd wake up and go out and get another bottle."

"Jim Beam?"

"What else?"

"Seems to be upright now, driving okay."

"Now? He's not drinking. Hasn't had a drink for two days. Feeling all right. Little bit all right."

"Ran out of money."

"Wants to be sober for church tonight."

We began to give other drivers and passengers nicknames. The Bishop. The Baptist. Muscle Man. Hotshot. The Bum. We nicknamed the woman driving a blue Pinto, Lady with a Dog, after the story by Anton Chekhov we'd read in Mildred Donne's class the year before. Lady with a Dog was sipping an Icee from a red and white straw, her brown bulldog watching everybody through the back window, panting, fur trimmed, standing out on his two paws, teeth out.

Muscle Man, with gray hair combed and trimmed, steering a black 280ZX, eyed us eyeing the Lady with the Dog. His goatee was clipped, and he wore a white tee shirt.

Salazar honked the horn. "Yo, Muscle Man," he called, "got a crease in your tee shirt. C'mon, man."

"Looking good there, Muscle Man," I called out.

He nodded upward to us.

"How much longer you think the Bishop's got to live?

"You think he's going to die in six months?" I said.

"We all going to die," Salazar said. "We all going out of this world."

"I'm living until a hundred."

"You what?"

"My great-grandfather, the Kansas City rabbi, that one," I said, "he was ninety-seven when he died. Got to beat that."

Salazar parodied a movie trailer voice. "For a thousand generations, the Wains have been America's rabbis. Now, in the city of Houston, 18-year-old Duke is the heir to their Jewish empire."

"Tragedy or comedy?"

"I'd like to make it to 33."

"Jesus year."

"My little brother says I'll never make it. I said, 'What's the matter with you? You want a big brother or don't you want a big brother?' He says, he's never going to work. Shit. He's going to be shoveling dirt."

"He's into magic, man," I said. "He's going to be a magician."

"White folks are magicians," he replied. "Chicanos, we dig our own graves."

"He's not going to like that, though I guess Ronald Reagan will insist."

"Motherfucker will definitely insist," he said.

Salazar rolled down the window and spit a wad of chewing gum into the wind. He appeared to be feeling easy, and he liked driving. He was drinking lightly. Kept saying his head and throat were sore. He needed to stay normal, just have another beer or two, was all, blow a bowl so his brain would settle. My throat, he kept saying, it's sore-red.

That year I was desperate for his recognition, although I'm not sure why, confident as I was at that age, refusing to be a supplicant to anyone, to petition for anyone's favor, much less love. My own family came from Meyerland, in a big house—compared to Salazar's—on the north side of Braes Bayou. The road to our house led out past Godwin Park, trimmed baseball fields, and Kolter Elementary School, a section of the city where the whole of the sky lifted from the flat roofs and widened toward the horizon. The roads were laced with willows, live oaks, and one-story houses. Only recently had houses been divided by fences, with hedges for windbreaks, brought on by the clouds passing over. Most of our neighbors were retailers, bankers, doctors, dentists, lawyers, executives, accountants. Many were religious Jews, though on other streets in Meyerland they were not. Those people went to synagogue only for High Holidays, and occasionally the bar mitzvah of a neighbor or relative's son, although the women of the house lit candles on Friday night, for the same reasons one does the dishes, my father liked to say. They were educated, comfortable, rooting for their college football team on Saturdays in the fall, with unshakable views about politics, Arabs, the state of Israel—but couldn't care much about Zionism. Israeli culture, yes. The working class, not so much.

We were not wealthy. My father's job at the synagogue and fees for speaking engagements provided a regular salary. My mother was a professional volunteer. I earned pocket money by ushering the early morning and evening minyan and Saturday services, and I sometimes taught kindergarten Hebrew School weekday afternoons. Ours was a house where conflict kept us close. If you weren't in conflict with someone, you weren't doing family right. Conversation among my father, mother, sister Rivka, six years older, was amiable, but punctuated with jibes. Don't press your luck. Don't get me started. What, are you stupid? You're going to wish you didn't say that. You need to be walloped?

Hardly anyone knew who the others were, truly were. Attempts to reveal who you might be, who you could be, who you wished to be, or longed to be, were cut off. *You are who you are*, my father said in one of his signature expressions, spittle on his lips, and that was that.

What was surprising about us, to Salazar, that is, he once told me, was the tenacity that kept us at each other, refusing all entreaties to get along, declining warmth, choosing contention, rivalry, as if kindness were irrelevant. There might be days when two of us stopped speaking to each other. The only photograph we had of us all together was from ten years back. It rested inside a silver frame on a side table in the living room. We were dressed for a wedding—two puffy parents, two lonely children, with our dark eyes, expressive mouths, and unblemished futures ahead of us. Ruthless Jews, never so much as once resting your feet, is what I told Salazar, when I showed the photograph to him one afternoon, the house empty, and he'd come over after classes let out.

I said, "That's Rabbi *Gadol*, Hebrew for Rabbi the Great. My mother, I call Batya the Rock. Rivka, my sister, she lives in Dallas now, finished up college, I call her, the Wounded One."

My parents valued everything American and Jewish. Israelis of course, were without flaws: brawny, courageous, practical, rugged. My parents were dyed-in-the-wool capitalists. The only socialism they praised was Israeli socialism because, as everyone knows, Israelis knew more than American Jews and understood more than American Jews and did harder labor than American Jews and wrote better poetry than American Jews and prayed more deeply than American Jews. If it was Israeli, it was good, from the Knesset to the machine gun. End of story. Western Europe was still on trial. As for Germany, my parents gave no ground, Berlin Wall or no Berlin Wall. After all, it was a country where people murdered Jews. No amount of admiration for fancy cars, cheeses, coffee makers, pilsners, or marzipan would change that. Praise for German belfries and flagstones and forests was forbidden. It was the land beyond what the light touches where you dare not go.

The place my parents saw as blessed was far from the

stench of Dachau. It was to be found under the shade of the leafy streets of Meyerland and in the halls of Meyerland's large synagogues, and in Meyerland's integrated public schools, where the children of well-mannered middle class Jews mixed with the children of well-mannered middle-class Christians, all of whom practiced piano, played Little League or girls softball, and later, at university, pledged the same cliquey fraternities and sororities as their parents had. Most of Houston's tight-knit population of Jews lived in Meyerland. They exercised along the bayou from Hillcroft to the Loop, they crowded Weingartens grocery store and Braeswood Square's little shops, all owned by Jews, where they bought gifts and music and jewelry, and they shopped at Meyerland Plaza's sporting goods and department stores, bakeries, beauty parlors, and movie theaters. Years later, when I read Issac Bashevis Singer, I was certain his characters lived next door to us in Meyerland or else across the street or on the next block. In the house behind our fence was Gimpel who made challah Friday afternoons and delivered two, wrapped in white cloths, for my mother. Yentl lived four houses down and frightened kids on Halloween with cross-dressing getups. The orphan Hindele taught nursery school. There was Getsel, too, living on each street, noisy and pushy. All this gave me a feeling of provinciality. Real life was happening far away. Affairs, broken hearts, sitting in all-night bodegas—all this, I was certain, took place far from the intersection of Braeswood and Chimney Rock, in Provence, Seville, Barcelona, San Francisco, Paris, Venice, cities where people lived recklessly, suffered, and fell in love, fought over ideals and poetry, brooded alone in rain-swept alleys or tattered coffeehouses. Nothing like that happened in drowsy Meyerland.

Salazar pulled the frame of the photograph of the five of us from the side table and studied it. Looking back was my muscular father with his square face, thick salt-and-pepper hair cut short, wearing wide black-framed glasses in front of his green eyes, his arm around the shoulders of my mother, her rouged face with lively dark eyes, and a lock of white hair straying over one cheek. Both of them holding discreet smiles. Same as Rivka with her soft skin and black bangs and good health. Last was me, stiffly staring into the lens.

He said, "These people are pathetically oblivious to the life of art. You're the family ascetic."

"In this neighborhood, it's Chagall meets Nieman Marcus," I replied. "The early months of my parents' marriage," I told him, "they were nearly broken up after four months because Rabbi Gadol, immersing himself in his studies, ignored my mother. Day and night he ignored me—this is her telling it—so I packed my bags and left for Bubbe's without saying goodbye. He says, I caught up to your mother at the Greyhound Bus Station, the one near Fannin Street, and I brought her home. She says: Only after much pleading and promises to rehabilitate. Yes, yes, he acknowledges, tapping his heart—you've seen him do that, you know that move—and, he says, I succeeded, did I not? You came home. Did you not? She says: That's how I gave your father a place in the world—then, always, whenever they tell this story together, and it gets more elaborate depending on who the audience is, sometimes with Borsch Belt absurdities thrown in, she ceremonially extends the back of her hand to him, like she's the Queen of Judea, to let him kiss her skin."

"Genesis 51," Salazar laughed. "*She made the husband she had dreamed of, not a man of solitary contemplation.*"

"Exactly," I said, "a husband who is urgent, indispensable, ample. *Gadol.* So, my father says, I was wearing tasseled loafers when I drove to the Greyhound Bus Station to retrieve your mother. I've kept them all these years. Going to be buried in them."

"Nine months later your sister was born."

"The crazy thing is, my mother was born on a street in North Dallas where the Orthodox Jews live. Growing up, she was practically lost in the world. She was born and raised on that Orthodox street. A dismal street. Her father died when she was little. We used to visit when my grandmother was alive. The pavement, paved with sharp gravel, was so cracked you'd have thought it was cobbled from the old country, in another time. Every morning and every evening, someone rang a triangle bell for services. Like we were on a chuckwagon calling in the cow hands for chow. Orthodox Jews riding their chuckwagon to the Promised Land. Once you went in, you stayed in. You weren't allowed to play, except in the backyard. And, only because Batya the Rock insisted. You can't keep children cooped in here day after day, she'd scold my Bubbe. It was a dreary, yellow, pale house where the air had died. As for news from the world? You didn't get anything. No TV. No radio. My mother said she used to dream of being a crown princess. Look at her now."

Salazar looked at the photograph in the silver frame and performed an elaborate bow. "Crown Princess of Meyerland."

WE BUMPED ALONG THE INTERSTATE, and I felt dour, unsettled.

Houston in autumn was like falling into a half sleep, a dim dream wanting to turn over and see what was in the next season. But it didn't have much strength. Stillness, ease, long muzzle of humid nights. An ether drifting along the Gulf of Mexico's currents. Somewhere behind the polluted clouds and the open window full of dark wind, the stars came on with total precision. That night, like most nights, I was wearing cowboy boots with duct tape over the toes, which I had wrapped there because the leather had come up from the sole. They were narrow brown boots and scraped my bare ankles. I was dressed in blue jeans and a denim shirt.

For a few miles, I had the impression I was far from home, on the open road, and wanted life to start. Soon, I'd be able to walk in any direction, look out over the sand and foamy tide, perhaps the sight of a sailboat under the moon. No longer carried by the past, is what I felt, but gliding over a gentle, timeless expanse, and the air I would breath had the sweetness of beauty.

Salazar knew who he was. The compact kid with a hairline mustache who I adored for his manner of not being handcuffed to expectations. He owed me no explanation, and expected none back. He could pose all the questions he liked, interrogate me without end. I no longer felt a need to hide anything from him. The ease with which we arrived from different wards of the city into friendship made me pleasantly euphoric. This night wasn't happening by chance. We were at the start, both of us, of a new life.

It was here that a green pickup came up fast alongside us, with a white girl alone in the bed and her long brown hair scattering around her face. Her two friends sat side by side in the cab, both of them white, the driver with a trucker's baseball cap—his arm looped around his girlfriend's neck under her short black hair—her cheek on his shoulder. I watched the girl in the truck bed blink at the wind, her hair whipping every which way. She was seated with her back against the cab, and shouting something through the open window of the rear windshield. Tube top, blue letterman's jacket, stitched with four yellow Ms, sitting demurely. Her eyes mostly fixed on where the truck had been, somewhere else.

Salazar was saying, "We got to get some writing done this weekend, Duke. We got to flip the letters into the slot. Pablo is calling us to the sea of renewal. We can't waste our time while we're wasted. We got to get us some words, man. Got to go deep underneath the breakers. The words, man, the words. Got to fill the page," he said, and swigged his beer.

What was so admirable to me about Salazar was his own tenacity, writing stories about his family. He liked to say, he was writing stories as if written first in Spanish inside the Centro Historico, where his ancestors came from in Mexico City, and then translating all that into English. These were stories that Mildred Donne raved about before reading passages out loud to class. Stories that typically did more than hint at being Chicano, about anxiety and orderliness, and feeling terrified. Stories where heroes kept leaving and then returning home, but always inside the dailiness of a fanciful sketch. Stories he refused to let the

Maple Street Journal, our high school's literary magazine, publish. Stories he declined to give to the *Bayou Review*, the undergraduate literary journal at the University of Houston, where his older friends from Gulfgate took classes. Ridiculous, he says, when his UH friends solicited one about an old priest riding a donkey through River Oaks who impales himself with a lawn rake so as not to return to the Third Ward. Absurd, he says, to want to publish that one. The most recent story he'd shown me was about two bullfighters, Abel and Marco, marooned on a cove along the Straits of San Juan de Fuca who practice stabbing their barbed spears against rows of hemlocks, and I had laughed out loud when I read the description of both of them having kissable faces.

"They're kissable now," I said, "but later in life, they're going to be jowly and bald."

"You should write your version," he said. "Jews coming out of the foam-capped waves and they meet my bullfighters."

"That's the story of the Jews in America already," I said.

"Same with Chicanos, Duke. Same with Chicanos," he said.

He had recently started to write his Telephone Road Trilogy, he called it, about being imprisoned with aunts and uncles and cousins, burdened with their anger of exclusion and their fetish—his word, *fetish*—for their status as Chicanos, as Houstonians, as Texicans, and always yearning for the homeland, *Mehico*. "Each character is thwarted by Texas. I'm going to hoist us all up," he said.

"That would make you Borges and Whitman all wrapped into one," I said.

"Márquez, Duke. Gaby Márquez, Mexican, man I'm talking kinship, man. What's an Argentinian know about Gulfgate?"

"Oh, you're trying to make legends, that's what you're trying to do."

"Shit, no. Legends are all about irony," he laughed. "Irony is for the weak."

"Cryptic lives."

"Moody. Life's terrors in Tejas."

"Nobodies?" I said.

"Sí. Very, very sí."

When I thought about what I might try to write, I just came up with glum imaginings about Jews I knew in Meyerland, Jews shackled to restraint, with a world that first denied, then gave them, freedom. Middle class wannabes for whom only when success was theirs for the asking, only when they reveal to themselves and others how obviously unsuited they are for that success, to have and to hold anything allowed other people, only then would they take their revenge on the outside world. But whenever I tried that, I couldn't get my characters to act. Not at all. No Meyerland Jew had anything unusual ever happen to them. No Meyerland Jew would destroy other people, any more than they would destroy themselves. They were loyal to one thing: self-love. Sometimes, like a soft whisper, they felt doubt. Wee bit of doubt. That was all. I was certain nothing Meyerland Jews did could possibly be of interest to anyone beyond that southwest corner of Houston, not even to the most courteous of readers.

One night, over the telephone, after Salazar had read a passage out loud to me that he'd newly written, he said, with a tone of melodrama, "I wish I knew as much about Gulfgate Chicanos as you know about Meyerland Jews. But, I know nothing. All I can do is make-believe. All I can do is fantasy."

"Would that I could do half of what you think I can," I said.

"You got to let the ugly in, man. Not going to happen in poetry. Poetry's all *Let us go then, you and I.* Big old blah-blah-blah feelings. That's all. Stories, man, novels, things happen to people, gets ugly. Novels go like this. Why? Why? Why? Why? Why? People get burned, people eat food, people fight over money, people die. Its not just *Let us go then, you and I.* You have to learn to tell these people of yours, *No.*"

"It's not them. They can't help themselves. Every one of them is afraid of being stupid and so thinks everyone else is stupid."

"No one understands themselves, Duke. No one. You got to work for it."

Softly, so Batya the Rock and Rabbi Gadol, sitting plump in their arm chairs in the living room while watching Dan Rather, couldn't hear, I said, "These people. Always wondering what's in it for them, what's good for them, good for the Jews. What do you do with characters like this, mi hijo? What's good for the Chicanos? What's bad for the Chicanos?"

"Mine are always on the brink of tears. You don't got that."

He was right. I didn't have that. Whatever I might have written about neighbors and family was merely what mattered to me as documentation, as if the life I lived weren't my own, but a simple composition of deeds and feelings. With nothing to confess, with nothing to clear up, with nothing to illuminate, with nothing to translate but impressions, all I had were facts, those mysterious things, and they remained.

Once, at the kitchen table, on a Sunday afternoon when my parents were attending a musical performance at the Jewish Community Center on South Braeswood, Salazar and I sat on stools at the long counter where white lilies and purple roses were arrayed in two vases beneath the windows, and we worked on a writing prompt together. The kitchen was a sunny, lively room, almost cheery. Beside the roses blooming were cuttings of herbs taken from clay pots in the backyard, and colorful, odd-shaped sizes of bowls with fruit and walnuts. The cabinets were shut tight. Nothing of the copper pots and pans, pantry of staples, or canisters of flour and sugar were left on the counters. Nothing of the special dishes and cutlery for holidays and another set for Passover, cherished crystal, or prized collection of antique Hanukkah menorahs could be seen. The only reassurance of untidiness was the morning's *Houston Chronicle* folded in a misshapen heap on the kitchen table. On the walls were small, framed woodcarvings of Hebrew letters. It was the domain of a woman who refused to reveal her wrinkles.

"Let's tell our stories," Salazar said to start the write-off. He pulled from a drawer the egg timer. "We each have six minutes to write. I learned this from the UH guys. You got to start each one like this: 'Behind the X house…' That's what you write, 'Behind the X house…' X is for somebody's house in your neighborhood. Each house is different. After that phrase you tell a secret. How about three times in a row without reading out loud. No, five. Let's do five" he said, and I nodded, while smoothing out the lined pages in my notebook. He twisted the nob on the timer.

"How about this?" said Salazar. "Winner decides whether we go or not."

"You mean down the coast?"

"For good."

"Self-judging?"

"You know it," he said. "Hard-nosed, bloodless self-judging."

"Best three out of five," I said.

Under the ticking, we began. After a half hour, we each had written our pieces, like flashes of light, taking turns reading them to each other.

Salazar read first:

Behind the Garcia house with the tapering willow, Alejandro Garcia once called his wife Socorro into the living room. He had a tequila on ice in one hand. They're sitting on matching red armchairs when he tells her about the affair with her best friend. She smiles back sadly. Do what you have to do, she wants to say, but doesn't. She will fight him all the way through court and tells him to sleep in the living room where, at night, a glow from the streetlight bears down.

I read mine:

Behind the Katzman's house with the baby swing hanging from an oak tree, a black cleaning woman next to the backyard swimming pool was once clearing out the flowerbeds and waiting for the afternoon rain to come down. She finds a page torn from a Playboy *in the hedges that's been tucked in there, no doubt, by one of the teenage boys, whether it's Daniel or Jared she can't tell. She opens the damp, folded paper and looks at the white, naked, pink-nippled woman who appears to be hesitating with her eyes, but who also feels suddenly hungry, gnawing, intrigued with the tightness in the folds of her skin.*

"Aw, Duke, you slayed me. *Playboy* in the hedges."

"Right?"

"That's what it all comes down to. 1-0. Your lead," Salazar said and read his next piece:

Behind the Martinez's brick house with a tan gate, two teenage sisters, Isadora and Lucretia, one night laid out their sleeping bags in the hallway to camp out, and if you had to come in through the front door you'd have to step around them—and so they didn't dare go to sleep but lay there, each propped on a pillow, each pretending to read, both imagining what would happen if the boy one of them likes saw them there, nearly asleep, arms bare, legs spread wide in their sleeping bags, letting themselves get carried away in the downy world.

'Downy world! That's good," I said, and then read mine:

Behind the Roth's house with a single star on the side wall, there's a cousin from Argentina once lived in the spare room, working on a dissertation on Eastern European Jews with the philosophy of Maimonides that he never finishes. He wears a gold chain around his neck where the collar is open, sprouts of black hair from his chest tangle with the loops of the chain, his round belly rising and falling. He won't take a job outside his uncle's downtown pawn shop. On the side he sells pot to the jocks who go to Westbury. He meets them near the ballfields at Godwin Park and hands small plastic baggies of weed through the cracked window of his Trans Am.

"Trans Am? Duke, cliche. Shit, man."

"I know. I'm out. 1-1. Where'd you find those two girls?"

"Not saying. Let's go. You first."
I read mine:

Behind the Weissman's house where the grass is cut sharp, a grandfather came out of his room where he lived with the family now and was thumbing through a picture album, saying in a Yiddish accent to his only son who works in insurance—he's taken over the family's firm—this is where I went to school before the war. It was a cheder. I didn't get to attend long, he says. A year, I think. I went to school here. He's fingering the slender columns in front of the brick building in the photograph. We had to abandon the school. We buried our books in the ground. We threw straw over the mud to hide them from the Germans. He clears his throat and coughs. Yellow phlegm stains his white handkerchief.

Salazar read his:

Behind the Romero's house with the gravel driveway a daughter just about to finish ninth grade once sat between her parents at dinner. The daughter says: My future is a blue cloud. The parents don't understand. She says, I can't convince myself to go up there into the sky, it's so uncertain. The parents squint at her in unison. They are sitting in the drab kitchen. We don't believe in meddling, Papi says. Do what you want, Mamá says, as long as you don't bring shame to this family. I want to be an actress, the girl says. What do you know of acting? Papi says. She watches a lot of TV, Mamá says.

"No one says, 'My future is a blue cloud,'" I said. "What is that?"
"Surrealism, man. Extra credit."
"Points for weirdness. You win. You can have it. 2-1. I'm first."
I read:

Behind the Bloom's house with dark flat windows, there was a grandmother who wore a diaper like a baby. Her daughter meets her in the bathroom to untie the diaper and says cheerfully, Good, Mommy, you are still dry, shall we go to the toilet? The grandmother doesn't nod, nearly helpless, but stares at the brown eyes of her daughter, who has her hair tied up and smudges of makeup around her eyes like wet petals on new flowers. She puts down the seat to the toilet and places the mother on it who slumps against her daughter's leg. The mother's thighs are bleach white and purple. There she sits, half-naked, only a wash cloth covering her, like a statue of Sarah, wife of Abraham, waiting for her husband to return to her after banishing Hagar and Ishmael in the desert. The daughter waiting, leaning on one foot, with a piece of toilet paper in her hand.

He read his:

Behind the Gomez's house with the wide red door, a son is sobbing in his bedroom. His little brother took his toy car. He knows he must keep his feelings secret. He begins to pray the Prayer of the Guardian Angel, over and over. He steals into his mamá's closet and stands alone there as the scent from her perfume and clothing are like a hidden treasure. When his mamá finds him there, she pauses, thinking to reproach him, and instead blows him a kiss and walks away. El maricón, she says to herself. He can hear her preparing tomorrow's school lunches and crinkling the brown paper bags on the counter.

"Uncle!" I said, and dropped my head.

"Already?"

"Five second penalty."

"Biblical allusion," he laughed.

"Blew that play."

"You fucked up." He raised his arms. "Champion! Writers are like pitchers, Duke. Short-term memory. Bullet-proof confidence. Got to move on. And, the decision is—let's go. Let's leave. Barreling down the coast, Duke."

Afterward, we stood in the grass in the backyard and shared

a joint, talking about books. Salazar seemed to have read three times as much as me, but he listened intently to my opinions, concentrating on each overblown insight, under the spell, not only of friendship and literature and the sunset falling heavily behind the trees and hedges, as cryptic and magical as ever, but of the warm sensation of the dwindling joint passed between our hands, all the way until we burned the skin of our fingertips as we gently passed the roach, as if we were handing to each other the singed wing of a moth.

COMING OFF THE HIGHWAY, I could see the beach, all its hard-packed sand seeping away as the shroud of night came on with only a red seam in the sky above the horizon, like the seam of an oven's flame, and the sound of the waves through the open windows looming. The lights from a dozen campfires a dull sulphur.

Next came miles of slender beach pressed between the surf and the seawall, figures fading in the distance, and, above that, the shrimp shacks, ice cream stalls and taffy houses, seafood joints and barbecues, glimpses of Stars and Bars and Lone Star flags hanging from awnings, aroma of woodsmoke and charcoal and grease and potatoes. All of it framed on one side by the seven-story Flagship Hotel on the Pleasure Pier and, on the other side, Gaido's Seafood Restaurant, opened before the Depression, with a giant blue crab on the facade and, inside, formal white table cloths and bow-tied waiters.

Above the water, the wind-blasted clouds began their advance, undulating swells rose and surged, thickened and shrank. Clouds wheeling high in the air. The arcs of the constellations through the smog sprinkled the air like a repeating question, a metallic ping. I studied what few stars peeked through breaks in the sky until I thought, Yes, I know this one. It's Orion. Tip of the bow.

I tried to keep a rein on my heart.

We were always meeting all kinds of people when we came
to Galveston at night, whether near the seawall, along the beach,
or cruising the bars and galleries on The Strand on Avenue B.
If you were to believe Salazar, most of Galveston was crazy.
Everybody there had a condition, a secret past, a troubled life.
There was Lee, the angry, foul-mouthed surfer. We'd met him a
month back on the beach. His girlfriend had run off that very
night with a football player from Texas City while Lee was waiting
at the Shrimp Boat for takeout. Other nights, people were living
their upside-down stories, their afflictions, neuroses. Craziest
of all were the college students, callous, brazen, disorderly kids
who thought the world was made just for them, what with their
unruliness and their pretentiousness and their silly ideas that
nobody could ever live by.

Salazar and I watched the waves from the truck as we
slowed on top of the thick sand. Wind stormed through the
open windows. The sky like miles of dark flesh exposed.

"Be careful, a night like this. A night like this. A night to
capture life in a word," Salazar sang in a whisper.

"Which word is that, you think?"

"*Charm. Charm*, man. Seems busier here than I was
expecting," he said, looking behind us from where we'd originally
driven onto the beach, and seeing only a fistful of people on
the sand, some fires blazing. "Tonight, we party. Tomorrow, we
drive." The daytime crowd was gone, the people of every race
and type and age—milling, pushing, laying out in the sunshine on
warm, dry towels, running this way and that—possessing every
peculiar quality, inheritors of all the secrets of daily existence,
from thousands of years back and into the future, all the motives,
rationales, passions, mainsprings, all the essences and distillations,
the work, the expense, the jockeying, contrivances, the lusts and
despairs, the clutching and hanging on, letting go, the ways to
begrudge, yearn, turn green, flout, refuse, all the avoidance and
hunger, and going for the jugular. The beach was narrow and
tilting into the mild surf. The sea itself was disappearing far into

blackness. You didn't need to be as drunk as we were to feel it. "Got to keep our wits," Salazar said. "I know we'll get separated. Right? There are some pilgrims out there—warm, lean, tall, lean, warm. May there please be a pilgrim out there for me. But, after that, back at the truck, first light."

I was warming myself by rubbing my palms together and thinking about heading south for as long as we could, just doggedly go south into the raw coastal country—wooden houses on stilts with screen porches, stretches of blacktop hot and growing hotter, sleeping on a strip of sand or empty jetty, looking out over the slinky, brilliant Gulf of Mexico, the water billowing, the dull sun rising in the mornings and falling unseen in the evenings beyond the gloom.

NIGHT BEFORE I HAD SLEPT on the living room floor at Salazar's house after days of drinking and smoking weed. There was a small, brown, side-table under which I softly laid my head on a wadded blue jean jacket. My boots splayed on the floor next to the sofa. Before dawn I awoke to a long shear of light outside. I could hear voices on the other side of the room, the voices of two women talking calmly. One I knew was Mamá Salazar's. I wanted to get up, but I felt crumpled on the floor, and I wondered if I was still drunk. It didn't feel like it, and the two voices talking on the other side of the room were reassuring. The other woman had a voice I didn't recognize. She was speaking about a letter she received at "the ministry," which I took to be Reverend Salazar's, and the other woman, I guessed, was his assistant of some kind.

"You got to read this one," the other woman said

"I hate those. Don't bring those letters around,"said Mamá Salazar, a tiny woman, soft black hair, and sharp lines across her skin, who struck me as a survivor, a woman who didn't let much—child-rearing or agonized loves—grind her down. I was to learn she had been near to completing a college degree when she got pregnant with Salazar, and then strayed no farther from this neighborhood where she lived and worked as an office manager at a dentist's office.

"Look at it," insisted the other voice. "They infuriate me."

"You read it. I'm making breakfast for the kids. They're going to the beach."

"I hate these," the older woman said. She read from the letter—

To Minister Salazar, I have just finished listening to twelve hours of your sermons on cassette tape. What you say about Jesus as a beggar, I couldn't help but notice your voice has a Latin accent. What are you, Mexican, some kind of wetback? You think this can of beans you are selling is Jesus? Go back to Tijuana! C. Jones, Bridge City, TX.

"Put that away. Please," said Mamá Salazar.

I heard Salazar close the door to his bedroom and pad into the living room. He was dressed in a long tee shirt down to his knees. "You crash on the floor?"

"Hey, mi hijo."

Mamá Salazar clapped her hands, and peered from the kitchen. "He's my mi hijo," she laughed.

The other woman left through the sliding glass door to the backyard.

"Mi hijo's mamá, hey," I said and pantomimed raising a glass in toast. "Thanks for the floor. Great floor."

Hours earlier, with my ankle sore, I'd limped into the kitchen. The lights were on, but no one was awake. The sliding glass door to the backyard stood open. The scraggly trees, holding still in the night air, splayed their short shadows from the street lamps onto the thick grass. The air thick, folding into the bark. It was a busy, ordered kitchen, with a dishtowel hanging from the faucet giving the impression it wasn't a room anyone fussed over. On the counter, beside the sink, there was a plastic drainer with knives, small pots, and a ladle drying, and a coffee maker crowded next to a dispenser of dish soap and paper towels. Next to the coffee maker were canning jars of oatmeal and flour, candles, cookbooks, a toaster. There were stains on the cabinetry above the stove from a grease fire. Lace curtains gave the kitchen warmth, especially when sunlight fanned across the tiled floor in the mornings and onto the checkered breakfast table. I walked to the sink and poured a glass of water, then returned to my spot on the floor and fell back to sleep.

Some mornings after partying I felt a heaviness, a burden, or bearing down. But, that morning, there was none of that. The sky was mysterious and fresh. I rolled over onto my back on the floor and began doing sit ups silently in a series of ten and caught a glimpse of the light through the picture window each time I heaved upward.

Salazar sat down in the living room, handing my boots over to me, and I pulled them on before we sat down for breakfast, molletes topped with beans and cheese, with pan dulce.

Mamá Salazar began talking about the serenity of the morning, the serenity of home, how much she loved starting each day in the presence of "His exalted and blessed Name, Father, Son, and Holy Spirit, always, now and forever." She was fawning over Salazar to comb his hair.

I did love the way she treated each morning knowing there were all the hours of the day to be loved. It was as if she saw life as an uninterrupted time to clear the paths that twisted before you for miles, with nothing falling back, nothing biting, that this very day, the one you shared with her, was an exhilaration, and all she could ever want.

"All the food in this house is actual Mexican food," she said, smiling at me.

"We thank you, Lord," said Salazar.

Clasping her hands, Mamá Salazar bowed her head. "Say it all, mi hijo."

"We thank you, Lord, for these gifts we are about to receive. In the name of thy only Son, Jesus Christ, Lord. Amen."

"You have a pure spirit, Yochanan," she said, using my full Hebrew name, to acknowledge my saying, with them all, Amen.

"Incorruptible," I replied.

Mamá Salazar frowned. "That's your problem. You don't believe it. You'll do your own thing in your own time. I've been a Bible-thumper since before I met Manolo's Papi."

"Don't try it," said Salazar.

"Come now. That's not becoming. He's my friend, too. My other mi hijo. I share him with Batya."

"I'm not saying he won't achieve something. I have a high estimation of you, Duke. You know your value."

"Don't you?" I said.

"I know where I can go, how far. It's not a surprise to anyone in this neighborhood. What's here? Really. What's here? You agree, don't you? No? What?"

"I won't listen to this kind of talk," Mamá Salazar said, and stood and left the kitchen to prepare for work.

"I'm just saying! Means of production!" he called to her, swirling the crumbs around his plate.

"Who was that lady here earlier?" I said.

"My aunt. She left for work. She works for Papi."

"Should have heard the nasty letter she read."

"Those come all the time, man," said Salazar. "Your old man gets those."

Shrugging, I said, "What he gets usually goes like this: "Dear Rabbi Wain: Hello! My name is Judy Danenbaum! I'm currently in mourning for my mother and saying Kaddish everyday, but I'm falling a bit behind as I'm having some issues outside of the shul. I wanted to ask. How I can catch up! I broke my back six months after I started saying Kaddish, and now I'm having violent grand mal seizures, and I'm still healing from it, and this is kind of my first time saying Kaddish...for anyone. I also just moved to Houston from Fort Wayne, Indiana. Nice to meet you by the way!"

"Okay, very funny," said Salazar "Come on. What you been

through? Mamá won't hear."

"I know who I am," I said, and we left it at that, though, without prompting, I relented and, without telling much of anything, I described how my girlfriend, Leah, found out about me and another girl. I told him only this much: A few nights earlier there was this girl, who I only knew as Nicole. We met at Meyerland Park where there'd been a gathering of high school students late at night, drinking, smoking pot near the empty ballfields, with the crickets loud. She was a senior at Episcopal, a debate champion, who had already been accepted to Wellesley. By the time we drove north to the outdoor swimming pool at T.C. Jester, it was after midnight, humid and foggy. We kissed and fondled, and all that, and then, sitting on the pool deck, behind the diving boards, while smoking a joint, we built a small fire with grass and twigs, and fallen limbs from a week of storms. Acrobatically, the flames twisted and rose. When a scrap of wind kicked up, it blew the smoke into our faces and burned our eyes, along with the chlorine misting above the pool. Slowly the smoke straightened into the shapes of long funnels, and we talked about a desire to reach for it, like reaching out to touch fiery wings. No one could see us, but we could see an old man alone in the park, which was crazy at that hour. He was sitting on a crooked lawn chair a little ways outside the fence. In the dark, it was impossible to tell if he was a white man or black, or what he was. I began to pretend to describe him—his gnarled hands, that he was chewing some kind of chaw, but likely he was only talking to himself, out of pain or boredom. A beer can in his lap, untouched.

The night was a hapless undertaking. Nicole lay down on her side and propped her head up with an arm, her black hair falling over her shoulder. The fire erratic. The teeth of the flames reckless in the little wind. Her eyes were glazed from being stoned. "I don't think you care for me," she said.

"Maybe you intimidate me," I said.

"I can't believe we never met before."

Above us the sky was moving thick as water. The doorways and awnings and brickwork and gutters of rooftops in that neighborhood swayed in silence, diffuse in the hard spaces that, as our little fire soothed us, loosened and took on a renewed spirit, like the wind. The door to a house slammed. For an hour longer we stayed there, making out, or groping, with our clothes on, as if we belonged to no time. All around was an aroma of cut grass and burnt gasoline, bits of sky a poisonous purple and red.

Mamá Salazar whisked by in low heels, blew kisses, and was gone.

We sat in the living room and shared a joint. I took a long haul, let the smoke settle in my lungs, and felt a glistening spirit whirl inside the room. The album was *Led Zeppelin III*, side B, the acoustic side. The music and the weed burning straight through.

Salazar was hunched in an arm chair. Woozily, he studied the white album jacket—tracking with his finger tip the butterflies, airplanes, flags, birds, spaceships, faces, blimps, stars, and hummingbirds. Normally, he loved talking about disasters— tornados, car crashes, suicide bombs, massacres. He was looking oddly at the way I was smoking. "Make sure you put that joint out. Okay? It's a cigarette caused that underground mine to blow in Tennessee a while back. Ten miners lost their lives. Investigation found that the explosion came after a miner's cigarette lighter ignited a pocket of methane gas. Fuckin-A, man. Ventilation. It was poorly ventilated. The company didn't even ban smoking in the mine."

"I'll put the joint out. Don't worry."

"I am worried. This shit happens all the time. Stardust Fire in Dublin? Valentines Day. 800 people in this disco. There was, I don't know, a thousand gallons of cooking oil in the kitchen. Some electrical shit broke. Boom! 48 people died. Shit happens, Duke."

I had settled onto the floor, looking up, listening to the soft music shift sideways, and I was thinking to myself, take these eyes, take this throat. Salazar blew out smoke he'd been holding in his chest, then lifted his right hand in the air, his fingers formed into the shape of a pistol, and began cocking and flicking his thumb, pumping invisible bullets into his head. "This is the cure. Duke, take it."

The slender joint came back around.

"Getting normal, man," I said, through my held breath.

A little cloud of smoke from my mouth swam up to the light in the center of the ceiling, twisted around the glass, and fell backward like a long sigh.

Sitting forward, Salazar was resting a hand on my knee. "Leah's a gem, man. You should fix it." He looked at me as he nodded his head back and forth as if to shake his eyes into focus. "Come on, man. Don't be a fuck."

He walked into the bathroom and came back with an aerosol can of Glade air freshener, spraying all around.

The music had stopped. Near the label, the needle scratched in the groove. It was the second time through we'd listened to side B. I looked at him, nodded, and took another drag. At once, Salazar put the needle on the first song. Sweet strums of the guitar picked up my spirit. I could feel the hollows of my imagination and all that had belonged to the past untuck and spin slowly, like I was in the invisible space you feel right after an accident and before you are thrown through the windshield.

"Been together a long time."

Behind my eyes were pinpoints of light that left small claw marks I was having trouble flicking away.

"Second grade. Then fourth grade. Since eighth grade."

"Practically married."

The high was pumping. It felt hot in the house, and I could feel sweat on my brow. I stared up at white paint on the ceiling. I could still see Leah from the day we broke up, two days earlier. I imagined her curled on her bed—she was soft and small and breathing quick, then squinted as if to see the future that was inches from her—even as I stood outside her house in the warm wind. Listening to the music, I felt I was trying to catch myself with my hands. My breathing was shallow.

I wondered what Salazar saw in me right then, my body swaying on the floor, the edges of my mind, crisp and dense, getting darker, stilled, then trembling, like a flame.

He began singing—

My, my, la de la, come on now it ain't too far.
Tell your friends all around the world
Ain't no companion like a blue eyed merle.

I nodded to the beat of the hard interlude, and tried to inch upward, my stomach tightening and un-tightening, taking a deep breath, a reminder of something, a prod, and joined in singing the last line of the next part—*You're the finest dog I knew, so fine.*

Salazar was rolling another joint. I waved him off, laid down on the floor, and returned to thinking about Nicole, the girl from Episcopal. At the swimming pool, her breath on my neck felt cool as a pillow. She was resting her cheek against the top of my back in between my shoulders. Her hair draped over my skin. I could feel her hand on my back. She was rubbing a circle down below my spine. I hadn't moved and let out a small sigh of gratitude.

"I love you, man," Salazar said, turning the music lower.

"You're my people, mi hijo."

"Why shouldn't you enjoy yourself? Who deserves it more than you? With your gifts? Because you happen to want to live doesn't mean you have to deny yourself."

"So I'm not going to be damned?" I remembered that I gave Leah nothing, not a word, no explanation, when we broke up.

"Damned? Shit, Duke. Soon we're going to be driving. I-45. Gulf Freeway. Right over the ancestral lands of the Karankawas. They were here before Cabeza de Vaca. 1535 AD. I can see by your face you've fallen behind on your research. You got to do your homework. You got show your math. All eight lanes are on top of burial grounds."

I reached over to the turntable to turn the volume up. "Yeah. We're murderers," I said.

"Can't be forgotten, man. Can't be forgotten. We're imprinted. Come on now. Tell me about Leah. She's a gem. I love her. What'd she do? Throw a glass at your head?" He was giggling. "Tell you she'd rather die? Was it that bad?" he said, and, enjoying the thought of it, he acted out throwing a glass at my face and blew shattering, explosive noises with his mouth.

The thing about Leah was, he was right, she was a gem, brilliant, planned to attend Bard. We'd known each other since we were in diapers. Her father was the cantor at Beth Tikkun, my father's home synagogue, and her mother was an officer in the Sisterhood. Sunday afternoons, Leah's mom and Batya the Rock played mah-jongg with their girlfriends. Leah could be romantic. When she learned something, especially about the history of Judaism, which she was obsessed with, the words came out of her mouth with an excitable thrust. Once, while she was at dinner at our house, at the kitchen table, Leah went on and on about *Toledot Yeshu*.

"You're reading about the Chronicles of Jesus? Look at you," Batya the Rock said.

"Ancient Jews didn't ever talk about Jesus," Leah said. "Totally avoided speculation about Jesus, his life, and all that."

"Or the origins of Christianity," my father said. "Pretended it didn't happen." We were eating baked chicken with rice and salad, and he was slicing the chicken into strips before stabbing into them, one by one, with his fork.

Leah agreed. "What are you going to do with all those miracles? Right? Because they're enticing. Best to shut down any talk."

"Exactly," he shouted.

"Anyway, I was reading in this magazine we get at home, *Ancient Jewish Lives*, it comes a few times a year, that Jews, after the time of Jesus, openly mocked Jesus and his" —she does the air quotes gesture— "church. Anyway, they kind of satirize Jesus in *Toldot Yeshu*. Probably it was shared by word of mouth. People like us, in the medieval period, sitting around making fun of converts from Judaism to Christianity. Do you know the one night of the year *Toledot Yeshu* got told in Jewish households? Christmas Eve! Isn't that funny?"

"See the problem with Jesus, I mean, the origins of Jesus, for the Jews of his time," my father joined in, delighted by what he seemed to hope were going to be many, many dinners with his future daughter-in-law talking about ancient Judaism, and he ran both hands through his hair, "is the question of the truth of who this young man's true father is." He slapped the table with his palm. "This remained in dispute, even as all Christians cited the Holy Spirit. The Gospel of Mark and the Gospel of Luke look the other way. And, Matthew says he's from the lineage of Joseph, Ruth, Bathsheba. Got to afford him royalty."

"That's what this article was saying," Leah said. "*Toledot Yeshu* focuses on how Jesus got his magic, his miraculous powers, how he fooled the masses with magic tricks, and that's how the rabbis came to excommunicate him, then the Romans."

"We know the rest, dear," said my mother, with an expression that said she didn't allow gruesome talk of crucifixions at her dinner table.

"You know, I had a great-great-grandfather," my father said, with his sermon tone, "a Rabbi Seforim from Odessa, who wrote a book defending Jesus. Said Jesus was a good Jewish boy all the way until he died, never meant to found a new religion. Rabbi Seforim asked, what kind of Jew wants a new religion? Enough trouble with the one we've got. Rabbi Seforim made the argument—nowhere to be found in your *Toledot Yeshu*—that Jesus was a righteous philosopher on par with Rashi. Made the argument that Jesus was downright kosher! Rabbi Seforim's family begged him not to publish such meshuggah. Did he listen? Of course not. Rabbi Seforim was the kind of nudnik who refused to hold his breath when he crossed a church or the cross. What can you say? Crazy Rabbi Seforim. He was a dreamer."

"Both Rabbi Seforim and Jesus!" Leah said, and the table laughed, and it seemed all of us felt aware that, with her eyes bright and her mouth moving fast, Leah made you feel there was a larger world that you belonged to, and from this you couldn't be separated.

"You should be the rabbi at Beth Tikkun," I said.

Rabbi Gadol guffawed. "Beg your pardon?"

"Benny, please," my mother said.

"It's going to happen, Rabbi Wain. In time, it's going to happen," Leah said.

My mother wiped her lips with her linen napkin. "Hear, hear, darling."

My father reached across the table for the bottle of white wine, filled my mother's glass and his. "If you say so, sweetie. If you say so," he said.

"Maybe not me," said Leah. "But, women. The millennium is nearly over. Jews are going to adapt. That's what we do. Women already do most of the work in synagogues and temples all over the world anyway."

Listening to Leah, knowing that everyone at the table, as well as her parents, assumed Leah and I were the future of our families, a golden merger of the son and daughter of the rabbi and the cantor of Beth Tikkun, I briefly closed my eyes. It was not long after that night I was making out with Episcopal High's star debater behind the diving boards at T.C. Jester Park.

The day we broke up, Leah and I had been sitting on the bed in her room. One moment she was looking away with hard eyes, a catch in her breath. She seemed brittle, but not delicate, when she breathed in, sharply, a caught breath, then dipped her head and looked downward. There came a gasp. Her eyes were dazed, as if she were trying to reassemble all our time together and hold it with a downward stare. After we sat quietly for a time, talking intermittently, finally I said, "I've got to go."

"Why are you saying this?" she said. "You're afraid? I'm afraid, too. How many people are we going to let down if we break up?" School books were spread out over the bedspread. A single yellow marker held my attention. "Remember that time we went to La Porte?" she said, and I nodded.

We'd driven an hour to La Porte one Sunday to eat at the San Jacinto Inn and returned in a foggy darkness. On the drive out of Houston, we joked back and forth about the family style menu they'd been serving since the restaurant opened during the Depression.

"Sticks of celery and bowls of shrimp," Leah said.

"Fried chicken, red fish."

"Hot biscuits and blackberry jam."

"Oysters or crab!"

"Or whatever's in season!"

On the drive home, as we crossed the San Jacinto River Bridge, the water rushed underneath us and the sky tightened with a riffle of stars. In the passenger seat, Leah sat with her legs pulled up, delighted as a child in a grassy field. "What is it you like about me?" she asked as we cruised past oil refineries near Pasadena, exhaust flames snapping and flattening against the night air.

"You're smart. You're intuitive. You stand up. I like that. I can't take my eyes off you. There's that. You make me laugh."

She was letting the praise rinse over her, with her eyes closed, like I was standing behind her and pouring a bucket of warm water gently over her hair and running my hands through it, slowly washing her hair, the suds on the skin of her forehead and over my arms. She opened her eyes, looking at me a moment. Then reclined her head back, eyes closed, face tilted to the window as I steered through traffic.

When I popped a Loretta Lynn tape into the cassette player, Leah sang along—*If your eyes are on me, you're lookin' at country*—and studied the twitching refinery fires, the stink hanging for miles. She shifted her weight so her back was leaning against the passenger side door and, after slipping her boots off, she rested her stocking feet against my thigh. The shadows from the refineries reached across the highway and speeding traffic and dropped over the asphalt as if to hold our throats. The downtown skyline, with lights on in several tall buildings, was ringed far off by clouds.

"Then we can go on like this. This right here. For a long time," she said, nodding with the intervals of car lights flashing through the windshield. By the time we got to Meyerland, she'd grown quiet. We wriggled out of the car outside her house. "This day!" she cried, and she jumped, piggyback-style, onto my shoulders.

That same night we'd driven to La Porte and back, when her parents and younger brothers were asleep, I'd snuck in through her open bedroom window. We were lying together on the narrow bed, the room dark but for a chain lamp throwing a light across the bed covers, both of us in our clothes still, whispering about friends and school, when she said, "I want to do something for you." She got up from where she'd been cuddled under my arm, her cheek against the buttons of my shirt, her face drowsy in the dimness, her hand resting on the buckle of my belt, and, with her hair still tangled, she stood at the foot of the bed and began to dance. No music, not singing or humming, but, silently, she wavered in and out of the dull lamplight.

Flirty, giggling, directing my eyes with her hands to her mess of hair, her neck, hips, pressing the palms of her hands against the outsides of her breasts, blowing kisses, she performed a slow, rumpled dance. Smoothing her fingers across her belly, up through whiffs of hair falling around her eyes, alongside her ears, and back into the tousle of hair, she pirouetted, plunging from one side of the bed to the other. She twisted her torso, again touching her hips and breasts and hair with her hands, her face reddening, then, generously, untucking her shirt, unbuttoning a top button, another, so that the lace from her white bra was exposed, her dainty skin, mouth open, letting me watch with my head propped on her pillows, as if this sinewy connection, this strip-less striptease, contained particles of a new secret between us, something we'd always remember, and tell no one. What, I wondered, was this offering, this calm, this arousal? She kept moving, kept saying, with her eyes and mouth, with her hips and legs, and her untucked shirt, with the exposed white lace of her bra, with her hips and legs, *I want to do something for you.* Unburdened, she danced. As if to say, nothing else matters. Only this matters, she said with her hands. This, she said with her eyes, is what life means. There was before, and now there's now, and then there's tomorrow. Look at you, she said with her hair. The world gives itself to you, Duke, she said with her flushed face. To how many generations will you say no, Duke? To how many will you say, Out there there's something else, Duke? Stay, Duke, she said with her swinging hips. Stay, she said with her reddening cheeks.

There I was, without any disguise, thinking, why am I enjoying this? Is it just what happens between people entwined with each other? Even teenagers who, with little prodding from the other, can imagine decades of life together? One in love with the allure of the other? Were we already in a place in our lives where one could persuade the other to do almost anything? Or, was there something in her, her chastity, clear conscience, that, even that night, after the long drive to La Porte and the long drive back, after the simplicity of my saying, 'You stand up," I couldn't reciprocate, much less measure up to her offer—because her dance contained the impeccability of love, and I was lying on my back, my head on the pillows, sinking onto the bed into wantonness, craving, appetite? Was there something in her spiraling hands and shifting hips and flush face? Something authoritative about her that made me susceptible to her ingenuity, more than my own? Or, was this performance a dance to prevent my demise? Something I was undressed by? So that I would have no route out of doing what she wanted? And, always? We'd been dating long enough that it was comfortable just to hang out like that, instead of trying to get our hands everywhere on each other's body every time we were alone, pulled along, impatient, swept aside, and both of us going along, shoving our hips with soothing jolts, the sexual blur that seemed like it would never stop, so that we would, weak and lost, be carried far enough along to make time last. Her legs around my hips, our heads side to side. Our dogged, timid, watchful, floundering pleasure meeting halfway our dogged, timid, watchful, floundering despair.

What I said to her, whispered so her parents didn't hear, was, "Don't stop, Leah."

She danced until she crawled across the bed, again stood on the floor, and twirled five, six, seven times, until, dizzy, she collapsed onto the carpet. "Hurry. Go," she called. "I hear my parents. Shit. Go." Then, "No," she said. "It's not them. It's okay. No. Come back."

The afternoon of the breakup she was slumped on her bed, the better to plead with me. Her face was blotchy and wet. A misery in her eyes. But she surprised me when, at last, before I walked to the door, she said, "When I'm certain I can't stand it, I'm going to remember that night we went to La Porte, how fine that was."

SALAZAR AND I SAT TALKING together in the pickup once we parked on the beach, each sipping a beer. There were stray bonfires. A couple dozen people on the beach, and they could be heard talking and singing, listening to radios from car stereos. Four teenagers threw a frisbee in the darkness. There was a green flag waving in the wind—conditions were calm. We sat looking at the dark swells, talking about *The Divine Comedy*, which we were studying in Mildred Donne's class, and I was feeling calmer, delighted. Salazar had fallen behind in his reading, and I was detailing the circles of hell that followed Limbo—

Lust, Gluttony, Greed. I reminded him who was in which circle. "Achilles and Dido are in Lust," I said, waving a hand out the window at the beach frolickers. "The everyday folk of Gluttony—like these people." I went on like that, not the least bit worried that I sounded like some expert. But, I still couldn't stop myself, under the nighttime spell, and the waves falling heavily beyond the clear windshield, rolling up and back as they did day and night, a new one every few seconds, whether we were present or not, or knew about them, or cared. I was losing all notion of time, thinking we had all the time in the world to get to where we were going. Nothing needed to be clarified. Things were simple in the pickup. I was tempted to suggest we leave Galveston, right then, and drive to Jamaica Beach or Surfside, somewhere quieter, fewer people, or go as far as Christmas Bay and Freeport, or farther still, down the narrow highways to Aransas Pass, or just keep driving through the night to Corpus Christi.

To be sure: No matter how long we stayed away, days, weeks, the same circumstances, the same faces would be waiting for us when we got back, like familiar stars in the night sky, like the waves slapping at the sand and murmuring to the foam something of its own never-ending lore. The beer and weed blended in with the last hours: Nicole from Episcopal, the breakup with Leah, sleeping on Mamá Salazar's floor, Salazar's praise at breakfast, smoking the weed, drinking, driving to the beach, even the fantasy of the girl in the back of the green pickup, her hair cinematically blowing around her cheeks, the traffic, the Lady with a Dog, Muscle Man, the sharp memory of the turkey vulture. It all came to me with total precision.

Salazar put out a cigarette in the ash tray, leaning back.

"Going to be tough, going it alone," he said. He turned to listen to the surf. "Story of my life. Because, you know. Pilgrims."

Pilgrims.

Pilgrims was our nickname for the secret. At a raucous house party at Leah's a year before, with her parents out of town, there had been more rolled joints and cans of beer than any of us had seen to that time. It was a hot June and the record player was cranked. By midnight, I drank so much Jim Beam I was nearly passed out standing in the doorway on the side of the house and getting a small breeze from the street. I sidestepped through the scrum of grunting bodies into a long hallway with rooms branching off from it, with all the doors closed, and stumbled up a staircase to the second floor, and more closed bedrooms, including Leah's. A great mass of drunken people were pressed along the walls and the stairs, sitting and standing, detritus of beer cans at their feet, people stretched out from one end of the hallway to the other. I elbowed my way through them as if parting a sea of flesh. Behind the closed doors, I knew, were couples making out, fucking, throwing up. I thought Leah's room, on the second floor, would be empty, and I could lie on her bed covers and rest. There was a banging noise, like a lamp falling, in the room next to Leah's. I shoved through the hallway until I reached the door. Opening it, I found Tina Brochstein and Lisa Nathan, two senior girls, both topless, and two guys, brothers, blonde twins, Todd and Pete Shore, dressed only in their white underwear and crew cuts. The boys' skin was so smooth and hairless you could ice skate across their lanky backs. I never could tell the Shore brothers apart, even when they were dressed, but one was sitting on the bed with a deck of cards in his hands, while the other was lifting the fallen lamp from the floor and setting it, askew, on the bed stand. I did not remember a time when I did not know Tina and Lisa. We had gone to nursery school together at the synagogue. The Shore boys I'd met in Little League.

"Want to play?" one of the twins called. The girls covered up their breasts with their hands.

"Strip poker," the other twin said.

"I'm too fucked up," I said.

When I reached Leah's room, the door wasn't locked, but a chair was blocking it from the inside, and, when I pushed it open, there was only the lamp on the side table shining. Salazar was lying on his back on the bed, his eyes closed, his jeans rolled to his ankles, and his hard cock inside another boy's mouth. This, I had never seen before. The mouth of the other boy, who I recognized as Alan Brooks, whose father was on the board of directors at the synagogue, was red and wet, and he had his eyes closed, and did not stop or look up. I held the door open long enough for Salazar to open his eyes to see me standing in the threshold, my hand squeezing the door handle.

Outside the room, in the hot hallway, feeling woozy, I was aware that I was holding my jaw tight, clenching my teeth, a lucidity tapping inside my heart, like the sound of fresh gravel tossed at a window. I tried to understand what I had just seen. It was like I had taken a strange drug and needed to arrange my mind and balance my feet. The feeling drew me into the unpleasant fear of my imagination, like a deception, and I had no way, right then, to understand the meaning of it. The mouth red, the wet mouth. Benign really, little disappointing. But, I'd never seen that. A nervous agitation gripped my stomach. But, also a thrill. I knew, nothing was going to happen. There were no sirens, no snarling dogs. I had simply seen it. But, why hadn't I known this about Salazar? Or, I had known it, and was unable or unknowing or too naive to recognize the very blood of it coursing brightly through the veins of friendship. Suddenly, I saw interactions I'd had with Salazar for years as markers I should have noticed all along. The way he often touched my face, hands, knees—and with me indifferent to him, if not, dumbly, disapproving, of those gestures of loneliness. I considered that I should walk down the hallway, downstairs, but, also, I was scared that someone else might enter the room and catch them, and so I remained outside the door, like a sentry. Same time, my legs felt like they were asleep. I rubbed my thighs. I looked at the skin on my hands—the knuckles seemed to me melting. The light in the hall almost soaking wet. Bodies crammed next to each other. For a time, I stood watch. Which meant what, exactly? I wondered how accustomed Salazar was. Had he had the feeling all his life? Is that what I thought? I had never imagined. If I didn't know that about him, how could I know myself? My father's synagogue forbade membership to gay people. I hardly gave it a thought. So, when Salazar stepped out of the bedroom with the other boy, who quickly hustled down the hall without looking at me, I thought Salazar was someone I might be able to save. But, that feeling evaporated. He seemed shaken. No, it was me who was shaken. He looked at my eyes—distinctly, we held each other's eyes—and he seemed, not devastated, but aggravated.

"I thought you knew," he said.

"No, mi hijo," I said, but my heart felt heavy, hurt that he hadn't confided in me, and I realized perhaps for the first time, that people are never who they say they are. They are, instead, what they hide. That feeling was comforting.

In the hallway, I felt alien. Loud music, thrumming bodies. Standing next to each other, both of us furtive, evasive, we were also, strangely, wordlessly almost, closer to each other than ever before, more in love, if that's the way to put it, safer with each other afresh, consumed.

"I hate when people say *fag*," Salazar said next morning over Pop-Tarts and a bong filled with ice water in Leah's Meyerland backyard, after we'd mopped up the house and carried plastic bags of empty cans and bottles and potato chips to a dumpster next to the Stop-N-Go. The three of us were sitting barefoot on the patio in the blazing hot breeze. Salazar looked content, his eyes shining with a new freedom. Gone was his usual—what, that morning, I came to see had been his usual—uneasiness, alienation, impatience, deference, social anxiety, whenever talk turned to girlfriends. "Do you like it when people say *kike*?"

"No," I said.

"Come on, guys," Leah said, turning to listen for her parents' car, though they weren't due home until evening.

"You are absolved, duchess," Salazar said, and he resumed eating, silently.

I turned to him. "Do you feel okay? I mean, I'm okay. Not that I need to be okay, or not okay. I mean, are you okay?"

"It's not a catastrophe, Duke," Leah said.

"Well, no," I said. "I don't mean that." But, what did I know? What had I seen?

"You weren't born in a cave," she said, impatiently.

Salazar took a long, studious hit from the bong. The ice water bubbled. He leaned his head back and closed his eyes, holding the smoke inside his lungs. One by one, he blew round smoke rings from his mouth that blended with a cloud of insects above our heads.

"You can do anything you want, mi hijo," I said.

"Really? You're a dumb rabbi's son, you dumb ass. Really? Can someone like me do anything that doesn't reek to the gates of Heaven of my being someone like me?" he said. "I've kept this to myself so long. I'm not happy about it. There are straight people who look down at people like me, and straight people who look up to people like me. Then there are the straight people who look down and up at the same time. The evil fuckers. No end in sight. First, it was me being a Chicano that was offensive, then what was hated was a Chicano fitting in. Now, it's gay that'll be disgusting. Sissy, fudge packer, girly man. I'm going to get the shit kicked out of me just for breathing the air and walking down the street. Hola! Fort Bliss! Know what'll scare the shit out of those assholes? A fudge packer with a rifle. No more frail faggots, that's my motto. But, when we're strong, muscular, bold, they'll say that's disgusting."

"Manolo," said Leah.

"I'm sorry, man. I'm with you," I said.

"Look," he went on, "you straight people can't live with gay people. But, you have to. We've always been here." He stopped talking, lifted his chin, and yawped into the sky. A scream that surely the neighbors had heard. He quieted. Rubbed his eyes. "Just don't say *fag*. Okay, guys? That always knocks me back," Salazar said, flushed, but spoke no more.

Leah put her hands to her mouth.

"I'm your brother, man, okay? I'm cool. Don't have a nervous breakdown. Not, that word, but—and I know you know what I mean here—we need some word, between us. You could have told me, then I could've made sure no one came into Leah's room."

Leah stood, when the phone rang, and started for the kitchen, asking, "Why do you need some word? What are you talking about?"

I said to Salazar, "You know what I'm saying. Right? You know what I'm saying. As your wing man." I gave it thought. "How about, *plug?*" I said.

"*Plug!* What the fuck is *plug?*"

"You know, 'I'm going with that guy to get plugged.'"

"You fucking idiot. That's stupid," he said.

"Sorry. okay. That was crude. First draft. I'm in some new region, man, okay. I'm in. It's uncharted territory. I'm a newcomer. Land ho!"

"Let me ask you a question," said Salazar. "You think I don't want to live as a normal human being? The last thing I want to be chained to is being the token neon faggot."

"Pilgrim," I said. "That's what you are. You're getting to your true self. How about that? 'I'm going off with that pilgrim.'"

"*Watch my back, pilgrim's coming.*"

"*I'm journeying to a sacred place.*"

"The pilgrimage."

THE TIDELINE CRAWLED AND SOOTHED, and after awhile I opened another beer.

"You going to be a Jew your whole life?"

"What?"

"I'm thinking, me and Jesus have come to an impasse," Salazar said and crossed his hands over his chest and rested them there.

"Go on. How you going to do that?"

"Well impasse might not be the right word. I feel like I've turned a corner. I think I just want to pick flowers in the moonlight. Or else, let me die in a war. That's what I'm talking about. The Doctrine of Atonement is trash. As I see it, Jesus ain't as great as Buddha."

"You think? That'd make a great country song."

"If the country was China," he said, and that made us both laugh.

"Got to be Chinese Country and Western music," I said.

"'Blue Eyes Crying in the Beijing Rain.'"

"'Devil Went Down to Shanghai.'"

"'I Walk the Line' would be 'I Walk the Wall.'"

"'It Wasn't Deng Xiaoping Who Made Honky Tonk Angels.'"

"Ha! I love it! Here's one: 'Mama, Don't Let Your Babies Grow Up To Be Pinko Chinese Commies.'"

"'Stand By Your Chinaman.'"

"Watch your mouth, Duke. 'Stand By Your Chairman Mao.' We got to write the lyrics for these titles down. Get out your notebook. Get this. *Commies aint' easy to love and they're harder to hold.*"

"*They'd rather give you songs than fortune cookies or gold!*"

We were laughing hard, too hard, and I pushed open the door and fell to the sand and rolled around, laughing, and singing. "*Mamas, don't let your babies grow up go to be Peoples Republic of China commie apparatchiks.*"

Salazar began tooting the horn to the rhythm of my voice as I climbed back inside. He said, "We could get famous at the Grand Ole Hong Kong Opry."

"All right, all right," I said. "Stop. Stop." Coughing out laughter. "No more. I mean it. What happened to Jesus? Dial it back. Dial it back to Jesus."

"The Father, the Son, and the Moo Goo Gai Pan."

"No, no. Stop. I mean it. Whew. What happened between you and Jesus?" I said, and reached into the glovebox to find the box for kitchen matches we'd stored a half dozen joints in, and, after pulling a bone out, and sucking one of the ends, I flipped it over, struck a match, and sparked it up.

"As the Buddha says, *Be here now*," said Salazar.

"Be here now? Somewhere else later. Not complicated."

"There is no *self*, Duke."

"Are you kidding me? Whose hangover did I have this morning?"

He nodded.

I said, "What are you saying? You're not Chicano?"

"Still Chicano, man. But, I'm getting away from Jesus."

"Reverse of your old man?" I inhaled the joint hard, passed it over. "He quit the priesthood to marry your mom. You know?"

"Fuck! Not just me. You're getting away from Yahweh. Going to be somebody else? That what you want?"

"I don't want to be anybody but myself," I said.

"How's grand old Rabbi Gadol going to take that?"

"Can't get a word in," I said. "He doesn't listen."

"What word would that be? You don't have faith? Is that it?"

"I have faith. I mean, there's old faith and fresh faith. Lustrous faith. Dull faith. Faith in sunlight and faith in shadow."

"Bring it! Bring it, my servant of the Lord! My man of fresh faith."

"My faith isn't fresh, exactly, but, you know, it's abstract. It's timeless, spaceless, never changes, disinterested."

"Like it has no consciousness," he nodded.

"Exactly. Faith that's aware of nothing but faith." I took several hits off the joint. "Rabbi Gadol wouldn't get that. I don't know. Maybe it is fresh. It's a faith that enters the soul and doesn't startle it, doesn't amaze the soul with itself. That kind of faith. Faith that's its own subject. Look at the waves. Okay? Would we love looking at them as much if they held up a big neon sign that said, 'Admire me! I'm the waves! Love me!'"

"I get it, man. For me, faith is recognized as faith only as it comes into being."

"Amen! Brother Manolo!"

"But, then, shit, poof, it's gone. Why can't it just be a wet pilgrim? We'd fall in love. Be happy. Not this existential shit.

"Yeah. Why not? 'The Lord is my pilgrim. I shall not want.'"

We passed the joint, giggling. "You're going to write about Jews. And me, I'm going write about lovers of Christ. Either way, we're fucked," he said.

"What are we going to say?"

"Money and blood. That's what books are about," he said.

"Living's not enough? Dying?"

"People make noise. That's it," he said.

"They make a noise? Like what?"

"Hear that car, up there, above the seawall? Hear it? Like that. Like a car driving past on a hot night." The joint had died out, and he relit it.

"Like waves."

"Like fire."

"Like ashes."

"That's it."

"Proving what?"

"You tell me, Duke. You tell me," he said.

I thought about it while holding what was now half a joint in my fingers, rubbing the bottom of my ring finger with my thumbnail, and looking at the wind throw sand against the hood of the car. "Yeah, I'm up against the old man, all right. Last week, we were working in the lawn. Mowing, edging, raking up. I just kept looking at him on his hands and knees, weeding, his rump in the air, and I thought, you could polish silver with that ass."

"Ah, man."

"I admire my dad. What he has to go through—illnesses and deaths and troubles and the board of directors and the lunatic congregants. He does the best imitations of some of our congregants. Oy, Rabbi, this, and I'm going to potchke my baby's tuches, rabbi, that. He's amazing at impersonations. Total recall. Then, there's all his famous friends, all his travels to lecture on the Old Jew in the New South. He's given that talk a thousand times. He goes, 'My friends, the old Jew in the new South has got springtime in his heart.' Who comes up with that shit? I love him. But I don't like him. Impressed by him? Yeah, I am. He's the Grand Rabbi of the whole fucking state practically. Rabbi Gadol. It's not easy."

"Not like my dad. No way," said Salazar.

A long silence fell between us, and I thought of Father Salazar, as we secretly called him, the defrocked priest-turned-Evangelical preacher, who lived in Bellfort, east of Mykawa Road, and did a weekly radio broadcast of his charismatic sermons. He was often at Mamá Salazar's house, I discovered, and they were oddly sweet on each other, even though they'd dissolved their marriage ten years earlier. Father Salazar usually had his white dress shirt unbuttoned, bare-chested, to keep cool, and gold cufflinks, slacks, and flipflops. He had deep black hair, like he'd spread shoe polish over his head. The effect was he appeared fallen but passionate. He was something of a middle-aged wolf, who could lure men and women to find their most spirited selves, who could ease the hearts of his admirers, who was, Mamá Salazar called him, with the wink of her eye, *el integrante*, a conniver obsessed with temptation, his blood aflame. Which isn't to suggest Father Salazar actually was a ladies' man. On the contrary, his personality was so colossal that you might miss the deviousness underneath it, not meant to protect him, but to seduce whomever he was talking to, then to move on. Who he truly was, was difficult to fathom. Sly and enchanting, he had the gift for beguiling, a bewitcher. He reminded me of a matador, flattering his charges, burning them up with swift *reboleras*.

One night, Father Salazar appeared at his ex-wife's house dressed finely in a white, three-piece suit, white cowboy boots, and a white silk tie and white shirt, and he introduced us to a high-heeled, black woman he called Annette.

"You're Manny's friend? I've heard so much about you

from his dad," Annette said when she shook my hand with more affection than I'd anticipated.

Manny? No one called him Manny. Did they? But, the reverend was now singing out across the house, "Manny! Manny! Manny!" When I asked Salazar about it, he said Annette had nicknamed him Manny when he was small. "She, Papi, and Mamá had gone to Yates together."

Father Salazar put his arm around Anette's neck. "These two trouble-makers are going to drive around tonight. Right? Westheimer Road?"

"Our Lord Jesus reminds us," said Salazar, "if you find a good thing, you get favor from the Lord."

Father Salazar giggled, clapping his small, plain hands.

"Where does it say that?" asked Annette, whose boldness seemed diminished.

"Proverbs," Salazar answered and bowed low to his father, the ex-*el sacerdote*.

Leaning against the doorframe of the sliding glass door to the backyard, Father Salazar casually spoke about the meaning of the proverb, sometimes speaking in English, other times Spanish, but it appeared, all in all, he was defending it, admiring its spirit of carnality. Talk like that surprised me, so open, in front of us, Annette, Mamá Salazar. It was unlike anything expressed in my house, where everyone stayed on message about three things and three things only: Jewish ancestry, Jewish posterity, and Jewish endurance.

OUTSIDE THE PICKUP, the wind and waves were hurling after each other.

I lit a new joint and held the smoke inside my lungs.

Here, a yellow helicopter came overhead.

"Noisy locust," said Salazar.

"Can't faze us."

The helicopter clicked around and circled off. There was

a siren. On the sidewalks people running. A black woman in a blue dress stepping outside her Oldsmobile station wagon, leaning outwards. She grinned and turned back inside.

"Ever imagine there's two guys sitting side by side in a pickup on the other side of all that water? Two guys, like us," Salazar said, "sitting side by side talking about helicopters. Way out there. Other side. Protestant and Jew, maybe. Or, maybe, they're Buddhist and Hindu."

"I do now."

"Which one?"

"Buddhist and Hindu? I don't know, man. Muslim," I said. "Muslim and whatever the Incas believed in. The Incas would be down that way."

"Aztecs, man. Mayans."

"Incas weren't down there?"

"Okay. Our dopplegangers are Inca and Aztec, sitting in an old Ford pickup. Not Protestant and Jew. Burning down some big, fat, soft Aztec gold," he said. "Not this cheap Godwin Park reefer some mama's boy grew in his closet with a grow lamp. Some kid who is going to end up robbing banks."

Something inside my head began to crackle, like a taunt, then went quiet. The traffic, helicopter, siren, people loafing on the sand amongst the cars and trucks. I inhaled them with another toke, gripped the smoke inside the narrow middle of my lungs, eyes closed, body at rest, skin smoothed out, eyes open, gone.

Salazar tapped his fingertips on the dashboard. "Yeah, now," he sang out.

"Yeah, now." I exhaled the smoke from my lungs.

"We're not easing away from the world, man," he said.

"Easing into it."

"Yeah, now."

The high began to flourish, a slippery, frisky, rapid high. Into my imagination came odd moments, crevices and shutterings, like the air before a storm, with an aroma, like long grass, shrinking away. The wind weaving in midair. The

beach like a mood, the sounds of the voices outside—gathered
near the surf between the jetties—a blood rush, such that this
whole sequence of unflinching moments seemed entirely true.
Here, the high tightened, snapped like wind. An enormous
wind swept inside of me. It was, at first, and only very briefly,
strange to emerge from the pickup just then: the click of tires
on wide Seawall Boulevard behind us, the call of honking and
beeping horns, the sound of Salazar fiddling with his keys as
he hid them up under the fender above one of the front tires.

I stopped and looked at him. He could make out what I
was feeling, how I was slowly hauling myself into myself. The
sky quavering, attached to everything that could disappear. I
stayed still, looking up ahead at the waves, wondering about
the secret world we were living in, the horizon beyond the
water an uninterrupted line of brightly lit offshore oil rigs and
shipping tankers.

The surf was pillowy and fresh.

The helicopter was gone.

Salazar said he wanted to go for a swim, and if I didn't want
to, not to wait, he'd find me, he said, "out there in the land of
the Texicans."

FIRST, THOUGH, HE WANTED TO CHECK the Astros game, and he
flipped the radio to KNTH. It was the middle of the fifth.
Nolan Ryan, who'd already struck out six batters, said the even-
keeled play-by-play guy Gene Elston, had yet to give up a hit.

We settled in and lit cigarettes.

Through the tinny truck speakers, the Astrodome sounded
like an alternate universe, but still finite, clusters of fans in
their seats, with a lot of bumping of knees and elbows and
hips. The city—that year of the Major League Baseball strike—
was mixed about the Astros, though the team was hanging onto
a game-and-a-half lead for first place over the Dodgers. In his
previous ten starts, dating back to May, Ryan had pitched four

two-hitters. Every time he pitched, especially at the Dome, the assembling crowd was hopeful that this might be the time he could get his next no-hitter, his fifth, and that would be the all-time record. His four previous no-hitters—against Kansas City and Detroit in '73, Minnesota in '74, Baltimore in '75—put him tied with Sandy Koufax for the most no-hitters ever. In the Dome, I was sure, people were probably feeling breathless—a no-hitter going for five innings. No doubt, there were plenty of French fries and hot dogs and double-patty burgers and people hurrying to and from the john or the beer stand. Since I was in first or second grade, I'd been listening to Gene Elston on the radio call the Astros games. Some nights, especially when the Astros played a West Coast game, I fell asleep to the sound of his Midwestern voice. I knew all the Astros players, and who the reserves were on the bench, and who was in the bullpen. I knew their names from listening, day after day, to the radio, and read their names in the box scores in the *Houston Chronicle* the morning after each game, and on their baseball cards I kept on my desk.

Salazar and I had seen Ryan's last home start, eleven days earlier, against the Reds. Parked in the pickup alongside Godwin Park on Balmforth Lane, listening to the early innings on the radio, while passing a joint between us, by the third inning, after Ryan had yet to give up a hit, we decided we had to drive over there. Inside the Dome, beneath the rumble, that night, near to us was a little black kid with an afro chanting, "Strike 'em out, Noly," and next to him a little white girl leaping from her seat to the ground and back, and her mother scolding, "Sit your rumpus down." There was a lady with bleached blonde hair who was scratching the Adam's apple of her neck, a Mexican old timer standing in a tucked-in, snap-button denim shirt and applauding alone as the Astros players milled in the dugout. Behind us: "You going to eat that?" a father asks a son, taking the rest of the peanut bag. Here, beer venders came through with rangy voices. *Cold beer here! Cold beer! Coldest foam in the Dome!*

Thousands of dusty shoulders. Hunters and lawyers and school kids and garbagemen, ex-cons and ladies from the Baptist choir and telephone linemen, cross-dressers, strippers, and high school sweethearts. Some rubbing the edges of their programs, others rumpling the wax of their hot dog wrappers.

The beach wind quieted.

With Ryan warming up in the bottom of the fifth, Gene Elston was saying Ryan appeared stiff, as if he was tired of his own body. Salazar and I knew Ryan was a student of the game, a thinking man's pitcher. Maybe he thought too much. But, it made him resourceful and humble. He played with restraint and discipline, as if he was still in awe of the game. With the Astros up, 2-0, Ryan made short work of the order in the fifth. Fly out, ground out, strike out. One, two, three. Down went the Dodgers.

In the sixth, Ryan struck out two more.

With two outs in the seventh, the score board flashed—

STRIKE 'EM OUT!
STRIKE 'EM OUT!

Dodgers catcher Mike Scioscia stepped in to bat. He'd struck out in the second and struck out in the fourth.

Ryan looked in. Delivered.

Next came the biggest scare when Scioscia swung at the pitch, a fastball, and he hit it deep to right center field. Terry Puhl, going back, running at full speed, nearing the wall, at the track, reached out and made the catch, trotting to a stop back on the green Astroturf.

The crowd cheered all the way through the seventh inning stretch.

In the eighth, the only fright for Ryan was wiry José Cruz charging in from left to make a tough catch on a blooper behind the shortstop. The crowd celebrated with the long, joyful, crooning anthem: *Crooooooooooooooooz*.

In that incredible moment when Ryan straggled to the mound in the bottom of the ninth, tugged his britches, bent at the waist to get the signals from the catcher, Alan Ashby, and the crowds' cheers began to rise, the din through the pickup truck's speakers like the sound of a seashell held to your ear, it wouldn't matter if I'd heard ten-thousand baseball games on the radio at that point in my life. I knew that when a man is pitching a no-hitter for eight innings, it's woozy stuff. I imagined, across the stands, all around, there was an unshaped mass of people. A blend of white hair and straight hair, cropped hair and big hair, big curls and small curls, looks of anxiety and distraction, the sudsy eyed, and bulgy eyed, the raised fists, spindly waists, the half-pissed and the entirely pissed, the boozy and the growlers, elbow to elbow, agents of salt and beer and heat and ready for anything, but mostly shock, while gazing down at the little hill where Ryan toed the white rubber. I, too, felt like standing, swinging and swaying.

The next six minutes began with Reggie Smith, batting in place of Davey Lopes.

Smith took his practice swings in the batter's box, then waved the bat in circles like a man swatting at a fly near his eyes. Gene Elston was saying that, earlier, taking batting practice before the game, Smith hit a foul ball up into the batting screen. The ball came down, bounced, hit him in the mouth, and knocked him to his knees. Well, he'd recovered, and, now, he was facing Nolan Ryan, who'd retired twenty four in a row and struck out ten, and not allowed a hit—though one came very close in the seventh inning with Mike Sciocsa's drive into right center, and Terry Puhl making the long running catch.

When Ryan looked in, the crowd rose to their feet.

Salazar and I opened another couple beers and lit cigarettes.

Fastball. Strike. 0-1.

Slow curve. 0-2.

No one was sitting in the stadium. Not even the players.

Third pitch. Swing and a miss. Down goes Smith. Strike out number eleven.

The players on the Astros' bench were pressed up to the top railing. All the Astros were cheering for what could become the greatest no-hitter in history. The Dodgers' bench was standing too. They can't like what they're seeing. But, it's historic, and they are a part of it.

Gene Elston sets the stage: Ryan circling the mound with his glove loosely hanging off his left hand, waiting for the next batter. Now, he bent at the waist and took in the signs. Two outs away from a fifth no hitter. The batter, the left-hander Landrieu. Struck out, walked, and grounded out.

First pitch. A high fast ball. Landrieu fouls it off the umpire's mask. 0-1.

Ryan is working fast. Circles the mound, bends at the waist. The sign. Rocks. Delivers. Fastball. Low. 1-1.

In between pitches, Gene Elston is talking about the crowd going quiet, as in a trance—even, at the beach, listening on the radio as the waves slunk in and slunk out, we know our role is to wait, to submit, to spin down into our seats and backspin up again when the action returns. We don't speak. Gene Elston, native of Fort Dodge, Iowa, always called the game without embellishment. He'd say: "Pitch outside. 3-0." Then, silence. Might not say a word, until— "Here's the pitch. Strike called. Three balls and one strike." No fancy home run call. Not: *It Is High, It is Far, It Is Gone*! Not: *Get Up, Baby, Get Up*! Not: *Fly Fly Fly Away*!

Just: "Pitch on the way. Swung on. Foul."

Then, Elston would pause, let the crowd noise seep in.

In the minutes of intense camaraderie, I tried to soothe myself by rustling the paper bag that held the beer, like I was rustling a bag of popcorn so the kernels filter to the bottom. Salazar was calm as concrete. But, he was blinking his eyes, as if calculating the moral force of the moment by lifting his face toward the roof of the truck, and holding his hands on top of his head and mouthing what might be a prayer. "I can't stand this. Don't let me blink," Salazar said and turned to look down the beach at the goings on, while inside the radio, in the crowd noise, we knew, were the roughs, the businessmen, the ladies with scorecards, the cotton candy guys, Bible hawkers, the beer guy—*Beer here! Sweet beer!*

Gene Elston: Ryan's 1-1 pitch to Landrieu, inside. Ball two.

Ryan paced around the mound and tugged at his sleeves. Retired twenty five hitters in a row. One out in the ninth. The last Dodger to get aboard was Landrieu, who walked way back in the third inning.

The next pitch to Landrieu. Breaking ball in the dirt. Ball three. 3-1.

Nolan Ryan had come so close to this moment many times. Since his last no-hitter, six years ago, in 1975, he'd pitched seven one-hitters. But the magical fifth no-hitter had eluded him.

Next pitch.

Ground ball to Walling at first, who steps on the bag, for out number two.

Now, thirty-three thousand fans inside the Houston Astrodome were standing.

I imagined the living rooms across the city. Fathers and sons, mothers and daughters—some watching and cheering at the TV screen, others leafing through a news magazine from inside the kitchen, the game on in the other room. Boys playing with their baseball cards. Men and women trotting back and forth to the kitchen to fetch margaritas from the blender. Salsa and chips. Or one has taken to his bedroom to watch alone. Or one has been sent to their room because it's past bedtime but is allowed to have a transistor radio going and doesn't close the curtains to feel closer to life as the bright light above the garage door, where the orange basketball hoop hangs lonely as a forgotten knot, and the gnats fly crazily around the solitary bulb.

Here, Ryan trudged up to the top of the mound to face the hottest Dodger hitter, Dusty Baker, standing in his way.

Baker, hitting .319, had grounded out twice and struck out.

I said, "Ryan, when he's on the mound, he's got a

weightless charm, that guy."

Salazar nodded. "Like he can feel his way through shadows."

A high noise from the crowd, when Dusty Baker stepped in and waved the bat twice.

The first pitch. High. Ball one.

What a sweet, beautiful moment—Nolan Ryan on the mound. Pitching no-hit baseball for eight-and-two-thirds innings. 26 outs, with one to go. Salazar and I—listening to Gene Elston's gentle voice on the radio—drinking beers, smoking cigarettes. The seagulls squawking.

Ryan sets, leg kick, and the pitch.

Breaking ball in the dirt. 2-0 to Dusty Baker.

Ryan walks twice around the mound, wipes his fingers under the bill of his cap. The crowd on its feet, cheering wildly. Gene Elston on the radio, saying: Ryan pitched his first no-hitter of his major league career on May 15, 1973, against Kansas City. He had twelve strike outs in that one. That same year, July 15, seventeen strike outs, no-hitter against Detroit. The next year, 1974, he no-hitted the Minnesota Twins, with fifteen strikeouts. And, then, in 1975, no-hitter number four, against the Baltimore Orioles. Trying to get another one today. Elston, the voice from Fort Dodge, Iowa, talking slow, very even, saying Baker was standing in Ryan's way, saying, "Two balls and no strikes to Baker. It's a ground ball to third! He has got it—Art Howe. He got it! Nolan Ryan! No-hitter number five!"

The crowd goes berserk. Explosive sounds of fireworks through the radio speakers.

On the scoreboard, inside the Astrodome, the Eighth Wonder of the World, we knew, was the head of a yellow steer. An American flag coming out of one horn, Texas flag coming out of the other. Smoke shooting from the nostrils in bright red clouds.

I imagined the Astros players rushed the field. Some pulled up to embrace Ryan like worshippers at the tomb of their God. Players quickly gathered around the scrum. Someone wrapped his arm around Ryan's head like he's a son returned from years lost at sea, and he kissed Nolan on the forehead. Players were hoisting the big right-hander from Alvin, Texas, onto their shoulders. He's waving his orange cap, glove in hand.

Salazar and I were now standing outside the pickup, arm in arm. My face ached from the tension. A record fifth no-hitter, and we'd heard it. Nolan Ryan, I was sure, was walking toward the dugout alone, breathing hard with a mixture of seriousness and joy, showing no trace of what the game might mean to him, and the stadium like a sheen, and the crowd of people pushing toward the stairs with their hair ablaze, wrung out, flushed, trotting down the narrow stairs toward the exit ramps, some stopping at the railing for one last look at the emptying field under the Dome, with business-suited men laughing and flapping their arms like birds, ghostlike, and people, already in the gravel parking lot, climbing up lampposts, slow-moving cars honking joyfully in the darkness.

For a few minutes we talked about how the game was now in our blood. We were sure this was the key to a sensation we could hold onto that could still dizziness. The broken shards of the universe seemed, suddenly, from the strength of Lynn Nolan Ryan, Jr.'s right arm, to have reformed into one swinging wholeness before all of it, just as surely, quickened into the past.

SALAZAR STRETCHED AND PERFORMED a half dozen awkward jumping jacks, stripped off his shoes and socks, but left his tee shirt on, wrapped a towel around his waist and switched out of his underwear for a pair of long, black swim trunks with pockets, and began walking toward the low waves. In the darkness, with lights from the cars fluttering over the beach, he looked like a guy entering the inner life of where the world had begun. He dropped to his stomach and did twenty push ups, each time smacking his face into the oncoming surf. Backed up twenty paces and returned to the open window on the driver's side, where I was sitting.

"Swimming in the sea is the greatest book I've underlined," he said and stared into my eyes as if that was all there was to it.

"The greatest?"

"As it must be. How else am I to know life?" he asked. "To know it and write it? Its substantiation. Its depth. It's the only way to live. That game, man. Got to celebrate. I feel free."

"There's always boot camp," I said, thinking it pleased me to see him return to the truck and do this pre-oration before swimming.

"And, what is greatness for Duke tonight?"

"I'm going to walk. Walk as far as I can, far outside this corner of existence, man. That's my greatness. That's it."

"Who you going to take with you? Because I'm going to the sea."

I was feeling very high. "You know, man, sometimes I like to imagine I'm on my last day. I look, for the very last time, at this beautiful Gulf of Mexico, at your beautiful pilgrim-loving face, and I could just leave it all behind. That's it. But, life would not be beautiful any longer."

"Or comfortable," he said.

"Let's get out of here. Fuck it," I said. "Let's go to Padre. Brownsville. I'll drive. Six months. Live on the border. We'll have long breakfasts in the sunlight. Get some golden bud, and, you know, figure it out," I said and wondered what Salazar might make of all that.

"Not asking for much, are you? You're not the type, to disappear and do nothing. You're not a beach bum. How much money you got on you, anyways? Not like we're outlaws. I repeat: Not like we're outlaws."

"What does that mean?" I said.

"You're going away from here, man? Away from all this? That's your destiny?" he said. "Padre Island, man? Not with me. I'm going to boot camp in El Paso. Maybe I get stationed in Puerto Rico."

"Not my destiny? Why?"

"Why? Why? Why not? What's with you, man? Come swimming."

"Why?"

"Because I want you to, Duke. You don't just leave your girlfriend because you want to walk away. You don't just leave your family. You, who thinks there's no middle ground. You think you're doomed. You're doomed to become a beacon of light. Oy vey, for you. Oy vey! You, who is terrified of being stuck with your beauties. You're a very beguiling motherfucker. Aren't you? But, also remote. Don't deny it. Duke in his remote castle. That's you. You're in a thousand-mile moat."

"I thought I was in the castle."

"Castle. Moat. Whatever. Fuck you. You're in it. You're in the castle. You think you're in the moat. You're not. Intersecting lines. Didn't you learn shit?" he shouted. "You don't get outside the castle, man. It's a box. You're the box. You are the box."

"Okay, Padre. That's some sacred geometric shit. In nomine patris, et filii, et spiritus sancti in a box with a fox in a moat with Sam I am. Amen," I said, and crossed myself.

"Duke, that's the Catholics. Jesus. Read the room. We're done here. I got to swim."

"I got to brood."

Salazar blew kisses with his hands. "Well you just wipe your little mind first. Okay? Wipe your little 45 of a brain," he said. "You're playing the same song over and over. Wipe the grooves. Wipe the edges. And play your beautiful thoughts. You think life is freedom. Freedom, freedom, freedom. That's all you want. Life is not freedom, Duke. It's not."

I watched Salazar trot toward the long waves, under the cloudy dark. "Don't drown, God dammit," I called, leaning my head back, and with terrible, meticulous detail, replaying the whole conversation—and yet I did want to follow him out there, unchained from what was waiting for me back at home.

LOYAL TO THE ROYAL

WHO COULDN'T SPARK UP another joint after that?

I didn't even wait for Salazar to sink his toes into the water.

I reached into the glovebox and pulled out a cigarette, plastic sandwich bag of weed, and a paper clip. Scraping out the tobacco from the cigarette, I mixed it with the pot, sank a pinch inside the sleeve, packing it full. I held the slender spliff to the light. When I sniffed at it, a fleck shook out. I could have tapped in more but didn't. Instead, I folded the plastic bag and paper clip back into the glovebox. For a brief time, I held the cigarette in my hands and stared at the cracks in the black dashboard that split, like dried mud, toward the windshield.

At last, I got out of the truck, walked around to the front, and sat on the hood. Lightly I ran my hand across the warm metal. In the distance I could see heat lightning flaring in the long sky.

Climbing back into the truck, on the driver's side, I looked through the stack of books on the seat, and held them in my hands, angled so the streetlights above the seawall shined on them. At first, I bent open the selection of Neruda poems, with its heavy gray print and read, without focusing on any of the words, for my mind was still on the tiff with Salazar. Finally, I flipped through the pages and stopped to read a stanza. I wasn't sure what to make of it, and wondered what Salazar was thinking when he'd underlined "Streets," circled "Became staircases," and double-underlined "your love, your son, your dinner plate," until

I remembered he had been reading a poem every day by Neruda, untwining phrases he favored and threading them through the eyelets of his own musings, which he wrote down as "poetries," as he called them, each night before he went to sleep. In the mornings, he woke early and typed out what he had and slid the paper neatly into a folder he kept in the bottom drawer of Monk's Island. This, he said, holding the wad of papers stuffed into a folder over his head one afternoon after school, is for when I'm no longer around—it's my voice turned to salt.

The copy of *Invisible Man* was dogeared. After spending nearly every day with Salazar for three years, I could understand why he kept folding and creasing Ralph Ellison's book. He took it practically everywhere. His favorite passage was, *I remember that I'm invisible and walk softly so as not to awake the sleeping ones,* which he whispered whenever he spoke it. Invisible? I teased back, I'd have thought visible is more like it. He'd whisper, Beware the sleepwalker.

The rest were school books, including the neglected Dante, underneath Salazar's paperback of *Leaves of Grass.* I spent the next few minutes reading the last sections from "Song of Myself," about the past and present wilting and folding into the future, and wondering who might miss me, or search for me, and would I stop somewhere waiting for them—until all of that and the argument with Salazar began echoing in my head, along with the high from the spliff, and the long buzz from the beers I'd been downing since morning that were cushioning a sore spot.

The lights from Seawall Boulevard had a pleasant flow to them that carried down to the sand and out into the water, then skimmed the surf and twinkled a ways out before going dark, all in one swoop. The beach was filled with echoes, like they were trapped in the sand. There were rustlings and laughter— laughter that sounded worn out—fading in the wind.

I pulled out my little notebook and wrote down details from the argument so I could think about it later when I was straight.

This I wrote on the pages that followed the words I most wanted to say to Rabbi Gadol when, late nights, I sat up in bed in my room and, with an ordinary pen, made a record of my life. I'd written a dramatization of what my father and I might say to each other, over and over, not the arguments we actually had, but arguments I would not have had the courage to say to his face. Inside my notebook, at that time, were all the things I'd been wanting to say to my father, from the moment I woke in the morning until I went to sleep at night, and perhaps even while dreaming. But, the words would fade once we were actually in each others' presence, and lived only in what I could get down quickly in my notebook—then the words were held there for all time on the paper, like mysteries from my mind.

I wanted, in those days, to get closer to what was most raw about my own existence with the same urgency someone else might want to forget a period of their life. On the top of each page I wrote in block letters: REMEMBER. If literature could be drawn from the sand hills of Judea, I figured, it could be wrested from the mowed lawns of Meyerland. That's why I kept the notebook. I remember there was a man I often walked past in the morning on Rice Avenue on my way to school. He was probably setting out for work. What I took notice about him was that he carried a yellow satchel and walked slowly. One morning, I did more than nod hello, but asked how his day was, and called out to him, *Beautiful day*! We struck up a conversation. He worked at an accounting firm. His name was Shaw, or Short, I wasn't certain what I'd heard. There were other details I couldn't remember, and that's when I determined to keep a small notebook that fit inside my pocket, and to record things like that.

Faced with my own words with Salazar, I flipped back a few pages to ease my mood and read what I'd written during the week, though it wasn't much. It was reading from my notebook that lead me to remember how much I was struggling to find the strength to explain to my father what had been keeping me up nights and causing me to want to leave home, as if, by some miracle, I could translate myself from son-of-a-rabbi rectitude to a fresh, exquisite earthiness, burdened by nothing more than adventure. Vivid adventure—allusive, capricious, tactile, exuberant, unchained adventure from three thousand years of well-heeled existence—and become a man, alone. Until then, my future had been engraved. What was my future but to follow him, my father, Rabbi Zebulun Benjamin Ben-Mordecai Wain, who was born in Jerusalem, in 1935, emigrating to America at the age three, ordained at the Jewish Theological Seminary and the University of Judaism, serving as a rabbi initially in Houston, then, briefly, Akron, Los Angeles, Dallas, until returning finally, again, to Houston? Him, who followed his father, Rabbi Mordecai Ben-Shlomo Wain, who was born in Hosel, Russia, in 1898, who worked his way through the traditional Jewish educational system from cheder to yeshiva, joined the Zion movement, graduated from City College of New York, and ordained at the Seminary, and was rabbi of several influential synagogues in the Bronx, Jerusalem, Chicago, and Dallas?

Two weeks earlier, after school, on a hot, sunny, humid afternoon, I was walking into the house when I found my father sitting alone in the kitchen with his sermon book open on the table and a silver Cross pen laid upon it. Even before I entered the room, I heard the refrigerator churning. I set my school books on the counter, grabbed a Coke, said hello, picked up my schoolbooks, left him alone, and closed the door to my small bedroom, taken up mostly with a slender bed, high boy dresser, and accordion closet inside of which I had squeezed a small desk, stacked with books, notepads, a blue mug with a broken handle for pens and pencils, baseball cards, candy wrappers. Our house was stuffed with books. They were stacked, wall to wall, in every nook and cranny, in the hallways and the bathrooms and the foyer and under windowsills. Whether they were paperbacks or bound with rough leather, whether they contained information

I couldn't understand or illustrated stories for children, whether they were written in Hebrew or English, Italian or French, whether the bindings held or tore away when you rubbed them, I loved to touch all the books, hold them, sniff their bewildering smells. Inside them, as inside scripture, were life's permissions and denials, the innocent and the outlandish, the conventional and the grotesque. The aroma has never left me. The dusty, alluring odor of landscapes and dialogue and the silences of lonely hearts, the seclusions of unrequited love, secrets of ghosts, moans of animals, murmurs of the elderly, ambition and cravings of those long dead staring out of mirrors.

Working on his weekly sermon usually gave my father deep satisfaction, sometimes a thrill. When he wrote a phrase he was proud of or found a nuance of interpretation that pleased him, he'd exclaim, *Now that's something!* Frustrated, he'd groan—you could hear him from the next room, moaning—*the subject, the subject, Benyamin! The subject!* Shouting, in Hebrew, *Sim lev*, pay attention, like a stern coach growling at a player, disoriented from exhaustion, to keep his eye on the ball.

Rabbi Gadol was often remote and mysterious, a broad-bellied man with a head of thick, gray hair. Points of view that veered from his own long-held biases as a conservative rabbi of a breakaway congregation—once located in West University and now situated near a strip mall on the border between Old Braeswood and Meyerland—aggravated him. His reputation was for rigor. He had established the first Jewish day school in Harris County, been president of the Jewish Teachers Association, reorganized the Texas Hebrew School system, lectured throughout the state on behalf of the Zionist Organization of America, and was president of the Texas Assembly of Rabbis. Of his sermons, there was never mysticism attached to them. He didn't go for obscure rabbinic legends, folk dramas, Kabbalistic tales, Hasidic yarns. The interpretation of letters or numbers had their place. But they weren't miraculous. He would never utter a sacred charm or hermetical formula. His answers to your questions came in short bursts. He had to be invited to tell his genesis story of becoming a rabbi, that it was the family trade going back so many generations: great-great-great-great-great, great-great-great-great, great-great-great, great-great, great-grandfathers, grandfathers, and father. He only spoke of the wild logic of the journey itself. Even in his directness there was little fascination with chance. What interested him was that his congregants—*my students*, he called them—remain far from intellectual and spiritual squalor. Not once do I remember him speaking of yearnings or disappointments. Even of things from when he was young. He preferred the ordinary breath to the magical potion. On rare days, he took me along on his hospital visits. We crisscrossed the medical district near Holcombe Boulevard. We sat bedside and said sh'ma with business owners and with paupers. As a treat, we sometimes stopped on our way home at Dino's in Bellaire so my father and I could sneak fries and a milkshake without Batya the Rock finding us out. No sooner had we ordered and sat in a booth than he began telling secrets about each congregant we'd met with. He'd say, "You'll need to know this. Take the Klaffs, okay? You're going to have your Klaffs someday as your students. Mr. and Mrs. Klaff, Ira and Rina, they've been utterly devoted to each other, but childless, forty-seven years. Lavish affection on each other. He's got the congestive heart failure now. She pampers him like an only child. When I go to visit him, at their home, she's got him swaddled in a black afghan blanket so warmly she has to set the AC to sixty-six degrees. It's freezing inside the Klaff's house. All so he won't catch cold. So, remember, always wear a warm blazer when you visit a family at home." And, things like that.

My father had by then been at Beth Tikkun almost all his rabbinic life. In shul, he was sometimes gregarious, other times tart, intensely sharp. Something of a Yiddish'y sweet talker. Something of a zealot. Something of a bureaucrat. Hardly the Hollywood caricature of the mumbling Rabbi Schlub. His revered study groups of Hebrew scriptures—known as TNT for Torah In Texas—was popular with congregants because he dealt with everything Jewish as a modern intellectual question steeped in ancient language. You know what's great about Torah? he'd ask—even as the class was still settling into its seats on the first day of the year-long study. It always comes down to letters of the alphabet, he'd say. Slanted lines interrupted by wiggles. That's where meaning begins. In the marks on the parchment. The genius of it. Slanted lines interrupted by wiggles. Like a dance. You and the Hebrew letters make up life. That's right, he'd say, and he'd hoist his black, hard-bound copy of the Torah above his head and bring it to his eyes and then read a line, at random. First, he spoke the words in Hebrew, then sight-translated them into English, say, from Psalms: *Our soul waits for the Lord; He is our help and our shield.* But that one line would be too idiosyncratic and not offer him enough, so, while closing the book, and laying it gently onto the table, he'd add, as if from memory, a phrase from the next line, in Hebrew followed by the English: *For our heart will rejoice in him.* And, why, he would ask, do hearts rejoice at all—which he pronounced, a'tall? Why does your heart or yours or your heart rejoice at all, he'd ask pointing directly at his students. Look closely at the word: *Yee-sh'ma.* Rejoice. Be happy. Be joyful. Two dozen times in Torah appears the word, *Yee-sh'ma.* Two dozen times. It would appear, would it not—his best known tic, *would it not*—it would appear, would it not, that the writers and sages of Torah want us to know that the good Lord does not want us to give up joy. When you suffer, when demands are put upon you, the good Lord insists you, finally, after all the suffering, after all the demands, turn from pain. *Yee-sh'ma.* Be joyful. But, you feel you need something in exchange. You're a capitalist. No? No? Don't you? Something in exchange? Thus, you reignite your pain. You become explosive. Your sense of your own self worth is an impulse that will not let you give up your pain. You feel alienated. You feel estranged, even from yourself. You isolate yourself. You defy society. We all know friends and family who have behaved thus. We all have succumbed ourselves. No? No? Don't you know someone? But, the good Lord is a generous protector. The good Lord is glorious. The good Lord has provided these slanted lines and wiggles, these dancing letters, as a shield, so that whatever brutal suffering you experience—and we all do, we all will. No? No? Yes, we all will suffer. But, we must return. *Yee-sh'ma.* To be joyful. *Yee-sh'ma.* To rejoice. And so, would it not be wise that we begin here today with this very question plucked at random from Torah? Why rejoice? What is the meaning of joy? And, as he posed that question, he patted his heart with the flat of his palm in order, he announced, to remind himself to keep ticking. It was a simple gesture, if one were needed, of all the little motions a body makes during an entire life, of the hurricane of details that fashion the trajectory of any single person's biography—a simple gesture to remind him that time was passing.

When he posed this kind of question, it was impossible not to notice the crevices carved deeply into his forehead, and in the brown eyes there was to be perceived the indelible energy he brought to everything. As rabbi, he had taken this quiet shul on the border between Old Braeswood and Meyerland by pushing out the board of directors' old guard and recruiting ambitious community men and women to remodel the daily and weekly services, as well as the education programs. Although he was still some years from retirement, already there was rumored to be architectural drawings for the Rabbi Zebulin B. Wain Study Hall, to be built adjacent to the gift shop. Already there were interior designs, shared privately among board members, of where on the walls would go the bookshelves and where would go reproductions of photographs from the rabbi's life—here he is, leading the Texas Jewish Museum's groundbreaking ceremony, leading the Texas Jewish Historical Society, leading the Society for Judeo-Crypto Studies, the Texas Holocaust Resource Center, leading the American Jewish Committee's subcommittee for Peace in the Middle East, and receiving the Exodus Prize from the Israeli Knesset for achievement in Jewish community building outside Israel, as well as photographs framed from his personal life, including a sepia image of his own father, as a small boy, during his harrowing escape from Russia, as well as bound editions of my father's sermons, many of which were collected in two editions, *Jews of the South and Civil Rights* in which, begins the Preface, "These sermons are the occasions of my own mind in conversation with the good Lord," and *Living Originally: Finding Meaning, Spirituality, and a Deeper Connection to Life in Judaism*, published on the occasion of his twenty-fifth year in the Rabbinate. And yet, on some of those occasions, after he had finished writing his weekly sermon, I would find him crying by himself at the kitchen table, bereft over something I dared not ask about, which he would have refused, anyway, certainly, to divulge. Was it that he feared the sermon would not garner the admiration he wished for from his congregants? Was it that he felt he had not written beyond his own ingrained habits and secretly despised himself for it? Was it that he was flush with desire to please the good Lord and, overcome by his failure, felt shame, indecent, transgressive?

Everything about what happened next is confused in my memory. For a long time, we both, through callousness or neglect, to avoid acknowledging what was looming between us, had not exactly toned down our conversation, but looked elsewhere. That afternoon, my father's breathy words, spoken in implosive whispers, had summoned me back into the kitchen, and, perilously, I had walked back down the hallway, while hearing the clank of the refrigerator, with my empty glass, and set it in the porcelain sink.

"Young man," he said deliberately, as if all that time he had been writing, not a sermon, but what he wanted to say that afternoon. But, he said no more, rubbing the pen with his fingertips, rolling it open and closed, before setting it down on his notepad. He sipped from his glass of iced tea. Wiggled the wrinkled slice of lemon until it sank below the ice, and returned the glass to the corner of the white placemat. He didn't seem to know what he should do next, both he and the glass of iced tea uncommonly still, and I knew not to expect sympathy. His wide mouth was closed, the outline fixed, and his brow and his sloping cheeks gave off the usual air of prestige, and, in the bright kitchen, I could see a few brushstrokes of black hair amidst the white.

He ran his tongue over his lips, looked at me with his drooping blue eyes, and his thick head of hair, and said, "What are we going to do about you? Something's got to be done. What are we going to do? What are you thinking? The things you're doing when you're out with your pals—your special pal and his quack preacher father—are disgusting. You appear to be making us all here at home seem awfully unloved. That's how I look at it. That's how your mother looks at it. We love you. But, you're turning into a *shicker*, with all this drinking. Are there drugs? Don't tell me. Don't tell me. I don't want to hear. It's nonsense. You're not part of any other world but this one. You hear me? The fact remains. You're part of this story. It's the whole story. The only story as far as I'm concerned. And, without you carrying it forth, there will be no story at all. Who the hell is Manolo? He's nothing but heartache to me. Maybe he's a smart kid, like you say. But, the father? Stay away from him. Nobody in his right mind would get close to that man. He's a broom pusher, not a man of the cloth. Couldn't keep his word to his God. That good Jewish boy, Jesus! Blowhard. What you don't realize, young man, is that in Jewish families, traditional Jewish families like ours, we are bound to each other by a series of responsibilities and practices. Revere your parents. Parents who provide for their children. For the future. Why?"

"To honor God," I said.

"Oh! You're still my son after all? Very, very good to hear it. Then you do know what parents are?"

"God's representatives."

"God's representatives. That's right," he said. "You're going to have blood on your hands." He slammed a palm against the white placemat and knocked the glass of iced tea, but it didn't tip over. For twenty-five minutes, no biblical passage he quoted, no hard stare, no crossing of his arms, no him saying "That time you…" ran away or "That time you…" hit your sister or "That time you…" had disappointed your loving mother, your good mother, was without its sway over me. In this small, bright kitchen, with its cuttings of herbs and bowls of fruit, with the cabinets shut tight, with not a crumb to be witnessed, I had learned to pour milk, to fry an egg, had celebrated my birthdays, had argued and loved, been slapped on the rear end, had my skinned-up knees bandaged, had got the news that someone had died. To take life for granted in this small, bright kitchen was forbidden, if only because life insisted. Life commanded. Life urged, stood firm, laid down the law.

I said nothing about what I wanted, nor anything I'd written in my notebooks, and I hoped, by remaining silent, across the chasm between us could be found the entrance to what I most wanted, to be turned loose and set free from this side of the bayou where Meyerland Jews lived in hope of being left alone. Oh, sure, my father would say, let them take their children to dance classes and Little League games, to grandparents and great-aunts and great-uncles' houses, but would it kill them to visit synagogue more often than on High Holidays, or, God forbid, while mourning? Would it kill them to observe any other rituals at home—except, out of fidelity to some mysterious force passed down by guilt, the mother of the house lights Friday-night candles?

"I'm going to do my homework. I have a test tomorrow in history and a quiz in physics," I said.

"You haven't answered me."

"Is that necessary?"

"All right. Calm down," he said, in a breathful whisper.

"You want to hear what I have to say?"

"If that's what you'd like," he said.

"Don't you have to write your sermon?"

"It can wait."

"You really ought to get it finished. Mother will be home soon."

"Maybe you should sit down and help me write it."

"I've got to study."

"It can't wait?" he asked.

A car revved past the front of the house to the corner where our street opened onto Wigton Drive. Neither of us turned to watch it. The mailman was coming up the walkway, hitching his bag tighter onto his shoulder, the bag so heavy it looked like it was going to break his neck. He dropped the mail into the box and, without any interruption, strode off, as if frightened by something he'd seen. He hustled across the street.

"So?"

"He's my friend. I don't have any control over who his father is. Anymore—" I stopped, not wanting to say the rest out loud.

"Is that it?"

"You know what I mean," I said.

"This makes me proud? You're going to wish you didn't say that. I will tell you something, Yochanan. Between you and me and the Lord God above. Then, you can go do your studies. You think it over, and you tell me when you're ready what you've decided. You're my youngest child. My only son. Soon, you will be out in the world on your own. This morning I emptied my chest of drawers of all the things I no longer wear to give to Hadassah. I had three pairs of shoes to give, as well, but first I sat in the backyard and polished them. I had trouble finding my shoe shine kit, with the brushes and saddle soap, but found it in your room. I don't know why it was in your room. But, I'll get back to that. It was a peaceful morning. I went into your bedroom and found the things you'd set aside to donate to Hadassah, to perform *tzedekah*, as I had asked you, and added them to the donation. Donating clothing to Hadassah is something I've

been doing twice a year since I was a child. I'm trying to tell you
things so you understand your place, to remember what matters.
I do not feel as my great-grandfather on my Bubbe's side felt,
that we are cursed, this family. Cursed because his father, and
I know you've heard this before, the troubled Rabbi Stein, of
Toledo, attended the *Trefa* Banquet in Cincinnati, and caused a
schism in our family. What the hell kind of Jews go to a hilltop
resort and eats little neck clams? Clams! In Cincinnati! And
don't tell me it was the Gilded Age. Refrigeration. Don't tell
me this was going to be a magnificent night with judges and
rebbes and professors. Don't tell me it was going to be part
and parcel of this new, American, excessive, culinary culture.
That was going to be second to none, the best. Don't tell me.
Best wine. Best foods. It was supper. That's all. With clams.
Littleneck clams. God-damned littleneck clams out of season!
In God-forsaken Cincinnati! And, then, from there, they begin
to roll out the crab and the shrimp and lobster bisque and beef
in cream sauce, pigeon breasts, frogs legs. I'd have gone home
hungry, that's what I'd have done. Ever since then, we have the
new Jews. Beware new when it comes to Jews. They say, new. I
say, cheapened. And, none of your little jokes about the precious
Jewish stomach. About kitchen Jews. A mark is a mark. When
you have a mark, Yochanan, it leads to one thing. I don't have to
tell you what that is. Did your forebears die in Bergen-Belsen for
you to eat little neck clams in their trefa shells?"

"I wasn't in Cincinnati. All that happened before the Nazis.
Father Salazar is harmless," I said, counting out the three points
on my fingers.

"Father Salazar! Is that what you call him? You can keep
your silly nicknames to yourself. He's not Catholic anymore.
But, I'll tell you what. I'm going to tell you a story about your
harmless Father Salazar that'll make you sick to your stomach.
That scumbag stole tens of thousands of dollars. First, he got
himself kicked out of the priesthood because he couldn't keep
his zipper closed. Then he ran a scam where the poorest of the

poor all over Texas sent him money for their confessions, which he swore to pray over, swore to pray to the Holy Trinity on their behalf. What'd he think he was? Some kind of Oral Roberts—that huckster? He was a defrocked Catholic priest. But, did he pray? No. He threw the confessions in the dumpster and pocketed the money. Then, all of a sudden, boom, shazam, look at him now. He puts out his shingle as an Evangelical preacher. What's he do next? He filches from the kitty. Thousands of dollars go missing. Bet that preacher swindled a hundred-thousand dollars. He had a position of leadership. His parishioners trusted him to handle their generous donations from all over Texas, all over the South, to his broadcast ministry or whatever the hell rug salesman scam it was. He cheated them for his own personal gain. I was on the multi-denominational committee that recommended he be sued. You see the dress suits he wears? You think every defrocked, evangelical, country preacher in Texas can buy five-thousand dollar suits? And yet, our beloved justice system couldn't find anything wrong. Nothing at all. After all the headlines and all the investigations and all the audits, they couldn't find one thing that this man of God had done wrong. What do you make of that pack of lies? Because that's what that is. That's your Father Salazar. Better stay far away from that swindler. Believe me. Next time you see him, if he kisses you, count your teeth. You hear me? So? What do you say to that?"

"I wasn't in Cincinatti, and I'm not Reverend Salazar's bag man. That's what I say."

"Now he's *Reverend Salazar*. Okay. You are listening. Tell me, Yochanan, you ever see that man preach? Ever listened to his recordings? You watch yourself, bub. I have. Many a time. He can bring Jesus to the bottom of your soul, all right. I give him that, all right. He's got the gift. No doubt. Could talk a fish to come out of the bottom of the oceans on the promise it's okay to breath the fresh air. Here's a classic from José Salazar. I'll never forget hearing him preach this one time." Here my father changes his voice from his breathy whisper to sounding like a charismatic preacher on Sunday morning TV. He goes, "'Nothing better than Jesus! Nobody's ever impacted the world like Jesus did. Nobody's ever had the influence over people like Jesus Christ.' And, the people shouting back, 'like Jesus Christ!' He goes, 'Out of all the billions of people who walked on this planet, he has more influence on more people than any other one single human being. I'm glad to be his servant. He's my brother, even though he's a king.' This is what he says, and the people are hooked. He goes, 'He's the greatest thing ever happen to me. Best thing that ever happened to me was meeting Jesus. You're never the same after meeting Jesus. You never are. I've not been all I could have been. I've not been all I should've been. But, I've never been the same since I met the Lord Jesus Christ. He changed me. He changed me.' And there's tears in his eyes now. He goes, 'Bible says if any man be in Christ, he's a new creature. All things pass away. All things become new. So listen carefully, as I read you the scripture here in John, chapter 6 and verse 35: *And Jesus said unto them, I am the bread of life. He that cometh to me shall never hunger. And he that believes in me, shall never thirst.'* Oh, and now your Father Salazar is weeping. Hailstone-sized tears dropping out of his eyes and bouncing on the floor. He goes, 'Buddha never said nothing like that. Mohammed never, ever even come close to making a statement like that. Mohammed never told his followers, *I'm the bread of life. You come to me and you'll never hunger for anything else.* Why that's preposterous. That's ridiculous for a man to say something like that—unless he is who said he was, the son of God.'"

"I don't know what to tell you," I said, laughing at him hamming it up. "If it helps you any, we all know to keep our distance, even Manolo. I'm not going to get wrapped up in some laundering scheme."

"Well I can tell you," he said. "You could. You could get wrapped up. He's a seducer." He does Father Salazar's voice again. 'Buddha never said nothing like that. Mohammed never, ever even come close to making a statement like that.' Listen to me. Anyone could. But you're not anyone. Are you? No. You're someone. You're someone who is the son of a rabbi, and who is the grandson of two rabbis, and who is the great-grandson of one of the greatest rabbis ever, and who is the great-great-grandson of so many rabbis and beyond nobody can keep count. You're someone. And, now, you're someone who writes things, as I read in that notebook of yours I found when I was gathering up your *tzedakah* in your bedroom and looking for my shoe shine kit, in that little notebook you keep, jotting everything down in it all the time like you're some kind of undercover spy. What do you mean when you write, when you say, *If there were any truth in religion, there wouldn't really be any need for politics?* When you say, *Why is religion back in such a big way? Hezbollah and Messianic Jews?* You think we're all the same? When you say, *Judaism can't even give comfort to those facing death.* When you say, *I am one of those people who cannot believe.* When you say, *God is a tyrant.* When you say, *The Ten Commandments are a monstrous fraud. What a missed opportunity.* Shall I go on? You're ripe for the picking for a cassette tape huckster like José Salazar. Oh, he can bring it. I give him that. He's got talent. I saw him many Sunday mornings during the investigation. It was a little shopping mall church over in Gulfgate. He was on fire. Again with the charismatic voice, this time as if he's in tears, my father goes, "'Whatever you need, He is. Think about that. Think about that. Whatever you need. Somebody said, Boy, I tell you I just need some things in my life. Well I know what you need, you need Jesus. Somebody said, Well I'm having trouble with this. You need Jesus. Somebody said, Well I'm not happy here. You need Jesus. Happiness is, to know the savior. Living a life within his favor. Having a change in my behavior. Happiness is the Lord. I don't say Jesus has the answer. I say he is the answer. There's an empty spot on the inside of every person in this world that only Jesus can fit.'"

The back door opened and shut with a thwack.

Mother was home, calling hello as she walked through

the hallway into the kitchen past the humming refrigerator, balancing in her small arms a sack of groceries. It was a thwack that brought my father and me both to sigh—mine, like his, rounded and coarse.

What, I wondered, was going on here? My father wanted nothing to do with my problems. Uninterested, or was it ashamed, and he was regularly at the synagogue or the hospitals, traveling to give lectures. I felt my mouth slacken with a sore on the side of my tongue. He expected me to do right, that was all. Fall in line. Maybe, he was right. I wasn't up to his ideal.

In a breathy whisper, I said, "Is there, in any religion, anything that can't be duplicated by people just being good to each other? A single moral action performed or moral statement spoken by a Jew or a Catholic or Hindu or whatever, even a preaching huckster, that couldn't be just as well pronounced or undertaken by an atheist? The new Jew in the Old South lives and dies for, what? To stay in the ghetto? Is that all we are?"

He clasped his hands together, looking quickly in my mother's direction then back at me, and pointed his clasped hands at me. "Judaism does not deny reason or science or medicine," he said. "My faith is putting all that I am and all that I have on the line for all the things I do not know about, that are mysteries to me, and, most especially, in helping others, including you."

"I'm saying, by my questions," I answered, "that we know how to think, and how to laugh. We know we're all going to die. And, then, you know, that's it. Over. I don't trust anyone who doesn't respond, while they're living, to music, or poetry, or nature. I just don't. I think we need to separate those—whatever you want to call them—impulses, or needs, desires, whatever, from the supernatural, and the superstitious, and all the little squiggly letters and slanted lines."

"For crying out loud, Yochanan."

He pushed himself from the table, stood, crossed the kitchen floor to hastily kiss my mother on the cheek, whispered into her ear, as she pushed strands of graying red hair away, grabbed his keys and hat, pulled on a blue blazer, violently shoving his arms into the sleeves, and hulked out of the house through the front door, leaving it open behind him.

After any talk of this sort with my father, I generally felt beaten. I knew he was dissatisfied with me. If only I could say, simply, I'm not chained to the curse from the *Trefa* Banquet in Cincinnati, and neither are you. You ought to forget it, I wanted to say. What can I say to make you move on? I'm not kidding anymore, I wanted to say. We're not stuck in time. But he wouldn't have it.

After closing the front door and returning to the kitchen, Mother gave me a look that could have burned the skin from my bones.

A well-spoken, proper-looking woman, barely five feet tall, whose unabated energy was matched by the way she spoke, always in a rush, she was healthy, smiled easily, and did nothing I was aware of to excess. From her composure, her attire, her posture, from the intensity she exuded even while seated, it was clear that she had disciplined herself to live inside the lines of social convention as a rabbi's wife. Hers was the personality of the go-between, the peace-maker. Hers was the nature of the sensible advocate. And yet, the aura of rigidity surrounding every interaction in our house seemed like one dogged, willfully aloof, reckoning with fortitude.

"I'll go to my grave wondering what all this fighting is about with you people," she said. I sat at the table, deflated, and began reading to myself my father's new sermon. "I'll go to my grave chafing under all this bickering," she repeated. "All this one-ups-manship. Every one of you so determined. It's going to lead to hatred. Breaks my heart. Once you get a taste for hatred, you people, you're going to get more than you dreamed of. My life is about the three Rs. Responsibility. Respect. Righteousness. Don't you forget it."

She was putting away groceries, while also wiping down the counter at the same time with a sponge, as if being a rabbi's wife had taught her to intertwine clutter and tidiness in a single sweep of the hand, enduring order with interruption, difficulty with romance, affection with disappointment, welcome-home-darling with don't-be-late-darling, as the ladders and the ropes life had given her to cling to.

The sermon was titled, "Does the Good Lord Answer Our Prayers? Will the Good Lord Stop Bringing Us These Terrible Rains?" After the opening set up, he got to his message: "If we mean, Will the good Lord do whatever we want, the answer is no, not always. If we ask for something we can already do ourselves, no. Defy natural law? No. We must eat, we must sleep, we must exercise. And the good Lord's not your bookie either. That's not God's job. God brings the rain our farmers need, and God brings the sun to dry up the floods, no need to pray for that. God is already working on that. It's a good question, 'Does the good Lord answer our prayers?' But it's not the most important question. Torah doesn't tell stories for no reason. When the good Lord speaks to us, it is not in this week's flood and next week's sunshine. The good Lord speaks in the small voice of conscience. Just as when the good Lord appeared to Moses. When God appeared to Moses in the desert, God didn't come while Moses was in a crowd or at home with his family, in the clatter of the marketplace. He came to Moses's heart when Moses was alone and was ready to listen. The Psalms tells us what Moses says. He says, *I shall listen to what God will say.* When King Solomon spoke to God, he asked for a listening heart. Only in the loneliness of our hearts do we hear God's voice. I do not mean you should withdraw from the world. When that tropical storm came last week, it was good for you to go out and help your neighbor. But first it was inside the safety of your home that your heart heard the voice of God calling for you to go outside. *What should I do now?* You might have asked God then in prayer. *Go out and help your neighbor*, says God. So it was with Moses. In his confrontation with God in the desert, he was called to free the children of Israel from slavery. You may have been called to cart away a carpet, bring dinner to a hungry widow, take care of a friend's dog or cat. Why then do we try to get away from that important silence in our lives, get away from loneliness, and instead seek the noise of others, seek the marketplace, seek the crowds? Because we want to escape ourselves? Escape the searching of our souls? Escape from confronting the eternal problems of life? Friends, the rain is going to fall. The floods are going to come. And also, they are going to recede. Do you have the strength and courage to face yourself as who you are? To listen to the voice of your conscience? To be loyal to the royal that is in you? More rain is coming. We can't all be like Moses."

Father Salazar, he was not.

"You're going to kill that man. And, then, where will you be?" Mother said, unpacking the eggs and putting them gently on the top refrigerator shelf, while wiping the handle clean with a cloth afterward.

I pushed the pages with the sermon to the center of the table. "How can you take his side?"

"There are no sides."

"He never lets anyone say anything. And, he read through my notebook. What do I have to have to do? Leave home in order to think my own thoughts?"

"Don't say such things."

"He hardly knows me."

"Oh, ridiculous. He's given you everything."

"He hates my friends. My friends aren't a threat to the Jews."

"No. No, they probably are not," she said. "But, to you, they might be."

"You are on his side."

She was tying on a blue and yellow, pin-striped apron. "There are no sides. You don't get to say anything and everything, darling, or write down any old thing you want. Even you make mistakes. Just, please, don't pull me into the middle of this. My life is about the three Rs. Your father takes care of you, and he always will. He's planned to set up a fund for you in his will, but the economy is so bad now, he doesn't know what he can do. He has to rethink all of it, because of the economy. When you're older, you'll understand. He's under a lot of pressure. There are bills to be paid. If you're not going to help me make dinner, go do your homework. Don't just sit around."

"That's all I wanted to do. I didn't want to talk to him in the first place."

In the face of my mother's defense, right there, in the kitchen, with the flowers and fruit and the bowl of walnuts, there swept through me a spectral feeling that, perhaps, all I had ever wanted was to be left alone.

"You two are tearing me in half," she said.

"In half, you say?"

"Oh, mister, please. 'In half, you say?' That's what suits you? To say that to me? Oh, I see it now. See it plainly. You'll just leave," she said, escalating everything. "Is that it? No father? No mother? No sister? What about my grandchildren? You're going to hide them from me, as well?" she said. "I'm never going to hold my grandchildren. Never know them. Is that it? That your plan? 'Papa, who is our grandmother?' Just going to be stone-faced when they ask that? 'Papa, do we have a Bubbe?' I'm not playing with you. Just up and say it suits you to walk away."

"Maybe it does," I said.

One by one, she put down the items in her hands onto the counter, a yellow potato followed by the potato peeler, clasping her hands together under her chin, closing, then opening her eyes.

"I will remind you, because right now you seem to have forgotten about life and fate. In Dachau, my uncle, your Great Uncle Reuben's cheekbones stuck out of his face like hill tops of burned-out forest. He'd been hungry for months, hungrier than you or I have ever felt in our lives, thank the good Lord. He used to dream of chewing, just chewing, while he was in Dachau, then Bergen-Belsen. When the British liberated the camp, he had typhoid. He lost his mother and sisters. He lost his hearing in one ear. He lost nearly a hundred pounds. He no longer recognized himself in the mirror. How he was able to keep that diary of his is one of God's miracles. Even when he worked in a screw factory inside the camp, he wrote down everything he saw. He wrote about exhausted prisoners singing in the camp orchestra. Don't you forget that. He wrote about artists. Emaciated, close to death. Funeral singers, their voices disappearing through the wretched German forest, all their messages carried by the wind, Yochanan. Anyone approaching the camp's barbed wire was shot. How he buried that diary underneath the camp grounds, four feet of digging, buried it in a hard box, and retrieved it after the end of the war, I'll never understand. It was too much for him. That's what killed him, why he took his life. You read it, Yochanan. Read it. It's not *Night*. No, but, the gun fire, the artillery, rifles, machine guns. Lying awake every night. One of the few testimonies actually written inside a Nazi camp. It's no *Het Auchterhaus*. It's not Franz Kafka. But, it's preserved in the National Library of Israel. Your uncle, of blessed memory, his diary, God rest his soul. I have held it. Its pages smell of filthy, wet German dirt. I think of him whenever I see you writing. He wrote in that book every night so that you would know, not his story, your story."

I said nothing, knowing both stories, and also imagining the kinds of books I dreamed of writing would be, like Kafka's books that, too, would stab and wound you, wake you up with a blow to the head, that I, too, had to be receptive, as much as engaged, with my own state of being, to feel, as I wrote, that words were not jewels, but door handles, not golden birds on golden paper, but recovered teeth found underground like Great Uncle Reuben's book. What else is a book for, but stirring up ordinary things, something, Kafka says too, that grieves us, like a suicide, like the death of someone we are told to love more than ourselves. To write, I knew even then, I must abandon myself into a chasm and cast my life into that cavity—and to accept the fate, bear its hardship, its splendor, without seeking reward. A book must fracture us into ten-thousand pieces, like the very origins of the universe. I knew that. And then put us back together, as yet, still broken.

She picked up a yellow potato and the peeler.

"Cut out your own mother? Your father? Poor Rivka? Maybe we'll cut you out first," she said, slicing skin rings into the clean, dry sink. "I can't believe we're even talking like this, after what I have lived through. This family has lived through. What do you think will happen to all of us when you waltz out of here? Describe that to me. Will you? Have you written that down in your notebook? You've written about your childhood—is it so bad? No, it is not. You've written about all this so-called pain, so-called anguish, how tortured you are. You've written about how you always have the answers. But, have you written about what I've suffered? Have you got a logical explanation for that? You think this is all fun and games? Always with you it's what you focus on, what you plan to do. No different than your father. Oh, but you have to murder him, too. What the Nazis couldn't do, the son will do. All the love in the world leads to this little nod of the head of yours: just up and leave. You have been allowed to struggle all your life, Yochanan Moshe Wain, with your 'tearing me in half' nonsense. You wish to be free? No. Put yourself back together. And, don't say it. Don't say it. Don't say, 'How?' You know how. It's the easiest thing in the world. Toughen up. Toughen up. Don't be so sensitive. Because if you go through with it—with that little nod of your head—it can't be undone."

"You're not making it any easier," I said.

"I should have known this was coming," she said. "I should have known. You acting like we're your jailer. Just damn it all to hell." She threw the peeled yellow potato and the potato peeler into the sink, and they clanked against the porcelain and rattled to a stop.

And then, I sat there at the table, staring at the pages of my father's sermon, and took it, all her intelligence and logic.

When she said I'd been overpraised from the time I was an

infant, I took it. When she said that people saw me as charming, but she knew me as shrewd, canny, secretive, I took it. When she said I was throwing away the entire family line, that I would forever be known as the deserter, I took it. When she said, one day we'll see each other on the street—"Maybe you'll be married, no? Maybe you'll have children, no?"—and I will not even so much as acknowledge her, I took it. When she said that if I followed through, that if I left as I had nodded was my threat, that I would be living too dangerously for her, that I should not even try to see her after that, no phone calls, no postcards, no letters, no telegrams, nothing, not a thing, ever, never ever again, never ever step through the door of this house again, do you hear what I'm saying to you? I took it.

TWO PICKUPS WERE RACING across the sand near the tideline, followed by another pickup coughing behind them that slowed and several people jumped out. There was the sound of the truck peeling off, swerving past the barriers meant to keep cars off the beach, and back up the sandy ramp to the street, its high beams on.

At first, I wasn't sure what I was seeing, and slipped back into Salazar's cab and shut the doors so the light went out.

It was her. The girl from the highway, with her two friends. Barefoot, in cutoffs and tube top, but no longer wearing the varsity jacket, she was making her way with her friends toward the surf, each of them carrying a can of beer. She walked ten feet ahead of them, winsome and mystifying. Anxiously glancing around, she looked at the clouds, billowing like silver ash, and put a hand to her cheek. All around us, couples or small groups of people carried by their own laughter were walking in every direction. Again, I looked at her. She was shoving her hands into her pants pockets and drifted off with her friends toward a nearby jetty where there were men in hooded jackets fishing for sand trout and croaker and bonnet heads, and beyond them a snack shack that during the day sold cold drinks, ice cream, and hot dogs. The girl with her two friends stopped when the boyfriend squatted like he was going to be sick. The girlfriend shook his shoulder, and he stood, waved her off and hustled over toward the scrub grass near the seawall. "You're never getting sober," the girlfriend called.

The girl in the tube top stood apart with an alluring silence. She pushed the hair from her face. In the vivid wind, I could see her nose and chin and cheeks as she shook her hair out, and, as she looked across the beach where the sick friend had fled and the girlfriend had followed, then they both returned. In a few moments, the three of them were a hundred yards away.

I climbed out of the truck.

By the time I got to the next jetty, in the direction of the Flagship Hotel, I had lost sight of her. I had lost sight of Salazar, too. Each time I looked for him, I couldn't see where he'd swam to.

A long-haired, stiff-necked guy on the opposite side of the rocks right then was gyrating with his lean hips, singing, in a cracked voice: *If drinking don't kill me, her memory will.*

He saw me, but he didn't budge, kept singing. I called the words back to him: *With the blood from my body, I could start my own still.*

"Yeah, buddy! George Jones!" the singer called out. "The motherfucking Possum!"

The traffic filtered behind us above the seawall.

He was fifteen years older than me, I guessed, with wide ears, and he wore short trunks and no shirt, beaded necklaces, his pink belly spilling over the untucked drawstring. He sang more, with an ineffable longing, his fist raised like a microphone to his mouth. Sometimes he arched his head back and put his fisted hand against his lips. We sang together, a ricochet of voices and splashing waves, out of sync.

Kicking wet clumps of sand into the foam, he flashed the "Hook 'em Horns" sign with his fingers, and tugged at the strap of the denim bag over his shoulder. His presence gave me a vibrant, exquisite feeling, and fitted perfectly, like a living emblem, inside my high spirit. The singer was strung out and swinging his long hair around, the beaded necklaces clacking. I was thankful to have a stranger with a happy face to sing with.

Wind and pieces of debris blowing around us, he waved over two of his friends, both white, a couple, a man and a woman, both in tight swimsuits.

"Everyone loves the waves!" the singer shouted.

"Fuck yeah!" called the boyfriend, rotund, about the same age as the singer, with a bulging neck, and mutton-chop sideburns, who was patting his hairy stomach like a bear.

"Fuck yeah!" said the woman and she leaned into the boyfriend, kissed him on the neck, and he put his arms around her and whispered something, while looking in my direction, and they both laughed. She was jittery, bony, with short blonde hair, and red polish on her fingers and toenails, and her voice was scratchy from smoking cigarettes.

I kept looking for the girl from the pickup, but didn't see her.

With the singer and his two friends, we watched the waves move in and out as if we were looking for someone who was gone.

White birds flew overhead, down the beach.

"You like the water?" the woman said, slurring.

"I do," I said.

"White on green on white on white on green, man," sang the singer.

"You mean, mud?" the woman said.

"White on green, babe," the boyfriend said, with an aggrieved smile, while peering up at the clouds.

"The waves are bearded, Randall," she said to her boyfriend.

"Bearded waves? Shit!" Randall said back and coughed, his eyes drifting upward.

"Just tonight," she said.

"Don't fall in love," Randall said

"I won't."

"I mean it," he said. "You can't swim, Marla."

They laughed and fell into each others' arms and collapsed on the hard sand.

"I can't! I really can't!" Marla shouted, her voice hoarse, over a flurry of honking from the boulevard.

"Oh, go ahead on in there, go on. Fall in love with the waves. There's billions of them. Fall in love with them beards," Randall shouted.

"But I can't swim," she cried back.

"We'll rescue you. Hey, yo, man, you swim?"

"I can swim," I said and looked at Marla to see if she would go into the water or not and noticed that her skin had blotches like rose petals.

"Fine enough," Randall said.

All at once she began running toward the receding waves until her ankles were wet, then turned and let the water chase her back to us, waving her hands in our faces, bits of foam blowing across the sand after her.

"I'm not your fucking charity case," she yelled.

"Here we go," said the singer.

But, she quieted, sat on the sand, scooted close to Randall, and I could see that her face was freckled.

"Y'all hear abut Ryan tonight?" I said.

"Fuck, yeah," said Randall. "Number five!"

The singer said, "You party, man? We got to celebrate. That liner Puhl snared nearly gave me a heart malfunction." He stopped speaking and stared at me, longer than I felt was right. "You look familiar," he went on. "What's with you? You look like a Jew. I know all about people like you. Are you? You live in your fancy house. What's your father? Lawyer? Some shit like that? Owns a business? Mom's a housewife? That it? Black cleaning lady named Clarice comes on Thursdays. You look like a Jew. You a Jew? Friday nights you eat that round bread tastes like eggs mixed with oatmeal? It's good. I've had it. Egg bread. I know all about Jews.

Knew some good Jews in the army. You can stay with us. Okay?"
said the singer.

Who is this guy, I wondered. The marbly drawl, saliva
dabbing his chin when he spoke. His voice thick, like a fence
post talking to a cow, sounding like he was always about to be
inconvenienced.

"I was going to swim in the billions of waves," I said,
thinking I've been away from home but a few hours and already,
here we go, as foretold, Jew this, Jew that.

"Take this," the singer said. "Blow this brick with us. To
Nolan Ryan! The big man from Alvin! Take that Sandy Koufax.
Hey, he was a Jew."

He fished from his denim knapsack a small white dish, like
you rest a teacup on, a short cocktail glass, and then unfolded
aluminum foil to unveil a pecan-sized, black chunk of hashish,
with a paper clip stabbed into it.

"Looks good," I said, wondering where these three had come
from, wondering, if I were to take a test about the identities of
these three characters, I'd have called them rednecks or hillbillies,
white trash, and wondering, too, if I were to take a test about
the look of the brick of hashish the singer unfolded, if I could
identify it as Moroccan, Bombay, or ear wax, Lebanese flue, and,
at last, wondering, if by saying, *Looks good*, I had indicated clearly
the impression, while untrue, that I blow ten pounds of blocko
everyday.

"It's okay. Come on. We're wasted," the singer said,
puckering his mouth.

"Fucking wasted," said Randall, and he lay his head, near
footprint puddles, on the wet sand.

Marla laughed and nodded and kissed Randall on the mouth.

One of them had a pink box of Bottle Caps and we passed
that around, along with an opened fifth of Johnnie Walker Red.
I thought to draw back from them, wondering, this time, if a
lifetime of hard labor was what followed several tokes from
underneath that cocktail glass.

"Don't get him worked up. He's unpredictable. Know what I mean?" Marla said.

"Nothing wrong here. I'm good," I said

"You a terrorist?" she said.

"I'm nobody," I said, and that caused her to laugh.

"Government knows all about you, Nobody," Randall said. "Surveillance."

The singer asked, "Where you live, Nobody?"

"Meyerland."

"Damn. I knew you were a Jew," the singer said. "You people in Meyerland hate Jesus Christ, I mean, you didn't murder the son of God personally. But, probably would cheer it on if it happened tomorrow. Am I wrong? The passion? The resurrection? What's that to someone like you, Mr. Nobody from Meyerland. Shit, don't get me wrong. I'm okay with Jews. I love Israel. I love Moshe Dyan, a bad ass, with his one eye and all, that black patch. Bad ass. Kinky Friedman. Love that guy. It's the fucking Arabs. They're the fuckers. That's why we need our troops in Lebanon. Keep the Arabs from killing the Jews, only allies we got. You a Zionist?"

Maybe they were undercover rednecks, I thought.

By now we were sitting in a circle around a crumpled sand castle—six bucket-sculpted turrets, with two of the turrets destroyed by the tide—unanimously enjoying the night breeze.

"Unlike you people in Meyerland, I'm a Reaganite right down to my scrotum," the singer declared, fisting his crotch. "The government should cut taxes 80 percent. If the libs and fem-bitches don't like it," he said, "send them back to the countries they came from. Put them on ships." He fingered the brick of hash and fixed it on the plate, then lit it up. Inhaling the smoke, and holding his breath, he went on, "Put them on ships, whether they want to go or not. I mean it. We got to mold a new American. I mean it." Sharply, he inhaled the toke, then blew the smoke into the humid air.

Randall agreed, while staring up at the few stars peeking

through the clouds, the waves crashing on and on.

"When I was in 'Nam," the singer said, "I had my fair share of fascists in the jungle. See, Marla, he's not offended. Bunch of angry, pissed off gooks.

"Not gooks," Marla said. "We don't talk like that."

"Excuse me. Shit. Excuse me from knowing a gook from a kike. Ain't that right, Nobody? You're not offended. Bunch of angry, pissed off members of the North Vietnamese Army. How's that? Marla? Better? Just as angry and pissed off as the Liberation Army Viet Cong. Fucking…"

Marla shook her head.

"…good old commie bastards, rhymes with pukes," he said and pretended to wipe crumbs from his lip in a dainty fashion. "Let me tell my shit, Marla. Okay with you? I was loyal. I served my country. Everybody feared my ass when I came back here, but I didn't give a fuck what they thought. In the jungle, life is cheap. You learn that, day one. Ears, tongues, fingers, balls, they come off with a knife blade easy as blasting with guns. You kill whatever moves, or whatever moves kills you. That's why I keep this bitch at all times," he said, reaching into his denim bag and pulling out a pistol. "Colt Cobra .38 Special."

"Whoa! Whoa! Put that down!" Marla hollered and ran off to a stop near the surf, and I ran in the other direction, shouting, "No, no, no, no, no."

He waved the .38. "Lightweight, aluminum frame, double-action. Same piece used by Jack Ruby to kill Oswald. One day I can smell burning skin, choppers blowing, grunts, my buddies."

He pointed the gun at Marla.

"Come on, man," Randall said, more calmly than was called for, his hands lifted near his ears, like he was being arrested. "Don't start that shit."

"You babies." The singer was walking toward me pointing the blunt barrel above my head.

This little leave of his senses was inexplicable to me—and, right then, with the singer walking in my direction, the .38 the only thing I can see, the life I had been living had come to a halt. Had I even had a life before this moment? Before being menaced by a Vietnam War veteran, with a Colt Cobra .38 Special, lightweight, double action aluminum frame who, minutes earlier, was belting out George Jones, the motherfucking Possum? What had I done, wandering after the girl from the freeway, to get here?

The singer raised the gun up beside his ear. "If you're an Orthodox Jew, why ain't you wearing that dark coat? The beard? Black hat?"

"I'm not an Orthodox Jew," I replied and acted, not like I was ignoring him, but that it was cool, everything was cool, guy holding a .38 Special, lightweight, double action aluminum frame next to his ear, accusing you of being an Orthodox Jew in gritty Galveston near the Pleasure Pier and the Flagship Hotel on a Saturday night. Cool. We're all cool.

Marla and Randall had gone silent.

"You're not an Orthodox?"

"Definitely not. What do you mean?" I thought, maybe I should reason with him? "What do you mean by Orthodox?"

"Keep kosher? I knew all these Jewish grunts. Kept Kosher. No pork. Lobster. That you?"

"Kosher, yes. No pork. No lobster."

"Are you an Orthodox?"

"No."

He spread his arms wide, the gun balancing loosely in his right hand. "How can that be?"

"Put the gun away, and I'll explain," I said.

He waved it over his head.

"Stop it!" shouted Marla. "Randall, do something!"

The singer turned to Randall and pointed the gun. "Oh, come on. I've been to war, motherfucker. Come on! Look at my eyes! You fucking chicken shit! What! What! motherfucker! What! What are you going to do? Sit there and cry?"

"Cry, bitch," Randall said, smoking his cigarette.

There seemed to be no one around us in any direction.

"You ain't going to do shit! Oh come on, motherfucker!"

Randall stared back, cigarette between his fingers, grinning. "Sweet."

"Make my day!"

"Shoot."

The two men seemed like they were going crazy now.

"Oh, you think I'm stupid? Go ahead," the singer shouted. "Lay your hands on me, motherfucker."

Randall took a drag off the cigarette and exhaled the smoke. "I do think you're stupid. I actually do."

"Come on, bitch."

"I actually do."

"Come on! Pull the cock out of your mouth!" The singer stepped back, hands in the air. "Oh, hold on, time out! Whatever. I'm not going to go ahead and make that decision for you." Another drag from Randall, smoke from his lips. "You can choose. Cock or pussy," the singer shouted. "Choose what you want. What are you going to do? So? What are you going to do? What are you going to do? Come on! I took an oath to this country. I took an oath to God. Does that still matter! Do you believe God still matters?"

"I do!" shouted Marla, one fist lifted high above her head. "I do! God first! God first!" she hoarsely chanted, pumping her fist.

I thought: This is what I get for sneaking off behind the diving boards at T.C. Jester Park with Nicole, the debate champion from Episcopal. This is what I get for saying to Leah, *I've got to go*, and she said, *When I'm certain I can't stand it, I'm going to remember that night, how fine that was.* This is what I get for not swimming with Salazar. This is what I get for trailing behind the girl from the pickup.

The singer waved the .38 at the sky, a headlight from a passing car on the seawall wavering like a halo behind his head. He turned from Randall to me. "So? Are you or aren't you?"

"I told you, man," I said. "Okay? I'm not Orthodox. Look at me. What do I look like to you?"

"You look like an Orthodox. What, I'm a motherfucker? Say something in your Hebrew," he said, with a grin across his mouth, as though I must now see what kind of motherfucker I was dealing with.

I imagined, if I stood there and said nothing, in no time, he'd run at me. He'd be shouting, a burst of gunfire, and we'd be dragging each other into the shallow waves. I didn't know what to be afraid of more. Thinking: Hebrew! Say something in Hebrew! It won't kill you. Where is your loyalty? Your whole life you've been trained to use Hebrew to motivate people. Any people. Don't get picky. Do it. Say it.

"Tell you what, man." I said. "Put away the gun, and I'll say, Thank you."

He lunged toward me and I flinched.

"Fuck it, Nobody. Fuck it. I'm no threat to society. See?" He opened the barrel. "No bullets. They're in the bag. I'm living my best life, right now." He fisted the denim bag and flung the gun inside, then dropped the bag onto the sand next to a crooked turret from the sand castle. "I've got my eye out for Sandinistas. Fuck them all. Ortega's a pig. We need to send in the Marines. Those people are threatening the security of our way of life. You think the danger's going to go away? It's going to grow worse, man. Come on back, Marla. I'm cool. Nobody, stay with us. Come on. Little excitement. All in fun. Don't have a cow. Take a breath."

Marla and I walked back to the fallen sandcastle where the denim bag lay crumpled near the turret. *"Toda raba,"* I said.

"What's that?"

"Thank you very much, in Hebrew," I said.

With his fist, he patted his chest above his heart, reached into his bag, pulled out a few white pills, flung two into his mouth and handed two to me wrapped in cellophane. "Keep them for later. Scooby snacks. You like ludes? Don't you? Here. No hard feelings."

I jammed the quaaludes into my pocket.

"Man, you missed it. Last night, we were hanging out at Surfside. Lot of people on the beach. Lot of parties. I was dancing to somebody's car radio, playing that J. Geils shit, with some dude's girlfriend. And then the dude shows up. Her boyfriend. Pissed off. Starts shoving me. The fucker. Couple times he pushes me in the chest. He's fucking wasted. I tell him, 'Stop it.' I go, 'Motherfucker, I served in Vietnam. Motherfucker. Motherfucker, I'm going to rip your throat out if you touch me one more time. Just touch me one more time, motherfucker. Do it. I'll rip your fucking throat out.' He backed off. The girlfriend pushed him out of there."

"You didn't pull out your gun, did you?" I said.

"I was thinking just now, I wished that dude could get that gay cancer. Know about that? All these faggots dying in New York and San Francisco. I read about that. Just thinking it. Don't look at me like that, Marla. Don't flip out, bitch. I've got a cousin that's gay. You know who I'm talking about. I love that kid. I'd kill any man that touched him, my faggot cousin. That'd teach that boy for shoving a veteran. But, that ain't going to happen. Only the gays have got it, so far. Africans. Jews, I guess. They're next. Dominicans. All those people. Not like you. You're not even Orthodox. You're going to be fine. See? I heard you. I was listening. What do we need all these cockroaches coming in from all these shit holes in Africa and Mexico. I mean, I'm a strong Christian man. But, I predict that the Mexicans and the Blacks will be fighting each other before they try to take on the rest of us. America's got to stand tall."

I couldn't stand him.

"Nicaragua?" said Randall, sitting on the sand, dazed, patting his hairy tummy. "Shit, man."

"Shit, man, nothing. Soviet-fucking ally, is what they are. They're on our mainland, only two hours' flying time from our own borders. You know how much money the communists send them? Do you? Over a billion dollars. A billion. With a B. So that Brezhnev can launch campaigns to subvert and topple El

Salvador, and then they're coming for Mexico. That's Mexico right there," the singer said, pointing at the oil platforms bright on the horizon. "Soviets are using Nicaragua as a base. The Soviets and Castro. They want to threaten the Panama Canal, interdict the sea lanes."

"'Interdict,'" Marla said. "Where you come up with that, man? 'Interdict.'"

"What do you know? Chicks ain't going to have to fight and die. I didn't see no chicks in Danang. No chicks in San Salvador. Those are vital seas lanes. Should that happen, desperate people by the millions would begin fleeing north into Texas. Can't let that happen. We're going to be the only free people left in the world. Fucking Russians are trying to get a beachhead down there. Thousands of Cuban military, East Germans, international terror cells, P.L.O. And, hey, Nobody. They all hate Jews."

"Because communists hate Jews?" I said.

"God damn right."

"Where's Qaddafi? He miss the memo?"

"Look, Nobody, I'm Baptist. All right." He cracked his knuckles by squeezing each hand. "I hate Arafat. I'm going to Heaven, motherfucker. Jews are holding the Holy Land. Where do you think Jesus is going to descend to? Astroworld? Moody Gardens? When you see me flying El Al direct to Jerusalem, that's because I'm getting ready for the afterlife. The Nicaraguan commie bastards are right on our borders. Right on our doorstep. All those Nicaraguans are just like people here on welfare. I'm not hurting them. Don't give me that look, Randall. Fuck you. It's all connected. The government hurt them. The government took away from those people on welfare something more important than money. They took away their initiative. They took away their freedom. They took away, in many cases, their morality. They corroded their morality, their drive, their pride. That's what communism does. And, welfare. I want to help them get that back. I want them to be Americans. We do that, and we stop Ortega, they're going to thank us. If the lion and the lamb are going to lie down together in Central America, Uncle Sam is going to be the lion. That's the way it has to be," he said. "That's why we come down here to this shit-ass beach," the singer said, re-inhaling the smoke. He took another hit of hashish and held his breath. "To escape their radar and cameras. Now, they know where we live. But can't find us down here. That's why we can't permit the Soviet Union to put a second Cuba, a second Libya, right on the doorsteps of the United States. Hear what I'm saying?" He exhaled. Smoke whisked above his head. "Light it up, Randall. Go ahead, you damn fool," whispered the singer, handing over the dish and glass.

"Why you call him a damn fool?" Marla said.

The singer looked at her like he thought she was an idiot. "Anyone who smokes hashish is a damn fool," he said, cackling, then stood and started to dance.

"Oh, Vince," Marla said to me. "That's his name. Vince Foster. He's a handful."

"Don't tell him lies, Marla," said the singer. "Then you're going to be telling him about my shitty home life. Aren't you? Listen, Nobody. Nobody's a good name. When you're done with it, I'd like to have it. My old man was a shit. Taught me one thing and one thing only: don't be a quitter. He was a junior high gym teacher. Every day he'd go to good-old FJH on Manison Parkway, dressed in the same shit. Blue shirt, gray shorts, white tube socks pulled up to his knees, whistle around his neck, baseball cap. Same thing. Every day. He used to take me to the batting cages behind the junior high. For hours, pitch after pitch after pitch, I was the all-American kid. Fastball, curveball, slider, changeup. He said I had to swing at everything. Can't expect to get good pitches in Little League. Fucking Little League. I mean, c'mon, man. Little League? But, if I didn't keep my eye on the ball, or my hands back, didn't keep my weight centered, pow, the fucker bean me with the next pitch. Bruises for a week. But, hey, forget that. Tonight is Nolan Ryan's night. Damn. Twenty-seven up. Twenty-seven down. Ryan better buy Alan Ashby a box of steaks."

Marla whispered "He's messed up a little bit. But, he gets the best drugs. Hawaiian, LSD, hash, ludes, you name it."

"Know why I can be Nobody, Marla? Because my old man beat my real name out of me. Then the gooks—Marla, the gooks—chopped my name up into ground meat and fed it to the dogs." He walked down to the waves and crossed his arms, eyes up, like he was looking for a lost star.

"Reagan's going to ban the roads from anyone who opposes him," said Randall, organizing the saucer, glass, and brick with both hands.

"Texas roads are state roads," I said.

"Reagan's going to ban the states, dude."

The singer returned. "Who gives a shit about the roads, Randall?" he said, sitting beside me, legs stretched out. "The Nicaraguan military machine is more powerful than all its neighbors combined."

"Yeah. Well, the truckers won't let him do it," Randall said, staring at the jetty. "Hear what I'm saying. That's probably what'll happen after Texas secedes," Randall was nodding, unsure what he was getting at, then wiping his nose across his arm.

"George Bush is a Yankee weenie," the singer said. He waved his arms to indicate he was done.

Marla fixed on me with her tired eyes.

I took the dish from Randall and looked in both directions across the beach. On all sides of us, little fires, like delicious cracklings, up and down the shoreline, were coming on.

With the dish in one hand, I lit the hard black rock, covered it with the cocktail glass and studied the smoke as it began to swirl. After I lifted an edge of the glass so a crease of air was exposed, I inhaled all the smoke, then stood, and lightly crossed the party and sat down on the other side, much to their amusement. I felt like I was in hiding, the smoke tight in my lungs. I exhaled. Smoke swam across the wind toward the foam above the waves. I felt false and true, lonely, my spirit padding soundlessly through my thoughts, down a long corridor. I stood, then slipped back to the sand, making my way on hands and knees. I rolled over, and collapsed, lying on my back, looking up at the clouds. "Yeah, now," I said. I felt astonishing, as if overhearing my own dreams, in love with my desire to feel the heat of this yearning for the future—Salazar out there in the water, or down the beach on foot, my notebook filled with words and sentences, the girl in the tube top somewhere. Leah in her mother's house, watching television, lying flat on her bed in her black pajamas like somebody I'd made up, and my parents undressing for the night—I could not have invented an hour like this one, nor invented this night's sky, nor coined one word about what I was actually living, and, even if I could, that word wouldn't be *charm*.

"Where to now?" the singer asked, taking the denim bag and wrapping the strap across his bare chest.

"I've got nowhere to go," I said.

Randall cackled. "How much farther is that?"

"Say hello to nowhere, Nobody," sang out the singer, "Nolan Ryaaaaaaan!!"

No hitterrrrrrrrrr!" Randall shouted.

"Say hello to mama when you see her," said Marla, then she sang, "*I was drunk the day my mama got out of prison.*"

"*And I went to pick her up in the rain,*" I sang.

"*But before I could get to the station in my pickup truck,*" sang the singer. "David Allen Coe, God dammit."

"Rhinestone Cowboy," I said.

Here, the singer dropped the denim bag on the wet sand and began wading hip high into the water, trudging his legs along, turning his back to break the surf, and bouncing above the waves to keep his head dry, like a promise going slowly into the veins of the gulf, his body lengthening and dangling.

Good Gosh A'Mighty

Salazar was still swimming.

When I went looking for him near the pickup truck, and to ask what could be done to ensure we left the beach at first light, I heard him shout from where he was bobbing beyond the breakers, waving for me to join, which I did, after throwing my boots in the cab, but without removing my jeans and shirt.

"What the hell you gonna do now? Dumb ass."

I said, "It's fine, man. Not like you got silk sheets in the back of that truck. Your truck's not the Ritz."

"You're fucking wasted."

He splashed toward the breakers, with his eyes peeking above the water.

I didn't tell him about what had just happened—Vince Foster, Randall, Marla, the brick of hash, the .38. "Let's get out of here," I called. "Let's get going. Let's go to Surfside, Freeport, somewhere less crowded, man."

But, when he swam farther out, I followed, ducking into crashing waves, swimming toward the flats, anxiously swishing my feet, while the pickup receded from view. We swam in unison, paddling out to where I could barely touch the sandy bottom with my toes, then floated on our backs, the salt water splashing near my mouth.

Salazar whistled. "This is the life," he said, and we stared at the fast clouds under the sky.

I said, "Not a whole lot of me left."

"Yeah, now. I'm toasted, man."

"Ubiquitously toasted."

"Out here, this is our commission on love," he said.

"Commission?"

"Yep. Commission, mission, power of attorney. A high commission."

"Totally high," I said and looked back at the waves tumbling into the beach and, above them, the bright lights from hotels and shops above Seawall Boulevard.

"Ever see snowflakes, Duke?"

"1973. Snowed three times. You don't remember? Once in January and twice in February. Went sledding down the banks of the bayou."

"1973. Wow. Gordie Howe was skating with the Aeros back then."

"Battle of the Sexes."

"Billie Jean v. Bobby Riggs."

"I remember that. My little brother says to me the other day, right before we had that tropical storm, he says, he can use magic to turn the rain to snow. 'I can make big white snowflakes sweep over the roof of this house,' he says. The sky was looking bad that night. Did you see that? Julian says, waving his arms around like he's some fucking Merlin the Magician, 'Rain in the sky turn to blizzard!' Fifteen years old, with that stupid peach fuzz on his chin, and he's standing in the living room, right where you slept on the floor last night, standing there dressed in a soiled t-shirt and track shorts. 'Rain in the sky turn to blizzard,' he says. I just laughed at him. I said, Good one, kid. 'Just leave it to me,' he says, not even turning, but staring outside the window. 'We're going to have snow. I know you want snow. Rain in the sky turn to blizzard.' He chants magic words, 'Hummunah-hummunah hummunah-hummunah-whatzeee!' That's when I had this fucked up thought, man. This fucked up thought. What if his magic words back-fired on him? What if they killed him, right in the living room? With him wearing that crappy t-shirt? Julian would be gone. Dead. How do you ever get over that? For the rest of my life, I'd be thinking, Damn, 'Rain in the sky turn to blizzard' are murderous words. My life would be Before and After. Before Julian. After Julian. I was thinking, I'd just be longing for him, suffering. He wouldn't feel any of it. Dead. That's all. The shock of it, and that's all. Dead."

"You're an interesting dude, mi hijo," I said, and floated on my side, weighed down from my clothes.

"What do you mean?"

"The way you see things. He was just pretending, and you're all 'What if his magic words kill him?' That's interesting."

"You think I shouldn't have these thoughts? Do you?"

"I didn't say that."

"You think, I just look at everybody and go, *that's an interesting story*. What if I thought this? What if I thought that? It's what writers do, Duke. Get used to it. Exploit people. You do it. Ever have some weird shit happen between you and the Wounded One, where she's a nuisance?"

"What are you attacking me for? You're an interesting person. I'm not saying I've never done something like that."

"Okay, then."

"All right. Here you go. Rivka. Okay. If you want her to run your life, you're set. She's trained her whole life to get married. Once, when she was in high school, she came to school to pick me up. I was in fourth or fifth grade. She comes to the synagogue, you know, the school at the synagogue where I used to go, and lines up with all the carpool ladies, honking her horn. A line of cars thirty deep, everyone patiently waiting to inch forward to the assigned spot where the kids can climb in with our hand-me-down knapsacks and Popsicle stick craft projects, or whatever, and she's the only one, about halfway back. Just laying on her horn. She can't wait. Turns out she's got a dentist appointment. 'I'm taking you with me,' she says. 'I don't want to go to the dentist's office,' I tell her. She says, 'Good teeth are my future.' Like that means something. She nearly drove into the car in front of her when she pulled her hand off the steering wheel and faked like she was going to smack me in the face. She says, 'What I have to do because of you! This car is mine,' she says. 'Don't get it dirty with your filthy tennis shoes.' 'What am I supposed do,' I say, 'keep my feet in the air?' 'Aren't you funny?' she goes, and she peels around a bunch of cars and we whip out of the parking lot. She starts honking at some other car that's not even in her way. Just because she's Rabbi Gadol's daughter, she thinks she can do whatever she wants. I mean, that's fucked up. One thing I know is true in this world is, when you're Rabbi Gadol's kid, you can't do whatever you want."

Neither of us said anything after that, but we floated on our backs, watching clouds scrub the blackness in the sky.

"Snow is falling," he said finally.

"Big white snowflakes."

I was losing focus. My eyes, my mouth, my focus. The hashish was beating wildly. Floating on my back, I could feel my blue jeans and denim shirt weighing me down, heavy against shoulders and thighs. No thought would stick in my mind. Images were flying apart, and the black sky and salty waves couldn't hold them together. As soon as I felt one thought come on, it got swept under. Whatever had been eating at me I couldn't shake. My birthright, my inheritance, I couldn't un-imagine. The gargantuan struggle with my father seemed already over. Meyerland? Was that my subject? Houston was no Jerusalem, that's for sure. Rice Avenue was no Ben Yehuda Street. Had I been Mark Twain, I could've written a book that begins, *You don't know about me, without you have read a book by the name of The Hebrew Bible.*" Or, if I'd been Saul Bellow: *I'm an American, Texas born—Texas that lone star—and go at things as I have taught myself.* There'd be no new controversy like the *Trefa* Banquet coming my way, not like the original one, with the come-ons and uprisings. Between God and son, the battle seemed over even before it got started—all the forms of existence were extinguished before they could be transformed, reconstructed, retooled.

The high inside my head was building.

I drew up my knees, fetus-like, and considered what it might feel like to flip over, and sink under the surface of the swells, my hair like tendrils. Sinking down, and down, and down to the muddy bottom, I could taste a briny tang from the seawater. Slowly rolling my body underwater in circles, I remembered the swirling eyes of the turkey vulture on the side of the Gulf Freeway, then my father bent forward at the kitchen table writing his sermon about the rain. I felt my skin ancient and thin, as if not only my skin but also my bones were shrinking. Like a primitive sea creature, I was oozing, saltwater sloping over my head. I let my body soften, as I sometimes did underwater in the deep end of the blue swimming pool at the Jewish Community Center on South Braeswood, while sitting cross-legged on the white tiles on the bottom, like I was having a tea party. Under the waves, I sank more, and loosed the tension in my neck and shoulders. I relaxed my feet, thighs, hips, torso, arms, neck, all in unison.

Here, I pictured Rabbi Gadol racing out from the beach in khakis and a white buttoned shirt to see me disappear under the flat water, patting his black yarmulke onto the back of his white hair, waving his arms—flapping them like a mysterious bird—and swinging a bright towel over his head, and I wondered if all my deeds were done. There was Batya the Rock, standing in a long white dress, like a simple wedding dress, barefoot, ankle deep in the surf's foam, her hands covering her mouth, her eyes unblinking. The night air like a blanket of black crystals. Its weight covering the dark. Under all the flat water where I'd sunk down to the bottom of the Gulf of Mexico, my body was a stillness, erasing the misery in my brain—like I'd entered a new virtuosity of being where I would not be found until the early morning sun, up the beach a mile, washed to shore, disgorged from the foamy waves. It took only hours after that for the family to gather inside the brick house at the corner of Runnymead and Wigton. Someone making funeral arrangements and placing phone calls. My mother talking slowly into the receiver, to each person she'd call, each member of the family living in Dallas and Oklahoma City and Des Moines and San Francisco. Her voice husky. My baby, she says into the receiver to Aunt Rachel and Uncle Abe in Dallas. Yes, she says to cousin Marvin in Oklahoma City, he wanted to be a writer, makes no sense. Yes, that's right. He did. He wanted to be a writer, she says to cousin Ruthie in Des Moines. What good is a writer now? Yes, yes, it's what he wanted. Of course, we knew he'd follow in the line. We spoke every day. Every day. He should have a had a full life. He should have. I should have been the one, she says. It makes no sense. She's dabbing her wet eyes with a paper napkin. After a stretch of silence, the ingrained look of sorrow on her face gives way to a pained smile. By early evening the house, along with the front and back lawns, has filled with hundreds members of the congregation, all dressed in dark clothes. Each one then comes through the front double-doors, having washed their hands in a porcelain bowl of saltwater that sat on the porch. Women stopped in the bright foyer to sign the guest book. Men put black yarmulkes onto their heads. One by one, they study the offerings on the dining room table: coffee and cakes and dips and sliced cucumbers and sticks of celery, bundt cakes, carrot cake, muffins, bagels, hard-boiled eggs, lentils, platters of finger sandwiches.

Flowers keep arriving all evening and filling the rooms.

Mother is wearing a dress she laid out on her bed and ironed before slipping it over her head, black with black lace. She roams the rooms to welcome the mourners. She walks through the rooms as if she's wandering through the house to water plants, and she keeps looking, in every corner, for the ones she missed. Every room is filled with people talking low. My sympathies, one says. It's so tragic, says another, impossible to believe. It should have been me, my mother says. May God console us, she says. She says, Blessed be the judge.

Air kisses and downward glances.

For a half hour, Rivka, who had immediately driven from Dallas, stands in the hallway and talks to a man whose jowly face is falling into his suit, a man who is an usher at the synagogue, who recently had been awarded Minyanaire of the Month, the paper certificate given to the congregant who attends the most morning and evening minyan services, a man I remember as Rabbi Gadol's driver the winter he broke his leg—and the man, Mister Something, Amos Something, Amos Somethingstein, I remember, would wait in his white Cutlass Sedan at twenty-past-six in the morning to take my father to lead the morning minyan service. Rivka, her black hair long enough to be damp at the edges of her eyes, says to Mister Somethingstein about how I used to sit in there, in the kitchen, and write in a little notebook. Right in there, she says. He'd sit with his head bent, she says, early in the morning and late at night, just like Papa.

Mr. Somethingstein clears his throat, twice, hard. "He was going to be a writer?"

"I don't know. That's what he said. That, or a bohemian. But, you know, Mother and Papa had other ideas. We all expected him to follow the line," Rivka answers with a wry scowl, looking past him to one of her girlfriends from college.

"The line?"

"Our line of rabbis," she says, but Mister Somethingstein is talking over her about how, at his own home five blocks from here, he lays out his socks and shoes and dress clothes on a chair in his bedroom the night before shul, so as not to be late for morning prayers.

Batya the Rock stands in the living room and people step back. She begins working her way out of the living room, avoiding the eyes and hands of the mourners. I don't have to see anybody, she tells my father where he's sitting, with his head down, in a straight-backed chair in the living room, and she walks out and waits in her bedroom, sitting on the edge of the bed. She sits alone on the edge of the smooth bedspread until her face falls into her palms. She can hear the people coming and going inside her house. But, she could no longer feel the wet tears on her skin.

All at once, my father looks up into the living room of muffled voices. So many had circled all over to reach him, to speak directly into his ear, to hold his head in their hands, with his hands on their hips, with helpless rocking, as he has done for them, so many times, with parents, grandparents, with children. *Toda raba*, he says, over and over, and adding, in a gentle tone, to some, *it can't be helped.*

He is fingering his jacket pocket, rubbing the edge of one of my little notebooks he's taken from the top drawer of the desk in my bedroom.

He stands with his chin down and arms crossed that sends the message: Do not approach me. But people do. Congregants keep coming. Shaking hands. Hugs. Air kisses. Blessed be the judge.

Hours earlier, he had read one of my notebooks in its entirety while locked in the bathroom, sitting on the toilet, with his trousers rolled down to his ankles, underlining passages with his silver Cross pen. Already, into his sermon book, by hand, in flat cursive, he has copied one of my poems, numbering the lines the way he numbers verses of scripture. With the letters squeezing smaller onto the page, he copied the one called, "Debts and Sorrows"—

1. Just as young birds can be taught
2. To make a song that people make
3. My body yielding to the rhythm of the music
4. And to the golden sunlight
5. Walked out into the wind
6. Of the sober day
7. And took my clothes
8. Down to the other end of the city
9. Near the cut banks of the bayou
10. Everybody was waiting to see
11. How I'd get back
12. They said if you look

13. At his pumpkin-soft head
14. And all its ragged points all over it
15. And holler to him in a voice
16. That repeats the old questions
17. The lightness will come back
18. Everyone near the water was walking steadily
19. And looked in my direction we were strangers
20. And not strangers
21. All of us going along steadily as before
22. Like we were the only angels
23. Of oblivion on the head and shoulders
24. As if we were all the blessed people
25. Who ever lived

Almost none of the mourners has ever before been inside our house.

No wonder they all are looking around, searching the mantles and side tables for clues, until realizing there is only the one, silver-framed photograph, the four of us looking into the camera, blooming with our strained smiles, because Rabbi Gadol, squaring his jaw underneath his prodigious head of gray hair, had just said, 'Make us proud,' and Batya the Rock and the Wounded One are holding hands tightly, and I am to the side with my eyes protruding. In a house of death, it's the keepsakes that become most visible to the callers. From where my father sits, he watches Rivka, his one remaining child, stand at the white double-doors in the bright foyer, shaking hands with each caller as they come in. He hardly sees the small nose and flat, wan cheeks of the single mother from Miami, recently settled in Fondren Southwest, who feels obligated to show her new rabbi respect upon the drowning of his only son. That's why she's alone, clutching the straps of her pocketbook, in this house of the dead. To pay respect. She was already taken in by Rabbi Gadol's sparkling presence in the synagogue, where she sat in a plush seat in the second row, the first time she heard him chanting in Hebrew. In a slow baritone, he chanted from the bimah as from a far-off land. His operatic swoons made the strange words familiar. The melody was composed for the spirit though it was nothing a spirit could join when he sang of things that exist in every congregant's life, and yet was meant to feel unknowable. He didn't sing as if he were in a trance. He was without ecstasy. Joining those of us gathered in Beth Tikkun's gloomy sanctuary, the woman from Miami, who that day was wearing a white hat with frills that resembled palm trees, had leaned back in her plush seat in the second row without a trace of disdain. The prayers belonged to us all, she may have thought, such that she might have believed we were nomads living in some desert outpost of an ancient village.

In answer to her shy question—"What was your son like?"—my father extols the grades, promising future, taking the next place in the rabbinical line. *I was hard on him*, he says. *He needed it. He was a pure, bewildering, marvelous, curious boy who had no knowledge of the world. I tried to protect him*, Rabbi Gadol says, crossing his arms, chin down. *Whatever he was going to do, it's a mystery now. He is gathered unto his fathers*, my father says into the collar of his shirt, and he turns his head from the young mother from Miami, newly settled in Fondren Southwest, who had been so taken by his baritone chanting, and, right then, Rabbi Gadol looks, his eyes tearing, into the overhead lights. Here, he can see in his mind something tangible. He can see himself seated at the kitchen table with the pages of his sermon book open before him, slanting rain outside the windows, leaves brown and flying in the wind. But, no sermon comes. Titles, is all:

"From Fear to Faith."

"Healing Loneliness."

"Listen to the Children."

"The Spirit of Emanu-El."

"Weaving Our Challah Together."

But, the words for the sermons are gone. He's forgotten what he's doing at the table, his silver pen scrolled open. Instead, he's sorting through an aqueous cascade of images, rolling this way and that, as if his mouth is filling with saltwater, as if he is ruptured, cleaved, torn, gouged, whipped in the riptides. The sea doing whatever it wants to him. The waves doing. Saltwater doing. What did it matter? What did it matter to my fearless boy? Who can I take revenge upon? Who can I mutilate like the water mutilated my son? Someone else should be the survivor, not me. Someone else should be driven insane, not me. Someone else should be crying a river in his sleep, wrathful, blighted, not me.

At last, he turns his eyes in the direction of the wide hallway to the bedroom where, behind the locked door, Batya the Rock sits, her small head in her hands, on the edge of the smooth bedspread.

The next day, after the funeral service at the cemetery, in the blazing heat, near the sounds of sprinklers watering the lawns and crooked rows of gravestones, alongside the rat-a-tat-tat of pneumatic drills from B & S Discount Muffler and Brakes across the road, one by one my mother, father, and sister step forward, identical to each other, each with thick hair, wet, heavy eyes, and rueful mouths, and hiding whatever alienation they normally feel, though even the worst the Wounded One can manage to say is, *Leave it to my baby brother to get us all to stop ripping each other's asses for two hours.* My father is dressed in a dark suit, white shirt, dark tie, and has spent the morning in the shade of the back patio, polishing his shoes with the brushes and rags from the shoe shine kit. My mother and sister are dressed in straight black dresses, cut below the knee, and black panty hose.

One by one, my mother and Rivka, wilting in the unrelenting sun, tremble as they fill their shovels until thick with dirt.

One by one, each ceremoniously marches to the center of the grave and pauses to consider how to dump the dirt over the casket.

One by one, each tilts the shovel to one side and lets the dirt slide off onto the pine box so that it crinkles across the wood into a sound none will forget for a long time.

My mother looks as though she is on the verge of falling to her knees and howling, violently overcome with pain. But, when she opens her mouth, nothing comes out, not even a gasp.

Rivka looks on in disbelief, as if she might scold her for not howling after all. Nothing in Rivka's life had ever matched the previous days of sitting *shiva*—with mourners gathered for hours among the arm chairs and sofas in the living room, so crowded for the evening Kaddish service, with our parents turning from each other with theatrics Rivka was accustomed to, and, as usual, repulsed by, with life stolen from her with calamity and confusion, and too, without daring to speak of it, a visceral taste comes into her mouth, down in her throat, infesting her heart, that she was thrust, no, restored, at last, to her position as the one living child. Nothing matched the power of all that. When she turns, for a second, two seconds at most, from watching our mother opening her mouth but not screaming, Rivka notices a cemetery worker waiting by an asphalt path, waiting for when the crowd disperses to cover up the plain pine box, and she notices the heavy belly on him, rolled tightly inside his tucked-in, blue work shirt, a man who she remembers from other burials, standing stiffly off to the side, in baseball cap and mud boots, his thick arms tattooed with crucifixes, with his spade laid down at his feet on top of the trim lawn, looking like he's dying for a cigarette, shifting his eyes from the assembled crowd to a black wheelbarrow he'd left in the pathway, but doesn't want to interrupt the burial to retrieve it. But, she doesn't want to think of that, any more than she wants to think of all the nearby dead beloveds: Sadie and Bubbe and Great Aunt Myrna and Great Uncle Sol. Even little Joshua—Sol and Mryna's first son, who six days after he was born, not even old enough for the bris—was buried fifteen feet from where Rivka was standing. Little Joshua, she thinks, with his wee fingers and pink toes Great Aunt Myrna and Great Uncle Sol had held and kissed for only days, was all, who missed growing up entirely, missed every Halloween, missed his high school prom, missed getting drafted and going to the Second World War. In that one second, two at most, Rivka imagined the unveiling of the gravestone to be installed over my very clean pine box in a year's time. She thought of how this section of the graveyard was meant for our parents, and realized I was being buried in our father's plot. In time, Rabbi Gadol would die, buried in the tasseled loafers he was wearing when he drove to the Greyhound Bus Station on Fannin Street to bring my mother home. Then, Batya would die. Then, the Wounded One would be the last of the Meyerland Wains. At Batya's funeral, Rivka would stoically hold the hands of her own children—a dark-haired son in short britches to her left, a dark-haired girl in a cerulean blue skirt and white socks rolled down to her skinny ankles, to her right—holding their little hands, like Jackie Kennedy held the hands of John-John and Caroline in that famous photograph, in the bright sunlight, not on the steps of the Capitol this time, but on Post Oak Road, with the pneumatic drills from the B & S Discount Muffler and Brakes shop rattling across the road and the ticking sprinklers watering the lawns. Rivka, the last of the Meyerland Wains alive, holding the little hands of her very own John-John and Caroline, and looking at the three of us buried under the freshly dug mound of dirt, and across the way from there, the plot where she and her husband would be buried, and perhaps their children, and theirs, and theirs. Rivka would let her eyes read the letters on my gravestone, darkened over the decades, the letters soft inside the granite.

Here, a stranger approaches her, someone who looks vaguely familiar, younger than her, five, six years, perhaps. He's a short man, with a wide bald head, enormous ears, whose eyes appear to have the weight of life in them, and he says, "I knew your brother. We went to high school together," and he introduces himself as Leon Wolf who, at Bellaire High School, took advanced classes with me.

She thanks him with a nod and smile.

"You lived on Runnymead in those days," he says

"Thank you, Leon. Nice of you," Rivka says, bending to scold John-John for pulling her arm too hard.

"You don't remember. It's okay. We were all so young. It's okay," says Leon Wolf.

"I know your family, of course."

"We lived on Grape Street. In those days," Leon Wolf says, "we lived on Grape Street. I moved to Memorial about twenty years ago, three-story house with a long pool out back. That's where I do my laps."

"That's right. Grape Street. I remember," replies Rivka, Caroline clinging to her, pulling her mother's black blouse, and John-John reaching around to pinch his sister's arm. "Off Chimney Rock," she says and doesn't waste a thought on the difference between Meyerland Jews and Memorial Jews.

"I remember your father from my bar mitzvah. Oh, boy, was he tough."

"Yes."

"Well that's all right." Leon Wolf places himself between Rivka and the soft letters of my gravestone. His skin is tan, as if he spent hours sunning by the long backyard pool at his three-story house in Memorial. "It's wonderful to see you. I'm sorry for the occasion, naturally. I remember you. You know, from a distance, because you were older than us back then."

"I'm still older than you, dear," Rivka says.

"It's okay. I was just a kid. Duke, too. We all were."

"Thank you. I must talk to the rabbi," says Rivka, stepping slowly on the bright uneven grass toward a slender man in a white tallit and—wholly inappropriate, she thinks—denim yarmulke, who had led the funeral, a protege of Rabbi Gadol's at one time, who stood talking to the worker from the cemetery, while holding his black siddur with both hands against his blue coat and tie.

"The new rabbi. Oh, yeah. Him," Leon Wolf says and, with his eyes, indicates he isn't impressed, that he's no Rabbi Gadol, that he's probably easy on the bar mitzvah kids. "That's a nice stone for Duke."

"Yes. You were in high school together?" says Rivka, patiently waiting for the protege Rabbi, while John-John and Caroline have slipped their fingers from hers to run to the waiting cars.

"Yes. Lot of classes. He was hard to know. A princeling in our world. Well, maybe not your world. To you, he was just your kid brother. But, to us, his friends, the boys especially, the boys his age, we knew he was going to be something. So sad. So pointless. He was actually a year ahead of me. He was between me and my brother Hal. I used to envy Duke. Don't mind saying so. If he were here, I wonder if he'd remember me or my brother. My brother, Hal. Not Kenny. He was the baby. Ha. Still the baby!"

"Yes. I remember your family."

"Hal died last winter."

"I'm so sorry."

"Cancer. Lung cancer. Smoked. We told him. He didn't listen. Never listened to anyone. I didn't sleep for weeks after. Didn't sleep at all. He was trouble. From start to finish. Used to say to me, he'd say, 'I don't care what you people do.' His own family. Can you believe that?" Leon Wolf was trying hard, focusing on what to say to comfort Rivka. "I remember that. Didn't sleep at all. Look at that headstone—what a beauty," he said, at last, and turned his head toward the sound of the pneumatic drills blasting from the muffler shop.

My headstone. What would it say, my headstone?

Here Lies a Beloved Son and Brother
Yochanan Moshe Ben-Zebulin Wain
5723-5741.
May his soul be bound up in the bond of eternal life

That would be it. Beloved son and brother.

The rest was empty. Everlasting tributes did not exist. The life I'd intended, gone. The flames unlit. Gone, my threadbare notebooks carried, decade after decade, from one apartment to the next, one city to the next. Gone, writing my first book that I once dreamed would drop into the world like an explosion of my psyche. Gone, my second book. Gone, the third. Gone, the fourth. Childhood mates like Leon Wolf thought I was going to be something. Instead, chiseled one inch into the stone, there was no future and no past. No threadbare notebooks. No explosions of consciousness.

Chiseled one inch into the headstone was not *Free Spirit*.

Not *A Gentle Man*.

Not *A Life of Beauty and Service*.

Not *Faithful Friend*.

Not *Dweller of the House of the Lord*.

Not *Gone But Not Forgotten*.

Not even, *Gone Fishin'*.

Not *He achieved success who has lived well, laughed often, and loved much, whose life was an inspiration, whose memory is a benediction.*

None of that.

Not *Into the Blind World*.

Not *Rabbi*.

Not, just for fun, just for laughs, *Abandon All Hope, Ye Who Enter Here.*

Not, *But I reckon I got to light out for the Territory ahead of the rest.*

Not, most certainly not, *Loving Husband*.

Not, most certainly not, *Loving Father*.

Rivka, the Wounded One, the living daughter of Rabbi Gadol and Batya the Rock, the last of the Meyerland Wains, who had scolded me for putting my dirty tennis shoes on the floor mats of her precious car, now the possessor of the photograph set inside the silver frame, with her younger self staring blankly, and, where her black bangs once tined across her forehead was now a gray cowlick cascading over her cheek.

In that moment, inching away from talkative Leon Wolf, looking at my gravestone, does Rivka remember, all those years ago, my funeral, that the last to approach the coffin, with his gray hair falling down under his yarmulke, was Rabbi Gadol, who always prided himself on his familiarity with the rituals surrounding death, and, with a grimacing smile, he does not use the shovel, but takes a clod of dirt into his bare hand? He hurls the clod at the casket. It thuds against the earth inside the grave's hole. He fists another clod, hurls it, harder this time, missing the grave hole so it lands up above the tarpaulin onto the grass. From his lips, he's muttering the Mourner's Kaddish. On his knees now, soiling his black slacks and loafers, he seizes fistfuls of dirt and slams them, over and over, against the casket. No one watching moves, no one steps forward to help him up, no one looks away. All his expectations that life has an order to be lived in the strictest cycle of beginning, middle, and end, is defeated, and, here, his concept feels, like the dirt in his hands, a moronic deception. With a last fistful in each palm, he stands, lifts his eyes directly into the sunlight and, with the pneumatic drills blasting from the B & S Discount Muffler and Brakes shop across Post Oak Road he uncurls his palms so the dirt sifts through his fingers onto the pine casket.

Arm in arm, Rabbi Gadol and Batya the Rock drift away, weeping. Protectively, behind them, is Rivka. They walk over the green lawn and disappear into an air-conditioned car, and I am left, with weariness and tears all that remain, to be lowered underground.

I CAME UP FOR AIR, and exhaled. Twinkling lights from the hotels on Seawall Boulevard. Revving traffic. The taste of saltwater on my mouth. Salazar, fifty feet off, drifting with the tide toward the Pleasure Pier, splashing away, parallel to the shore, his stocky body bobbing.

Scissoring my legs under the swells, not so much treading water, but being pushed by the waves into shore, then shallow enough to get my footing on the muddy sand, trudging.

The cool sand felt good against my toes when, at last,

I slogged onto the beach underneath a steady breeze, water dripping from my eyes.

My arms flung wildly, and the wet clothes clung tightly to my skin. The waves fell back, leaving foam to fill up footprints where the surf washed in. Up and down the beach was laughter and shouting. I took comfort in the buzz of rock and roll mixed with country-and-western stations cranked up through open windows of pickups and car stereos.

That's when I saw the girl from the green pickup truck on the interstate sitting with her two friends.

"Now that's a merman if I ever saw one. You fall out of a boat?" she called.

I rubbed my eyes, and shook my hair like a dog wagging its body.

How far past midnight was it, I wondered, and noticed a swoop of gulls fling above the foam, while sanderlings sprinted.

The girl was laughing joyfully. She stood, inviting me to join her and her two friends, and laughed. "I love to swim as far out as I can. How far out did you go?" She twirled, until she fell over, in a tipsy heap. "Swimming makes me feel purified," she said.

She had sharp cheek bones, homey eyes. What impressed me as much as her believing that anything made her purified was the remark—*You fall out of a boat?*— with a look in her eyes like she could imagine the circumstances of her life changing in a moment's notice.

"My name's Caroline" she said, waving with her fingers.

"Hey. Caroline. Duke."

Her friends had walked off and quickly returned dragging armfuls of brush they'd found near a jetty, left behind from the daytime crowds. They got a fire going and set about stacking the wood to keep them for the night.

"Jim Bob," said the affable boyfriend, with a reddish face, like a nectarine, tipping the brim of his black Texas Tech baseball cap, pulled low over an unshaven face, and sitting on the sand. "This is Cassie," he said. She said hello with a drowsy voice, swallowed hard, and began at once to look cozy, with her palms reaching forward for the fire. They resembled each other, like siblings, the longer I looked at them. Both heavy and solid, dressed in Red Raiders t-shirts.

There was a crashing of waves.

"No matter the time of day or weather," Cassie said, affecting a yawn, staring into the flames, "the waves will be here."

We stoked and watched the fire, and drank the last of a fifth of José Cuervo, passing the bottle, hand to hand. The wind shifted and then it was silent. A rich smell of woodsmoke hung over the beach. Jim Bob turned the logs over with another stick of wood, put his bare elbow into the sand, and rested his cheek on his hand, where he could see the fire and the waves at once. For a moment, his eyes seemed to be lit, above his plump hand, speckled with white and yellow paint. Sitting cross-legged, Cassie stared into the fire, too, without much curiosity, much the way one looks into a window display, and her hands dropped between her thighs.

"This fire is a beautiful creation," said Jim Bob, dreamily, not taking his eyes off the flames. "A beautiful, beautiful, beautiful creation."

"You're drunk," Cassie laughed.

There was another rumble of waves. Jim Bob lifted one finger, then another, on the hand under his cheek, like he was playing the piano. He began to sing—

I've seen liars and I've seen pain
I've seen windy fires that I thought would never end
I've seen lonely fires when I could not find a friend
But I always thought that I'd see Galvez again

"That's not how it goes, Jim Bob," said Cassie. "You idiot."

"Sure, it is," he said. "That's the lost verse, Cassie. Nothing on earth can keep that song away from my heart. Nothing on earth. Most songs are dull, drab, most of them. Like church ladies on a Tuesday afternoon, walking into church to meet about the upcoming Saturday baked bean supper, walking in with their big white pocketbooks held by those little handles."

Caroline laughed. "Got fifty lifetimes crammed into those pocketbooks. No one has ever been able to find all those lifetimes. Got husbands stored in there. Ex-husbands."

"Ex-ghosts?" said Cassie, without surprise.

"Ex-strangers," Jim Bob said, making a gesture toward the bottle planted in the sand. Cassie handed it to him. All this time Caroline had been staring at me, and I enjoyed it, like the way Leah and I looked at each other when no one was at home, and we sat on the sofa in her living room and hardly spoke.

"This fire is a bloomer," said Cassie.

"Who are you?" Jim Bob asked, turning to me, his voice raised only slightly above an idle.

I was feeling very high and loose. "I'm a commissioner on love," I said.

He gave a vague smile. "A what?"

"What's a commissioner on love?" said Caroline.

Cassie swiped the bottle of tequila from Jim Bob's hand. "I want to be that. Right, Jim Bob? Commissioner of love."

"On love. I am the commissioner who looks out over all the love lives in all the lands on all the continents in every language," I said, and looked at Caroline. "I am the commissioner that everyone knows is watching. I see all you do. I have watched you every day for three thousand years, and I think we are nothing but ghosts in this year, 1981, the year, this very, very special year of the high commission."

Jim Bob raised his eyebrows. "How do you become a commissioner?" He had a thin drop of rum spilling down his chin.

"We're all commissioners," Caroline said. "That's what he means. Aren't we?" She turned to me. "I'd like to ride in your boat one day, Commish. You got a boat? I could lay on the deck and listen to the waves lapping against the sides," she said with a coyness, in a deep, warm, southern way of talking.

"The hull," I said.

"The hull, then," she repeated.

For an hour, we stole glances, without embarrassment, with Jim Bob and Cassie watching us, and we fast created a devotion with our glazed looks, titling closer, elbow touches, and tapping our legs, kicking sand onto each other's bare feet, playfully, giggling, drunk. The tequila and the hashish high were full on. She glanced at me, and I glanced back, alert, interested, furtive, or, at times, feigning neutrality, staring—I was staring at her mouth and how she held her lips open when she wasn't talking.

"Jim Bob, pull out Little Blackie for us commissioners," said Cassie.

He reached into a paper shopping bag and revealed a durable, black, plastic bong, with a glass downstem held in place with a rubber grommet. I was offered the first toke. The smoke came into my lungs cool and clean. Cassie inhaled hard and lifted her mouth with an oddly cheerful look, as if with each swirl of smoke inside her lungs strange feelings came her way and made her quieter.

"I'm going to study this here fire, people," Jim Bob said. "Each flame has moved further and farther apart."

He waved his hands toward the coals.

Cassie stared at the sky, and pursed her lips, then got to her feet. "Come on out there with me, James Robert. Let's walk to the jetty." He screwed the top to the José Cuervo, stabbed and twisted it into the packed sand, and the two disappeared toward the twinkling lights.

It was a quiet fire, and, above us, slipping in and out of clouds, the arc of the black sky was suspended. Caroline's mouth and eyes curved downward from her narrow nose, as if she had brushed them that way. She said little. Our eyes met. Drunk and high, I liked it. Did she say, *I could kiss you?*

Soon, my back was pressed against Jim Bob's green pickup truck, against the passenger's side, with the door open, and we were kissing. I could taste the burnt stain of cigarette smoke on her tongue, and not, as it had been with Leah, a bubbly flavor of lip gloss. Whether I was rubbing her breasts, at first delicately, then harder, or she was cupping my crotch underneath where the zipper stopped, we shuddered. When she pressed my head into her nipples after she'd pulled her tube top down to her waist, I licked and sucked, and I heard her sigh. Kissing around her breasts, I felt my mouth had taken up my whole body and the buzz from the spliffs and beer and hashish and pot and scotch and tequila all swirling. It's not that I thought I could have had those feelings only with Leah, though, in that moment, I was imagining the fine lines of Leah's face, and the delicate hair on her arms, breathing in the smell of her, sensing the weight of her and the contact of her skin, the looseness of her stomach, her firm thighs, the numbness of our closeness. But, leaning against the side of the truck, I'd also forgotten everything else I meant to be doing, meant to be thinking, except that an hour earlier I had been imagining my death while treading water and, here, I was making out with a girl I'd only glimpsed on the interstate hours before. The likelihood, the synchronicity, was baffling. And yet, too, I knew, even then, that, days later, wherever I was—in the truck bed, on the beach, Corpus Christi, or Padre Island, wherever Salazar and I managed to drive before we believed we'd made ourselves disappear—I would, very slowly, go over and over this feeling. The thought of it, just the thought, of what it felt shaking back and forth against the pickup truck, was something like the endless, intimate, pure, enlivening pursuit of secrecy.

"Duke, man! Duke!" called Salazar from fifty feet off, with his feet in the water, waving me over where he was standing with a black girl with a white Stetson.

Caroline and I tugged at our clothes and walked back toward the fire.

Salazar's shorts were mostly dry now, I could tell, and he explained he was going with "Mac over here" to the Strand downtown for a bit, to meet some guys she knows. "I've told you about her. She's a friend of Alejandro's. She goes to UH. You stay with the truck. Can you? Look at you!" he laughed. "You're still sopping wet. I told you, man."

"Hey, Mac," I said. She was stocky, smiling, in shorts and a loud shirt and red cowboy boots. We both looked over at Caroline who ran off to the scrub to pee.

"I remember the first night I came to party at this beach," Mac said without prompting, in a tone a substitute teacher might use with a sullen student. "I thought I'd never get through. Beer, rum, bourbon, all the shit people were smoking and sniffing up their noses, fires, couples fucking inside their cars. Whole island stank of fucking. Then breaking into some argument, the girl crying, storming off, the guy standing outside the back door with his dick in his hand. My first time, I couldn't even make it through the night. Passed out in the dune grass, right over there where your girlfriend is. Or, maybe it was farther down, by the fishing pier. Somewhere. Face in the sand. Granules and shit up inside my gums and nostrils. The people and cars and radios blaring. I thought I was going keel over. My friends had to carry me home, cause I couldn't walk on my own. Puking my ass off. But, look at y'all. Ya'll found your stride. So, you're the Duke? Your royal highness," she said, with a theatrical bow. Her hands were shaking when she spoke.

"Just Duke," I said.

"Watch out. We black communists are going to overthrow you and your royal highnesses' white means of production," she said. Her eyes were bloodshot. She was drunk, or on something. I thought, some kind of speed.

"I'm just a rabbi's son."

"Jew. Capitalist. Same opium. I won't detain you. But you should know a few auspicious points. Here today, gone tomorrow. The masses fall for that shit. It never ends. From the Dark Ages to the funny pages, capitalists demonize the workers," she said, talking to me, Salazar, and, it seemed, no one, all at once, and I thought, who is Mac? Who talks like this?

Who just starts spouting off a bunch of Marxist-Leninist BS? She wasn't done either. "Now, it's our time to demonize the capitalists. Terrorize you, if we have to. You will be rejected, if you will. So sorry—you might get murdered. Look at me. Somebody's got to pay the gravedigger. Not me. I lost my chains a long time ago. I'm a descendent of slaves, I'm a locomotive of history, and I'm a dyke."

"Trifecta," I said.

Here, I bowed to her, and we slapped our hands, up, down, then bumped fists.

"Don't think just because we're in America it can't happen. I mean, that's not what I came here to say, not what I'm here to say. No, sir. No, sir. In a nutshell. No, sir," Mac said.

"What can't happen," I said.

"Nationalize banks? How's that sound to you? You think this is a beautiful world? Full of happiness, over here? Happiness, over there? Look, right now, today, you have a handful of people who control our entire economy," she said, and began coughing, repeatedly sniffing hard, and shaking her head side to side. "You have, maybe, two percent of the population that owns one-third of the entire wealth of America, eighty percent of the stocks, ninety percent of the bonds. And these people have incredible power. They sit on the boards of huge corporations. The race is not to the swift."

Salazar, walking back from the pickup where he'd put on a shirt and flip-flops, called out, "Chase Manhattan Bank."

Mac said, "Multinational corporations. All of them. They determine the destiny of our entire country. You, me, boys, girls, that lumpy pair up there on the sidewalk taking their sweet time. Three cheers for them! If there's one thing I can't stand it's ignorant people."

"Wait. What? You hate free enterprise?" Salazar said.

Mac was looking up at the sky, catching her breath. "We don't live in a free enterprise society," she answered, and she play-acted slapping Salazar across the face. "We live in a corporate capital society, where virtually every single industry you have giant, multi-billion dollar companies competing—driving the small businessman out."

Salazar whistled. "You don't believe the profit motive is fundamental to human nature?" He gestured like a bullfighter stabbing a bull, then, for my benefit, said, "Her uncle, he's HPD. He worked with the Chicano Squad. José Campos Torres, and shit."

José Campos Torres was a twenty-three year old Mexican-American and Vietnam War vet who was beaten to death by the cops in the East End near Salazar's house.

"You go to UH?" I said to Mac.

"Obviously, the answer is yes. Obviously, to you, Manolo, the answer is no. I don't believe in the profit motive. It's not fundamental to human nature. Think about it. The spirit of cooperation, that you and I can work together, is better, rather than having to compete against each other and destroy each other. Now, then," bellowed Mac, continuing with her point, "take a good look at that lumpy couple standing up there at the back—leather jackets, torn jeans—you can't make up the make-believe shit those people got going. I tell you, I despise them. And, why do I despise him? Because, Mr. Jew and Mr. Chicano, they are optimists. Their attitude is 'We're the winners.' Don't try to dissuade me."

"She's got a point," I said, and he flipped me the finger.

"Fifty percent of our entire population doesn't even vote," Mac said. "So, I guess we're stuck with it. Those are primarily poor people. Eighty percent of them, the people who don't vote, are the Blacks, the Mexicans, the Asians. That's why my peoples are going to invade your peoples. It's happening in Texas, as we speak. The Black, the Mexican, the Asian, hell, even the Indian. We're going to out number you white people. Give us time. It's happening. As we speak. You ain't going to like it."

"Look at you, Duke," said Salazar. "Now you're a Jew and a white."

"Nobody told Goebbels, I guess."

"Whites are going to turn on you, too, Manolo, once they

find out your interest in you-know-what." Mac said. "They're going to turn on you, Duke. But, first, we're going turn on her people." She was pointing at Caroline who was sitting alone, the fire brightening her white face. "White folks aren't going take that shit lying down. You know who's going to be first to get it in the ass in this history lesson of class struggle? You know who: rich folks like that pretty white-skinned girl right there, who I saw you bird-dogging by that pickup truck, are going to want to get off their backs first? Not going to be the white trash. Nope. Marx didn't know shit about race in America. Know who's going to be first? Who's going to feel the first knife?"

"Who?" said Salazar.

"You're looking at it" Mac said, coughing, bending over, in a fit, and then she flicked her entire body into a pirouette, while shouting, "Hooo baby! They're going to try to fuck the Blacks. Always do. Not this time. A Marxist revolutionary black? Now, that's some fired up motherfucker. Hear what I'm saying? When that's done, then we going to give up on God."

Salazar shook his head. "No way, Mac. Marxism is cool. But, it's not going to stop people having faith."

"Reduces crime, too," I said. "Compliance with the laws."

Salazar shouted, *"Thou shalt not kill.* Ever heard of it? *Thou shalt not steal."*

"You two are the last of your kind. Scientific knowledge is dispelling religion throughout the world, as we speak," she said. "What do you think is going to happen when economic and technological improvements take place all over the rest of the world? People escape. That's what happens. They can leave home. Goodbye, starvation. Goodbye, disease. Fuck you, violence. Suddenly, no religion. Gone. Once you get rid of all that shit, there's not going to be a need for religion. Especially, for women. Keeping women in the kitchen and gay people in the closet. That's going to be a thing of the past. Women going to control their own bodies. Right, white girl?" She waved at Caroline. "You don't believe me? I can see it. For many centuries, the masses assigned to women the role of producing as many babies as possible. Abortion, homosexuality, contraception, any shit not linked to reproduction, was out. Religions emphasized fertility. Average woman had to produce five to eight babies in order to simply replace the population. That's going to be a thing of the past." She began coughing, whooping, bent over, lung-deep hacks. But, still talking through it. "Workers are going to unite, going to lose their chains, and when the means of production reach a sufficiently high level of economic and physical security, younger people are going to grow up taking that security for granted. The riddle of history will be solved, your royal highness. Religion will be dead."

As she talked, I felt the most high I had since we arrived at the beach. My eyes itched, throat sore. Caroline was stoking the fire, and offered a wan smile. I looked at Mac. She was turning in circles. Very high. Stoked up. I looked up and down the surf, among the stray fires and parties, for the singer. Where is that guy? Got to introduce Mac to the singer. That'd be a show.

Mac was tap dancing in the foamy drifts of the waves, singing under her breath: "Workers are doing it, doing it! Workers! Doing it!"

The indirect light from parked cars with their beams on showed the intricacies of her high forehead, sharp nose, her trimmed eyebrows, her eyes. She was bowlegged. Waving her hands and arms over her head, her painted fingernails flashed. Was she honest about all that stuff? There was a mesmerizing power in her eyes, but it came and went, and I was unconvinced.

"You haven't shown her your little ministry gift shop. Have you?" I whispered into Salazar's ear, as Mac ran over to try to hear what I was saying. "Your *Hope Saves the World* t-shirts and beer cozies."

Salazar was quick to speak, pressing his palms down in an everybody-calm-down mode, "What you need to understand about my friend Duke, here, Mac, is his people pre-date modern bourgeois society. I got news for you, Mac. You don't know who you're talking to. This guy snaps his fingers, and he's the next Grand Rabbi of the State of Texas. Snaps his fingers, and he's giving the benediction at the Governor's Ball. He's not just some average dude on the beach. He's been raised. Reared. Ambitious, educated. Look at him. He's the Duke of the Jews now, but he'll be King one day. You want him on your side. Our side. Look how he dresses. Denim on denim. Look at that cowboy shit. That's no capitalist. He's got no relationship to the means of production. Jewish mamas don't let their babies grow up to be cowboys, but they do let them grow up to be socialists."

"Good for fucking you, douche bag. Don't roll your eyes, Duke. I know who you are," Mac said, putting her face up near mine. "I know who you are. Affluent. Upscale. You never revolted against nothing. You think I'm your worst bullshit nightmare, don't you? I bet you your mama hires my mama to clean her toilet. Say it. Say it. *Schvartze*. Tell me I'm wrong. You can't."

She turned and kicked at the tide.

"I'm going with her for a while, Duke. Chill out, Mac," he called to her. Salazar stepped closer. "She's on something. Snorted some shit. It's okay. She's cool. I know her. She's Alejandro's friend. She's wound up. She needs someone to keep an eye on her."

"She's going to suck you in, mi hijo," I said. "You're part of the Chicano invasion?"

"My people get fucked in this world."

"My people have gotten away scot free? Your people? My people? Hate to break it to you," I said, letting the drunkenness overtake me. "Your old man spends more in cash on fancy suits than Rabbi Gadol gets in his yearly paycheck. Does Mac the Knife over here know about you, Mr. Son-Of-The-Evangelist-Seargant-Major-Charlie-Chaplain-To-Be-in-Full-Cahoots-With-Our-Capitalist-Overlords? You going to be the shepherd to the masses? That it? Send $3 every week to the P.O. box at the bottom of your screen."

"Look, just because my old man likes fine clothes, just

because he's engaged in earning what you call a few shekels, doesn't mean I embrace it. I get what she's saying, Duke. I get it. People like her, people like me, we are living in a violent world," he said, and I thought, oh, sure, we all love looking our very best in thousand-dollar suits in the eyes of a violent world. This was a moment of reckoning. It was a moment, I thought, on which he and I would face the facts. He sighed heavily, thinned his mustache with finger and thumb, and made a surly look. Salazar was as good a talker as the old man—no, he was better, less the charlatan, more able to tantalize. I had always known this about him. He appeared confident that this middle-of-the-night dispute, like anything else confronting him, would blow over. Gotten through rough spots before, plenty of times. I realized, of late, I had been up in his face—talking about spontaneity and lighting out, being free, and he, consistently, countering. There was gospel in what he had to say about hardship being the only fact of life we are all sure to have. Can't be quit. Or you might have nothing at all. He knew what he was talking about. Yes, he could be something of a hypnotist. But, even a conjurer can tell the truth. Suffering, not charm, was our burden. "Duke, look. Dude, you've been sleeping through your old man's sermons about community and charity," he said. "We're living in a world that wants my face in the dirt. To survive, we got to rule. I know you're one of us. I don't want to crush rich people or white people or Jews or Muslims of Hindus. I just don't want to be crushed. I thought you'd understand that. You, of all people. Look, man, look, I'm going with her for a little while. Not too far. She wants me to meet these guys. Pilgrims, Duke. She's winging me. We're going to the Strand. Okay? You stay here with this fine group of people." Jim Bob and Cassie had returned, talking with Caroline by the fire, not looking at us. "I'll be back. We'll shake it out. Blow us a fat one. You and me. Watch the truck. Tomorrow, we'll drive all the way to Padre. Wherever you want to go. We'll get away from all this shit, this whole fucked up condition of existence. We don't have to be our fathers."

The meeting was over.

Salazar and Mac turned their backs to the waves and walked up a set of concrete steps to the sidewalk on Seawall Boulevard.

Near a black pickup truck, Mac was shouting, "Labor in the white skin can never free itself as long as labor in the black skin is branded. That's *Das Kapital*, for those of you keeping score at home."

CAROLINE AND I WALKED UP THE BEACH to Salazar's pickup where, after I took the keys from above the tire and pulled on my cowboy boots, I turned the power on, tuning the radio to KIKK. On came Charlie Pride.

"You want to dance?" I said, and tossed the damp notebook from my pocket onto the dashboard.

"What's that for?" Caroline asked. She was swinging her heavy backpack along the sand and set it down next to the truck.

"That's where I write down the words to what happens."

"What do you do with them?"

"And the life I live. That's all. My entire mind is in there," I said, and I felt numbly drunk.

She passed her hands through her hair and tugged at her tube top, tripped barefoot over a sand heave before she let me catch her in my arms, and we two-stepped near the yellow side lights of the truck. "Kiss an Angel Good Morning" crooned from the speakers.

"'You want to dance?' I bet you say that to all the girls."

"No. C'mon," I said.

"That so? I'm really wasted," she said. "That's what I am. I'm that angel, just like those tankers parked out there. See them?"

She pushed strands of hair from her face.

We stood there, looking in the direction of the tanker lights and tumbling waves, weakly dancing, her arms wrapped around my shoulders, mine, around her waist. Soon, we scooted under the truck bed on top of a slender beach towel I'd pulled from the cab.

"Making out is dancing," she whispered, and she lay across

the top of my chest. At first we kept our clothes on but they were shifting around. I fumbled at her tube top to pull it down to her belly. I took her hand and led it to my lips. A groan came from my throat. When she pressed her palm against the bulge in my pants, she watched my face, and kept moving her hand. I smoothed my fingers along the skin of her shoulder. A gasp when my mouth found her nipple and stayed there. Lying above her now, both of us underneath the truck, beneath the tail pipe, I looked up, over her freckled forehead, past the underside of the truck to see the gray water lunging. Our skin goose-bumped by the wind. When I undid my pants and she hers, almost at the same time, I reached between her legs, but her arm pushed my hand away. So I lingered near her hips, then glided my hand, slowly and quietly, back to her breasts, neck, forehead, alongside her cheek, around her ear, into her hair, as if my hand was straying on its own and instructing my sense of touch. We kissed more. Her mouth tasted of cigarette smoke and tequila. Shards of car lights showed up on our arms and on Caroline's face. Our breaths deeper and shorter, and we pulled tighter. My skin came down warm on her warm skin. For a moment we were still. Her face against mine, her hips cradled in my hands. When she clutched my neck, I brought one hand up from under her to roam through her sand-filled hair. Gripping. Sighing in huffs. Her face held a look I couldn't read.

The high inside me was lush and deep, deep as a dark root underground, stiffening, then the sloshed muddle was blowing away what focus I had, like scattering sand. Here, she stood. From behind the truck's gate, she looked around to see that no one was near and considered pulling the tube top over her head, letting it drop to her feet. I remembered how Leah would stand in the same way in the little bedroom of her parents' house just before she reached both hands behind her back, to unclasp her bra—pausing, looking at my mouth, and her arms still behind her as if holding a gift, hesitant, as her breasts toppled out. Briefly, I thought, why? Why was I underneath the pickup truck? Why was Caroline so persuasive, more than Leah? Sincere, honest Leah, good-hearted Leah, serious Leah.

"Good gosh a'mighty. I don't know what's gotten into me. You swimming out of the ocean," Caroline said, shivering, noticing people walking on the beach, pulling up her tube top, and crawling back under the pickup.

I didn't know either, as I didn't know much then of the furtive pungency and saltiness and mysteries of much of anything. And yet, still, I tried to act as one might when seeing a lightning bug for the first time—with an intense alertness, but also calmly, nonchalantly, as if I was in the habit of seeing fireflies a thousand times a day.

So far, it was as long a night as I could remember.

Aside from the pitiful sight of the two of us surreptitiously intertwined underneath the chassis of Salazar's pickup truck, rolling over the crumpled beach towel, aside from the strange, watery, drowning fantasy still sloshing inside my mind, aside from the beer and pot and hashish and liquor and the frail day turning to night and turning more outrageous, with more and more churning, more and more spilling— aside from all of that, and the crazy singer waving his Colt .38, there was only a shadowy sensation underneath the truck. The strain of being on my knees but not lifting my back. The jolt of abandonment.

Here, two small Toyota pickups raced past, circled, honking their horns, and flashing their brights at us, five, six times.

We rolled off each other, hunkered on our knees, underneath the corroded muffler.

The high beams wavered. Both trucks spun doughnuts and figure-eights on the packed sand, blaring their horns, until we clawed for our clothes and struggled to dress, fishtailing our hips to tug up our pants up to our waists—I was pressing my erection down to zip up my jeans—while lying on our backs in the scratchy sand underneath the truck. We began to notice that more people had gathered on the beach during all that time. Crawling to our feet and standing side by side, looking at each other, having poured ourselves over each other, with knotted admiration, we were suppressing smiles conspiratorially. Caroline put a hand over my mouth. Lights flickered over the water. My ankle was throbbing. She stepped aside, moved her arms like a ballerina, tripping drunkenly, forward and back, over the hard-packed sand, as if being blown in the wind, the waves breaking in heaves before dissolving back into the flats, again and again, heaving and dissolving.

By 4 A.M., Caroline Cahill had told me her whole story.

Words had come out of her mouth without interruption, while we sat with our feet dangling over the gate of the pickup truck and, later, while she lay on her back in the truck bed as if she were talking to the clouds, amid inconsolable weeping.

Afterward, we were sitting side by side in the truck bed, with Caroline wrapped tightly in Mamá Salazar's serape. She was reaching into my knapsack and tossing out the inventory—pens, pocket knife, spoons, cassette tapes, chocolate, a bolo, sunglasses, black notebook, bottle of Bayer aspirin—until she found the box of matches and cigarettes she was hoping for. I took them, smacked the bottom of the pack until a cigarette popped up. Lighting one in my mouth, I handed it to her. There came from her mouth a long exhale of smoke.

There were wet streaks on her face. She wiped them with a flat palm, and considered something I might only guess at after she eyed the cab of Salazar's pickup, frowning, tilting her mouth. A frail melancholy descended. We sat at the edge of the endless tide, our hair flapping softly, and waited for the sun to come dripping out of the horizon, but we didn't move. It felt like, somewhere, time was being borrowed out beyond what we could see in the gray, desolate waves. Here I was, at last, free. Or, something.

Opening the cooler inside the truck, I found a beer, snapped open the tab. "I don't think we have any water," I said. "Want to drink it?"

"You have some," she said.

I took a sip, offering the can to her, and I felt, for sure, she was giving me a gentle glance, as if she could see me plainly.

"Oh, yeah. I need that," she said and took the beer from my hand, lifting the can to her lips, then froze halfway to her mouth, looking as if she could take it or leave it, twirling the can. Drops of liquid leapt out to stain the sand.

I took the pack of cigarettes and shook another one out, cupped my hand, and lit it, and then put the match in the ashtray. A gust of wind was grainy in my mouth. I ran my tongue alongside my teeth. My eyes fell on her face, as if for the first time. I thought, she's a performer. Yeah, she's a performer. She could make you believe she felt the wind cold through to her bones. She could convince you with her trembling that she was continually amazed, that the amazement of life was always coming into her eyes.

When she handed the can of beer back to me, I lifted it to my mouth and drained it in one gulp, then I lifted the collar of my shirt and wiped my lips.

The story Caroline Cahill told started when she said: I want you to write this down in your notebook, my whole story. Cahill was not her given name, she said, but the one her mom had taken to hide from something, her mom said, I never want to tell you about, sugar.

Mom and daughter were living in Presidio County, near Big Bend, close to the Rio Grande River, in a house like a barracks, something squalid. Caroline slept on a slatted, iron cot, with Army supply blankets. After a time, they moved, then moved again, then again, and then again, in and around Alpine and Fort Davis and Marathon. It was in high school, after she turned sixteen, that Caroline finally came around to understand what her mom's situation was, and what happened to the money she made working nights at the Buns 'N Roses, a diner on the highway on the way to Marfa. Here, too, her mother used something like an alias. "Lynn Myles" everyone at the restaurant called her—just a lean, dark-headed, left-handed waitress.

Caroline's mother had decided she and Caroline would hide out in West Texas until Caroline graduated high school, then move to Denton, where they had a cousin, and put half of Texas between Linda Cahill or Lynn Myles, or whoever she actually was, Caroline said with a caustic laugh, and whatever it was we were running from. Her mother spoke with excitement of going to Barton Springs to get baptized. Caroline learned about what happened to the money while waiting to get her cheerleader's uniform in the high school office in Marfa. She had been sitting alone in a straight backed wooden chair, when she heard a woman on the other side of the door to the principal's office talking about her mother's situation. What had happened was, during the previous year, Mrs. Cahill, along with a girlfriend from work, had begun sending donations to a local TV ministry in Midland. First, it was just two or three dollars a week, which she slipped into a stamped envelope only on Sundays, when she kept the ministry's program turned low on the small TV they kept on the formica counter in the kitchen, while her mother was scrambling eggs or frying pancakes, under a naked light that hung down into the room with a long, twisted cord, before the two went off to church at One Assembly of God. Mrs. Cahill next began donating ten dollars twice a week to a P.O. box somewhere in East Texas. Caroline was seventeen that year. When the manager at the restaurant found out what the two waitresses were doing with their money, she pulled them aside and began taking them to Alpines' Catholic Church, the one called Our Lady of Charity. Caroline went on and on about that priest. She liked him, so did her mother. He was a lonely, middle aged, Hispanic man, Father Sanchez, who had a dreamer's twinkle in his brown eyes. Most Sundays, Our Lady of Charity was filled with deep silence, while faces of saints in a series of cheap paintings were moaning down on them. Caroline said it was the first time she felt a valley come into her when she prayed. But, for her mother, it was something more: she had found well water after years of dry land. Week after week, the saintly Sunday light inside the church, light that poured through sixteen stained glass windows with crucifixes in each one, filled her soul with fresh testimony. Father Sanchez implored his parishioners to be diligent with their money to provide for their own—and those who did not, as it says in Timothy, he liked to say, are deniers of faith and worse than unbelievers. Of debt, Mrs. Cahill learned from Father Sanchez, no one can serve two masters. One afternoon, before she went to work at the diner, Mrs. Cahill returned to Our Lady of Charity and told Father Sanchez she would like to come more often, but, since she wasn't Catholic, was there some way she could learn from him while staying true to her Baptist faith? Faith requires a journey, Father Sanchez told her, and he gave her a pamphlet for an Evangelical ministry in Houston, from a preacher who called himself, the Man of God. The pamphlet was titled: "The Real Meaning of the Cross." Readers were said to be greatly moved by the Man of God's generosity. He had a winning record, the pamphlet put it, with how believers could carry on—despite lapses, despite their fears of giving up the religions of their upbringing. Alongside the call to belief in an article titled, "Sin No More Alone," was an inset photograph of the Man of God himself. He stood alone in an blue silk suit, Caroline said, with a white tie and shirt. He was standing in front of a one-story brick ranch house.

This was the part of the story that Caroline Cahill told while lying on her back in the pickup, with her eyes shut tight. It may have been she didn't want to feel she could be seen telling her own story, that, worse was to come, that by closing her eyes, she had become invisible. She said, it's true, every word, and I mean it, and whoever claims I'm not telling the complete honest-to-God truth about my life is as good as dead to me. Was it so far-fetched, she said, inconceivable, that the last couple years she was not being fully alive but—here, she raised her hands into air quotes—dead? I've been dead a long time, she said.

The Man of God was the one who really took our money, Caroline went on. She said: We first began listening to cassette tapes of the Man of God and his sermons. They were mailed from Houston. One, I'll never forget, we listened to over and over and over. It went: "Twenty years ago, when the Lord called me from a Texas cotton patch, I stopped at the cow pen and picked up a little Jersey cow, and she and I went off to the University of Houston together. And, she knew, this is the truth, she knew as much scripture as I did. Twenty years ago. And, to think here we are today, because of the faithfulness of God and the grace of our wonderful savior. I love to hear scripture sung. Don't you? 'God in My Life' has been sung in so many places, in the jail, out of the jail. We all should be screaming, Joy to the Lord! To me, praise is the lubrication system that keeps Jesus, that keeps him from burning out of our hearts. You lose the joy, and you've had it. Now, friends, I'm glad that during these precious years when we've sought to be good Americans, we've taught our people to respect the flag. I love the flag. I believe in what the flag stands for. I preach that truth every Sunday. I preach that truth into this here tape recorder. I preach that truth, the truth of the flag, of Jesus Christ, son of God, into the hearts of all. Is your heart with me? Is your heart listening? Every time today—and I'm a grown man—every time today I sing 'My Country 'Tis of Thee,' I feel like I'm still that little old country boy going to school, just a one room school house, with one teacher who taught eight grades, and I'd stand and sing 'My country 'tis of thee, sweet land of liberty.' I never knew then that someday the beggars will come begging in this great nation, this great state of Texas, for freedom, for justice, for love, for God, for Jesus, the son of God. Amen. That's the cry that comes. I believe that this will go down as the decade of destruction for America. You want my text? Second Chronicles, 36:16: 'They mock the messenger of God.' They despised his word, they misused his profits, until the wrath of the Lord was sent upon his people, until there was no remedy. That's where we are today.

I believe three things happened. Number one, marijuana spells doom for any nation. America is now a wasted nation. And these people, these drugged-up people, they wouldn't talk to you and me for nothing. Won't listen to Jesus for nothing. Won't weep at the feet of Jesus for nothing. I say to these people, give up your marijuana cigarettes. Give up your bottled liquor. Clean up your homes for the homecoming so they don't look like hog pens. Well, you say, I don't like you saying that about my home. Well, I already said it. Ain't no way to un-say it. Well, you say, I'm not an addict. No, you ain't an addict, you're a pothead. What I'm telling you is give your life over to Jesus. And, before you get ugly, before you get mad and tell me I can't say what I'm saying, remember that no one has a track record better than Jesus. American, Olympic, world record, our Lord and savior, Christ Jesus. Before you get critical and ugly, and miss the blessing, and God has to whip your britches off you, you better pay attention to it. I'm sick and tired of these wet noodles coming in from the Jell-O Seminary with their tapioca pudding on the power of positive thinking. It's too late for that kind of junk. The only way we're going to keep our children off the marijuana cigarettes, is if you come back also for help. My soul! You need to get back in the prayer closet. Men and women, boys and girls, get back in the family altar. Get back in the gospel."

I loved that one, she said, *The only way we're going to keep our children off the marijuana cigarettes.* I can't remember the other two things. *Praise is the lubrication system that keeps Jesus!* Oh, we would sit at the kitchen table on Saturday evenings. Aside from being mesmerized by the Man of God's voice, a voice that was like a whoop wrapped inside silk, I was also frightened. Really, it was awful, the mix of pain and joy. But, then, my mom caught a fever, and I took a job, part-time, at the Buns 'N Roses, working as a counter girl. My mom was sick a month, maybe two, it's hard to say, and she was wiring more and more money to the Man of God. I said to her, Mom, stop giving all our money to that reverend. You must stop. She goes, money? What money?

Out of our savings, I said. Don't wet your britches, she said. He doesn't want money. That's not what the Man of God wants. Then, what does he want? I said. He wants us to have our sins cleansed, sugar.

One Friday night, Caroline went on, she and a girlfriend snuck out after dark and went to Creekside, a dance bar with a juke box, and got drunk. Bartender didn't even ask for their ID's. That's Marfa for you, she said. They drank four beers each. Couple of ranchers bought them two more and asked them to dance. Dancing, she said, that was what I needed. Though I didn't need that rancher's rough hands on my ass, and I told him so. But, there was no quit in that one. When Caroline came home, her mother was waiting, and she wasn't happy. I screamed at her, I want to live my own life! Then, I slammed a door. Fine, she yelled, live your own life, dad-gummit. And, she stormed out of the room we were in—in the kitchen, the living room, whatever it was. Good, I said, I want to. I said, You won't let me. I said, I need to dance sometimes. All right? Is it so bad? Dancing? Going to a dance hall? It's not like we're Pentecostals. We're Baptists. Or Catholics, or with the Man of God. I don't know what we are anymore, I said. And, my mom goes, You need to dance? Is that what you're saying? And now, she's really pissed. You can't just sneak around like this, she says. Then she was on me about my room. She goes, It's a pig sty. But, it wasn't. Just some clothes on the floor. But she goes, none of your things are ever put away right. You treat your clothes like this, sugar, how you going to treat other people? And, I said, Why do you care what I do? Oh, she says, now I'm the bad guy? I'm the bad guy? No, I said, I'm not saying that, you're saying that. But, she wasn't done. No. She says, it's such a shame, a damn shame, what you've done to us—and then she left my room—me shouting behind her, I guess you want it this way! And, she's out of the room. Just like that. I'm seventeen years old, can you believe that shit? And, I say to her, Stop yelling. And, she screams back, she screams from the other side of the house, I'm not yelling!

But then, then, she's suddenly right back inside my room, and she goes, Sugar, a dance hall? Sugar, a dance hall is where a man takes his wife. Creekside ain't a dance hall. It's a honky-tonk. And, a honky-tonk is where a man dances with somebody else's wife or with a seventeen-year old girl the same age as his own daughter who snuck out her mother's house through a window!

Next night, Caroline went on, my mom pulled out a Rand McNally map of Houston and tried to find the address where she sent the money. Sunday morning after church was the last I ever saw her. She was gone. That was in the middle of my junior year, in January, late in January. Or, I don't know now. Winter, anyway.

What happened next was Caroline kept going to school without telling anyone about her mom leaving. For a week, she turned in her Math 3 homework and Texas History project and took a test in biology. For a week, after school, Caroline practiced her jumps and cheers with other cheerleaders, and she cheered at the football game on Friday night, where the home team Shorthorns played Odessa's Permian Basin Renegades, six on six, with the colossal sky purpling in the dusk. Halftime, nearly all the boys on the football team, and all the girls in the cheer squad, threw down their gear and picked up instruments to march across the field in the marching band, including Caroline on the piccolo.

For a week or more, she said, I slept alone each night in my bed. No one to hold my hand. I kept thinking about those ranchers at the Creekside. So I went. And—you're going to hate me for this. But, you know. I found one, she said, and she opened her eyes and stared into mine, appearing like she might cry, but not crying. I realized, she said—closing her eyes again after a hard sigh—my mom taught me three things and three things only: God loves me, and I'm going to burn in hell.

The other thing? I asked.

Caroline laughed. Sex is horrible, dirty, filthy, and rude, she said, and I should save it for the one I love alone. She laughed again and, after lighting and cupping a match inside her curved hand, lit a cigarette.

After that, Caroline began living in Big Bend under a blue tarp for a lean-to, sleeping on the bare ground. Some days she went without food. If it rained hard, with high wind off the open desert, the lean-to blew off its stakes, and she slept exposed. She said, I kept thinking, I'm not fit for love. I'm just not fit for it. But that feeling made me feel free. You see? Because I'm not a bump on a cucumber, Duke, okay? And, now, that's how I live.

So much of what she told me was hard to reckon, from where I was sitting, from the life I was from—and my father assuming I'd follow in line into the rabbinate, with my iron-willed mother taking his side as briskly as she wipes clean the kitchen counter tops, with Rivka never giving an inch, and lately I could hear Rivka screaming into the phone from the other end, from Dallas, "I'm not a baby—I'm twenty-four years old," and with an entire section of Jewish Houston devoted to our comfort, every lawn, driveway, and streetlight flashing its power over us to fulfill—once and for all, deep down in the Old Confederacy— the covenant between Abraham and Yahweh.

Last year, when she was nineteen, Caroline Cahill had been living in the pickup with Jim Bob and Cassie. They'd met at Bastrop, she went on, and there was a band they wanted to see playing soon in Marfa, so they drove out there, and, while she had a chance to slip off, she went to the last house she'd lived with her mother. Thinking, maybe she'd returned. Thinking, maybe she was in there right then behind the peeling wood clapboard siding. Thinking, maybe she would just be sitting in the kitchen under the naked light that hung down with the long, twisted cord, listening to her tapes from the Man of God, and his voice like a whoop wrapped inside silk. Listening to Caroline, I pictured a shabby house but with odd touches: a balustrade, black tar roof, and in the yard, behind a tangle of cotoneaster, abandoned, a rotted bathtub, a slab of concrete. But, the lights were out, Caroline said, the house dark, rooms empty. She could only imagine the pine paneling, dishes in the cupboard, cups hanging from their hooks, television set surrounded by stuffed furniture with throws. Scattered on the enclosed porch that was covered with years of leaves, she said, there was a pile of bills, political brochures, church flyers, grocery coupons, unopened mail of every size. There also were three letters from her mother addressed to Caroline, but with no return address, which Caroline picked up, after hesitating, wondering how wan the circle of red ink of the postmark stamp appeared to her, the postmark from Houston, beckoning from the envelope, rubbed pink by the weather, and she tucked the three letters, unopened, into her shoulder bag.

Living with her friends in the truck hadn't been that bad. All along she resolved to tell everyone she met what she had been through. Determined to tell anyone who listened—not just guys like you, she said, opening her eyes, with a self-deprecating smile, then shutting them tight. How else could she live free? Free, she cried softly. I admit it, she said, I was also lonely.

One of the millions of reasons she loved living in the truck with her friends, she said, was they made money by stopping at rest areas and cleaning themselves up to a Christian shine, then driving slowly through the wealthy suburbs of Austin, San Antonio, Dallas, Houston, wherever they were, and collecting glass bottles for, she said, what we called our church's Sunday school where we said we worked teaching the children, doing Bible guessing games, making Bible book marks, and, you know—we'd tell them people—that at Easter time we'd teach the children to make open tomb clothespins. Got a lot of bottles that way, all cleaned up, and we redeemed them at the grocery. That, and selling weed to high school kids in those fat-cat neighborhoods.

Did you ever open the letters, I asked.

She had. One day, months after finding the letters on the concert trip to Marfa, while the truck was parked near the campus of the University of North Texas, in Denton, and her friends were collecting bottles and cans from the Greek houses, and she had just returned form the laundry, and had discreetly changed her clothes in the bathroom at a gas station on the way back, she realized the torment she was feeling from not yet opening them. Need to break out the Oreos, baby, I said to myself. Calmly, she reached her hand to the bottom of her shoulder bag. Here, she studied the postmark: Houston, TX 77023. The date was a year earlier. She studied her mother's clean cursive. The tail in the "l" of Caroline looped like a slender rope attached to the little "i." The "i" topped with a thick dot. Carefully, she opened all three envelopes at once ever so slowly, she said, and laid the letters in her lap in the order they were written. It was ceremonial, and she was feeling lightheaded. For a moment, she said, opening her eyes to me and putting her palm on my leg, I simply stared at the ink and rubbed my fingers on the paper, just as I'm touching you now——and it seemed to me, as I listened to her say, just as I'm touching you now, as I felt her fingers on my damp jeans along the inner part of my thigh, that this was not the first time Caroline Cahill had performed this story, and not the first time she had described how she unfolded the paper, ever so slowly, so not to tear it. 77023, she said again.

Gulfgate, I said.

That's what it said in the letter, too. My mom was living in Gulfgate, not with the Man of God, but nearby and they had, not fallen in love, but were companions. Because he had a wife. Or, an ex-wife. I don't know. Oh, Duke, she said, he had such a beautiful voice, the Man of God. Truly did. You could tell from the cassette tapes. But, it was better in person, my mom said. You could feel belief in that voice. My mom went on and on in one letter about his voice. She wrote: *Sugar, he is pure ecstasy, he is always of his audience.* My mom wrote that she often gathered in his backyard, listening to him record his cassettes. She wrote that she would lean back in a folding beach chair and feel the prayers belonging to her. The Man of God talking on and on, nourishing everyone, like a dream. But, those letters were just more of my mom's lies, Caroline said, her voice turned bitter. She said, all her days living with her friends in the pickup truck, all her time on the road, the beautiful, wide open blacktop, she called it, taught her that religion is the cause of everybody's suffering. Her life had been robbed from her, she said—by her mom, by the Man of God.

"IT'S A RIDICULOUS STORY," Caroline said.

"Ridiculous? I don't think so," I said.

"My talking like this. Don't know why I'm telling you all this. I just met you," she said. "I'm wasted, that's why. You're wasted."

"I don't know what you mean. It's not ridiculous."

"I want you to write this all down in that notebook of yours. My whole story, okay?" she said. "One day you're going to be a famous writer. Write it down. There's a story for you. An Alpine girl comes all the way across Texas, makes out with a boy she just met on the beach in Galveston Island. Which beach is this?"

"Well it's not Stewart. Not here. Porretto, I guess," I said.

"Alpine girls gets chased out by assholes in pickup trucks, those fuckers, and then, before morning, she cries hysterically, like a fucking little girl, telling him her runaway saga."

"Doubt I'll be famous."

"So this is me," she said.

"You probably should go home," I said.

"You probably should go home," she said and rolled to her side with her head in her hands. Long silence, then sleep.

What was the point of all that, I wondered.

To tell herself how hardened the world is, how indifferent? To tell herself that pious people abandon their children? Or, to tell me? Or, to tell anyone, whoever she'd told and retold this wild story to, to how many guys she'd sauntered up to while drunk and high, no different from me, and pressed them to her pickup, guys, like me, who were happy enough to be pressed up against? To tell them, me, whoever else, about her mom abandoning her to the desert nights of Presidio County in far West Texas? About taking up with the Man of God? In Gulfgate? The Man of God with his ex-wife?

I thought, to some people, the trouble of Caroline Cahill living on her own in the back of a pickup truck, cruising all of Texas collecting glass bottles to survive, might not mean a thing. To some people, it might appear she was a bad seed, is all, a fallen girl, worse, a fallen, white Christian girl. Did she tell people this story of hers so someone might take her home? Mother, Dad, this is Caroline. Caroline Cahill. Alpine, Texas. Orphan, waif. I was thinking, maybe Jewish Family Service can help her. The Sisterhood? Hadassah? She could stay in Rivka's room for a time.

Still, Rabbi Gadol would look at her, then me, then her, and he'd know within two minutes time what we'd done together on the hard-packed sand, under the chassis of the pickup truck. It would not take him even that much time.

Was this the power of her story?

Or, not my house. But, Mamá Salazar's house.

By now, I had rolled a spliff and lit it, removed my boots, and stepped away from the sleeping Caroline inside the pickup truck. I was walking in the drifts, the foam up to my ankles, leaning forward every few steps to get my breath. I squatted and scooped a fistful of wet sand when the tide fell back and let the grains fall onto dark puddles, as if to bury my thoughts. A black-masked seagull circled. I stood watching the waves curl and eddy.

Thinking of her tale, I had to wonder: Who was the Man of God? I wanted to know for sure. The strength of the feeling bewildered me. I seemed, at that moment, to have an urge to orient myself as I had never before felt oriented. Not when I was dating Leah, and she dazzled my parents with her interpretation of *Toldot Yeshu*, and how Jesus got his magic, his miraculous powers, how he fooled the masses with magic tricks. Not when I was making out, behind the diving boards at T.C. Jester Park, with Nicole from Episcopal as she lay down on her side and propped her head up with an arm, her black hair falling over her shoulder. Not when I sat in my father's shul every morning before dawn, passing prayer books to the jowly men come to say Kaddish before going to work, and listening to him begin one of his miniature sermons with the words, *My friends*. Not when I spent day after day with Salazar, who was determined to invent his own existence, and, if not that, write a new one with originality and intoxication. But, at dawn, on the beach at Galveston, the tide pounding, without forbearance, I let the perplexity get to me.

Your Father Salazar.

Gulfgate? 77023? The ex-wife? Was he the Man of God?

Even if he wasn't, when he met Caroline Cahill, the cheerleader from Marfa High School, piccolo player in the marching band, the diligent student who turned in her Math 3 homework even when she was living outdoors underneath a floppy lean-to under the harsh elements of rain and wind that winter, he'd take her in, research where the envelopes to Marfa had come from—he knew all those ministries—and at last, reunite mom and daughter. He'd get as big a kick as I did with her patter, too, the way she salts her story of the beautiful open blacktop with expressions that could steal your heart. Break out the Oreos, baby! Don't wet your britches! There's no quit in that one! Like a bump on a cucumber!

Still, if I returned her to her mom, if I took her to Father Salazar's or Mamá Salazar's, or even brought her home, to my parents, what then? Would Caroline Cahill's suffering—having sex with strange boys, and partying, lying about doing Bible guessing games—simply go away? Could she make herself afresh? Could anyone? Can one? What about Leah? What would I say to her? There were whole days, when Leah's parents or mine were away from home, we had been naked together for hours, hardly a foot apart from each other. This was not like when we were three years old, when we'd run around the back yard stripped to nothing, innocent as Eden, in the blistering heat, spraying water hoses at each other. But, hours on end, when I had looked at her skin, and she had looked at my skin. We concealed nothing. Gone, the shyness. Gone, the secrets. Both of us absorbed. Both of us, hands and teeth, hair, lips and tongue, fuzz, cock, vagina, fingers, salt, neck, hips. Both of us seen clear through. Muscle and skin, clear through. The meanings of boy, girl, Jew, clear through.

Here I was, a new life almost tasted, almost felt, smelled, heard, almost seen. Wouldn't I, by helping Caroline Cahill, be right back where I started twenty-four hours ago? Back to my future as the Meyerland Jew who asks the right questions? The Meyerland Jew who improves mankind? The Meyerland Jew who is responsible to the living and the dead? What, then, of my purpose? How much of life was to be lived for that ever afterward? Was my future one of reading the newspaper every morning, cutting out articles about notable Jews, leading the early morning minyan as, what else? The inheritor of a long line of serious rabbis, one by one climbing the ladder up to the world headquarters of Yahweh? Was that my destiny after helping Caroline Cahill? If seeking escape were not enough, if liquor and weed were not enough, if imagining one's own drowning were not enough, what was the route left to me? Who was I pretending to be, if not myself, had Caroline Cahill not intervened? A ghost living in some undiscovered time? And, was she even Caroline Cahill, who, only the evening before, had sat alluringly in the back of Jim Bob's green pickup as it cruised southward on the Gulf Freeway, who had shared Little Blackie and José Cuervo, who stood, half-stripped naked, from under the pickup truck and thought about pulling off her tube top and crawled under the chassis to rescue both of us? The Caroline Cahill who spooled out an epic of the soul's journey worthy of "Song of Myself?"

My longing, as I paced barefoot across the foam from the splashing waves, with lights from the tankers and oil rigs dotting the horizon, and as she slept in Salazar's truck, exceeded anything I had anticipated this day would have become when I'd awakened, hungover, on the carpeted floor of Mamá Salazar's living room. Yes, Caroline Cahill was young and charismatic and living an adventure, and her every word meant she was alive. Was I to turn her in? Like she was a fugitive? To Father Salazar? To reunite with her deserter?

Mrs. Cahill or Mrs. Webber or whatever her name is?

No one would believe her story anyway. No one who didn't want to. Nor, believe my story.

Mother, Dad, this is Caroline Cahill. She's come to live with us.

From then on, everyday, she'll walk through the living room, same as me, and she'll look at the photograph on the side table in the silver frame. She'll look into Rabbi Gadol's eyes and Batya the Rock's and the Wounded One's eyes, and my own, as if she could tell all of our futures. She'll coo, *Good morning, Rabbi Wain.* Coo, *Good morning, Mrs. Wain.* She'll walk through the same hallways as I, eat breakfast at the table my father writes his sermons with his silver Cross pen, turn her head toward the sound of his voice when he writes a phrase he's proud of or finds a nuance of interpretation that pleases him, and exclaims, *Now that's something!* Or, when he groans, *Sim lev!* She'll ask him questions about Proverbs and Deuteronomy and Psalms, and, patiently, tapping his heart with his hand, he'll dutifully answer with his orderly, accurate, shorthanded way of characterizing all of life as an emanation of slanted lines interrupted by wiggles. Yes, no longer would she be bereft. And, I? Wouldn't I mean every word of my capitulation, of my submission, my surrender? Good gosh a'mighty, she was an open book, all right.

Of course, I did not say any of this, nothing about who I was, or who I thought the Man of God is. Saying nothing explained it all.

Already, thick morning fog had settled over Galveston with blasts of wind from the east.

I peed in the scrub, walked back to the truck, pulled on my boots, and looked at the freckles on the face of Caroline Cahill, asleep inside the cab. This surprising mermaid, this West Texas magician, this fabulist, this spieler, asleep, with her mouth open, under Mamá Salazar's rumpled serape.

His Great Name

Bells.

They rang from church steeples through the morning's fog.

Beginning from a distance, at first lumpy, moving slowly, growing lighter, the bells brightened, then dulled, then scattered, freed from a lofty tower, high up, winging above Sunday, then hung in the air, as if at any moment, like pelicans, they might swoop down toward the sand because they caught sight of something moving, erupting, and dive down to snatch it, or else linger more and zero in on a soft wave beyond the jetties and then, finally, come to rest on the water, bobbing on the tide, like a gathering of surfers.

Soon a black pickup swung past, coughing and bucking, kicking up sand. From the back of the bed, Salazar leapt out, fell to his knees, and rolled until he was crouched on all fours, braying. Mac waved her Stetson. "Hey, yo! Duke! Your Highness!" She spun the truck in a single doughnut before driving up the ramp onto Seawall Boulevard.

Proudly, Salazar waved a piece of paper, pulled from his back pocket, filled with ink marks. It was not like him to tell me immediately after he'd written a story, and the way he waved the paper under my nose, the way he refolded it, first in half, then halving that, returning the piece, which he'd written during the night, he said, into his back pocket, held my attention. He smoothed his thin mustache. "They kidnapped me, man," he said. "No, not kidnapped. No. Snatched." He was smiling. "I was snatched by a fine pilgrim. *Cities of orgies, walks and joys!*"

"You all right?"

"I'm fine. Fine. All right. *Cities of orgies, walks and joys!* That's Walt Whitman, Duke. Been saying that all night long. *Cities of orgies, walks and joys!* Like I'm in a trance. Like I was starving. I've been licking salt off my fingers. *Cities of orgies, walks and joys!* I say my mantra. *Cities of orgies, walks and joys!* Blots out the waves and blots out the clouds. Oh, I met a fine pilgrim. Fine wet face. Fine wet eyes. Let me say no more about him. Another time. Another time. But, a fine mouth. No, no, no. I couldn't blot you out, Duke. One pilgrim was very sweet. Hmmm. Sweet. Just like my honey. But, he's long gone. Back to Sharpstown. Anyway, that doesn't matter. Duke, I knew you were out there. I knew you were out there. You needed me. I could feel it. I could see it, just thinking of you. I could pick up the scent of you. Same as I remember all the prayers for the Apostles, and each Apostle, always. Peter, Andrew, James son of Zebedee, John, Philip, Bartholomew, Thomas, Matthew, James son of Alphaeus, Jude, Simon the Zealot, and Judas. Like I'm pulling two thousand years of Christ Our Lord out of the black night. I could smell you out there—like two thousand years of our own fucked-up bliss. Mmmmm. Bliss. Mighty pilgrim. No, no. No one around me to say where you were. No one to tell me the last prayer of Saint Paul. No matter. Know it from heart: 'I thank God, whom I serve, as my ancestors did, with a clear conscience, as night and day I constantly remember you in my prayers. Recalling your tears, I long to see you, so that I may be filled with joy. I am reminded of your sincere faith, which first lived'…shit….'first lived' something, something, 'persuaded,' something, shit, man I'm fucked up. Wait. 'For this reason I remind you to fan into flame the gift of God, which is in you through the laying on of my hands.' That's how it goes. And, this ending. I could cry for this ending, Duke. 'For the Spirit God gave us does not make us timid, but gives us power, love and self-discipline. So do not be ashamed of the testimony about our

Lord or of me his prisoner. Rather, join with me in suffering for the gospel, by the power of God.'"

"Amen."

Up and down the beach were a few sad fires. We sat on the hard sand, his hand on my shoulder. He closed his eyes.

"It goes on from there. Goes on and on. Now, Duke, you tell me, Duke. Why was I sitting there doing that? *Cities of orgies, walks and joys!* Why? Because I couldn't stop. *Cities of orgies, walks and joys!* That's Walt Whitman, baby! *I long to see you, so that I may be filled with joy.* That's Christ Jesus."

"Were you with Mac?"

"I've been on a walk with Walt Whitman, the son of Manhattan," he said.

"Dude, what are you on?"

"I had me, well, I'll tell you. We shall name it, we shall sanctify it: 'When Mushrooms Last in the Dooryard Bloom'd.' Hear what I'm saying to you? I am cooked, man. I am toasted, roasted, fucked up, high as a kite. I am big-ass blown away. But, my bingo card is filled, this foggy, foggy morning, with my Father, my Son, and my Holy Spirt. Can't take my 2 Timothy 1:9 away from me. 'He has saved us and called us to a holy life— not because of anything we have done but because of his own purpose and grace. This grace was given us in Christ Jesus before the beginning of time, but it has now been revealed through the appearing of our Savior, Christ Jesus, who has destroyed death and has brought life and immortality to light through the gospel. And of this gospel I was appointed a herald and an apostle and a teacher.' That's us, Duke. Just like these bells you're hearing. 'That is why I am suffering as I am. Yet this is no cause for shame, because I know whom I have believed, and am convinced that he is able to guard what I have entrusted to him until that day.' Amen. Amen. Amen. Say it."

"What kind of weed did you smoke?" I said.

"Not weed, Duke. These pilgrims had shrooms. Not fine as you. But, they had fucking shrooms. You had a mere spliff. Do the math. Show your work, Duke. Hey! Hey! Hey! What is this?" he said, when he saw Caroline sitting in the driver's seat of his truck, sleeping with her head thrown back, and Mamá Salazar's serape around her shoulders.

I wanted to think of what to say. All this time, though, while listening to his vision, I was still stuck on what to make of Caroline Cahill's strange story, transported by her desire thumping into my desire. My mind was drifting: Caroline Cahill, her mom, the little house in Marfa, Mamá Salazar, Batya the Rock, Rabbi Gadol, and the Wounded One, even Leah, were all getting mixed up in my head. I kept seeing myself explaining to Salazar who she was, the girl asleep inside his pickup truck with his mother's serape around her shoulders, and that we had to drive back, that we had to do something.

Salazar yawned, stretched. "Let's get normal, man. I keep thinking about Ryan last night, that last play. That last out was a beauty. 'Two balls and no strikes to Baker. Ground ball to third! Art Howe. Got heeeeeeeeem! Nolan Ryan! No-hitter number five!' Whaaaaaaaaahhhaaaaahh! Whaaaaaaaaahhhaaaaahh! No one's going to break that. Except Ryan. Guy's a magician."

Without waking Caroline, silently Salazar pulled bones from the box of kitchen matches in the glove compartment, and sparked one up.

"We smoke too much," I said, as he inhaled and handed over the thick joint.

"Still, this half-lonely joint is what must never be given up, man. It gives us nourishment. Patience. It's our literature in exile, Duke."

A couple passed by, braced against the wind and wet fog. The woman, white, in a one-piece bathing suit, shouted something at me, her words broken by the wind. The man, also white, bare chested, in shorts, said nothing, and seemed annoyed, taking her by the arm, pulling her along. She was drunk from the night before. They appeared not to have slept. She tried to get away from him, but he wouldn't let go. He turned to me, open-mouthed, but said nothing.

"We may have to go home, mi hijo."

"What happened to lighting out for the territory, Huckleberry?" he said, and I took a drag from the joint. "What do we got to face that's so bad? You know? Know what I'm saying? In ten years, you'll be junior rabbi at B'nai-B'nai-B'nai, junior to your old man. Family business. Same as mine. We're fucked, Duke. God and Sons."

"Incorporated."

"Incorporated. Praying your *ru'chah, ru'chah, ru'chah* morning, noon, and night, man. I'll be Master Sergeant Manolo Antonio José Luis Martín Salazar, and thinking, Shit, man, I should get me a radio license and make some fresh cash preaching the Gospel of the Lord."

Would he? Would I?

Here, Caroline, her head out the opened window, while reaching two, lean fingers for one of us to bring her the joint, shouted, "You're going to be a rabbi? A stoned rabbi!"

"Oh, man, Duke," Salazar whispered. "Our time is up."

"Caroline Cahill of Alpine, Texas, meet Manolo Antonio José Luis Martín Salazar, future Master Sergeant of the United States Army."

"Can't a girl get a hit before breakfast. I'm going to wet my britches."

"At your service, ma'am," said Salazar, saluting.

"You should have breakfast with us, Mr. Master Sergeant. I mean, it's your truck," she said, opening the door, stepping out, and jogging furtively into the scrub.

This meeting of Caroline and Salazar gave me a chance to wonder what helping her would be like. For all I knew, Caroline Cahill's mother lived on Mamá Salazar's street, or Father Salazar knew Mrs. Cahill's anguish about leaving her daughter, and he knew Mrs. Cahill's nights crying for her missing teenage daughter, her precious Caroline, wondering where in the world she was. If any of that was even true, I thought, as I watched the two of them pass the joint, once Caroline returned from the scrub, dodging the kelp. Father Salazar would proclaim it a miracle. Rabbi Gadol would pronounce, *Ru'chah, ru'chah, ru'chah*. Mother and daughter, reunited, both with their brown eyes identical, hugging and crying.

"I need some eggs and sausage! I'm starved," said Caroline, and I thought, how mistaken I was to think this could work. *Oh, hey, Mother, by the way, can we get a pound of sausage from Weingartens?*

Salazar fiddled in his pocket for a roach clip, but couldn't find one. He walked to the pickup, reached into the glove box, and found one there, snapped in the last scrap of the joint, handed it to Caroline, and rubbed his palms together.

"I was thinking about what my future is, Duke and M'Lady. Last night, while you two were getting, shall we say, acquainted, I was thinking it out. After the army, after I become a preacher, family business and all. What else do we have, Duke? Duke and I will have weekly cross-denominational breakfasts at Alfred's Delicatessen. That place on Stella Link near the Pizza Hut. It'll be my Jew ally training. Evangelical bagels smeared with cream cheese."

"You're stoned out of your mind," I said.

"Can't you see us?"

"Thought you were done with Jesus," I said.

"A pleasant affair, crowded diner, elbow to elbow, with the intoxicating, strong blend of smells: salted meats, smoked trout."

"Matzo brei. Chopped liver," I said.

"Pickle plates! You should see this place, M'lady. Servings of pancakes with syrup and cheese omelettes, Belgian waffles. And, what it's called? That Jewish one? The pastry."

"Jewish one? It's a deli. It's all Jewish," I said.

"Blinkies."

"Blintzes," I said.

"That's why we need our cross-denominational breakfasts. I'm a novice, man. That's why we need an exhilaration of burnt black coffee, the aroma lifting from the tables like, if I may, Christ from the tomb. The little Jewboy Jesus steaming out of the coffee to remind you of all the farmers and roasters and truck drivers and waiters, the true workers of the world, the good Christians of every continent."

"Oh, shit, here we go," I said.

"Interrupting, man. The true workers of the world who had brought the coffee all the way from coffee mills of Bethlehem and the birthplace of cute, little Baby Jesus, all the way to Alfred's Deli on Stella Link Road, situated beside God's greatest glory, Pizza Hut, and then waitresses slopping it into ceramic brown mugs. I'm telling you. In the dense, savory womb of my mushroom delight, I found Jesus, all over again, last night. I haven't even come down yet. I'm on a fine, soft glide. I'm cool. I'm very cool. Fine. So fine. Fine indeed. *Cities of orgies, walks and joys!* Alfred's deli." He patted the back of his head. "Going to wear my Jew cap. Be one of the tribe. Honorary degree. I'm going to join the army of four star General David C. Jones first, however. Followed by five-million star chairman of the Joint Chiefs of the Bethlehem Branch of Heaven on Earth, Jesus Christ himself. Big house, Blue Cross Blue Shield, full protection. Parishioners throwing money at my feet. I know my apostles, motherfucker," he said. "Be nice to me, Duke. I'm having a revelation. Look, fog is burning off. Look at that beautiful, beautiful burnage. Not giving up my writing. No way, man. Going to work on Monk's Island. Write twelve *New York Times* bestselling masterpieces. In fifty languages. I'm going to need that many to afford my style of living in my sweet one-story off Telephone Road. Near the great Mamá Salazar. Near my little brother and his wife and their nine children. My brother the magician! Hummunah-hummumah! I'm going to have a lot of air conditioning in my house."

"Going to steal people's money? Is that what you're going do?" said Caroline. "I can't stand Amen Hallelujah bullshit. You're having a good old time. Aren't you? Look at you. You crush people, you people. You're a Marxist? Shit. Whatever you are. Home-fucking-wreckers." She was up on her high horse.

We were nothing to her but a wall she wanted to sledgehammer. A wall between what? Purity and turmoil? Better not be. Purity and turmoil was everything I knew, my whole life, past, present, future. Five Books of Moses in three words. Purity and turmoil.

"I'm with Jesus, Lady Caroline of Alpine. I'm an angel from the Good Book," Salazar said, and flapped his arms like a hummingbird near a feeder.

"Shall we rise?" I said, knowing what Manolo Salazar could do, cashing in our birthrights, knowing how Manolo Salazar, too, could bring it.

"Yes, we shall. All rise for Jesus!" he shouted, and raised his arms to the sky. "Yea! My bones will tell the stories. Yea! My bones will be indestructible. My bones will not abandon the spirit. I'm gone to Heaven. I'm riding atop the Galveston seawall to Heaven. Will you join me? How can you not? Jesus is with you. Or, will you say, Shame on me? Shame on me? I say, shame on you!"

Caroline lit the roach in the clip that had died out from the wind. "You guys are weird."

"Get out the whip!" Salazar laughed. "Off you'll go to rabbi school, Duke. Me, I'm going to doughboy school, a grunt, a dogface. Four years from now, we're going to collide into each other outside the Astrodome. Astros versus Cardinals. Summertime. Home game. Nolan Ryan going for his twelfth no-hitter. We'll take each others' hand and talk, share a beer. Coldest foam in the Dome! I'll have been at war. Got a limp. You're home visiting from Jew School and there'll be, well… well, we know, something—"

It seemed he was going to say Leah's name, but held back.

"Theological seminary," I said.

"Theological seminary, man. You with your words. You're home visiting, okay?" he went on, "But, already gigging as a sub at some little shake sugaree B'nai-B'nai-B'nai in Texarkana. A wooden palette for a lectern, okay? What will we awaken in each other? Tell me that. You'll have your secrets. I'll have mine.

We aren't what we think we are. None of us is. We are what we hide. How beautifully our lives go from one thing to another, and never change. How easily, how accidental. Even Jewish Jesus knows that!" he said, shaking the high from behind his eyes, looking at me with a shrug, as if about to cry. "You hear what I'm saying? No. You hear nothing. We understand nothing, Duke," he said.

WEED AND SPLIFFS AFTER BREAKFAST before we drove to the beach the previous morning, beers, spliffs, and more weed in the pickup on the Gulf Freeway, warm hit of hashish, Johnnie Walker Red, José Cuervo, tokes from Little Blackie, more spliffs since the sun came up, a fat joint, and I was hanging tough.

Every time my determination waned, and I told myself that I was lighting out, lighting out for nothing that made sense, nothing that promised happiness, lighting out from the impossible past into the impossible future, I felt ensnared by the memory of a dinner with Leah back in July at China Gardens that I'd never told anyone about. Not even Salazar. And, now, on the beach in the brightening morning in Galveston, that dinner terrified me.

China Gardens sat at the corner of Leeland and Crawford, downtown, near St. Joseph's Womens' Center and two asphalt parking lots. Originally a Chinese foods import store, the concrete building was painted beige with a green roof and red columns to give it a temple facade. Inside was a bright dining room with cheap prints of serene ponds, white, arching bridges, and lush gardens. Along the wall near the bar was an enormous oil painting of a stampede of brown and white horses.

Leah and I were dressed as casual as could be. Me, in cowboy boots, jeans, and a blue work shirt. Her, in jeans and a white cardigan. The sweater cost her father a hundred dollars, she'd told me. Because Leah worked part time at Saks Fifth Avenue in the Galleria, she'd likely got it on discount, after going on sale. So, he said he'd buy it for her. There were a couple dozen formica tables, covered with white table cloths, with red chairs spaced in three rows down the length of the room. Only half were occupied, and all of those far enough away so that none of the other customers seemed to have noticed Father Salazar, dressed in a thousand-dollar suit and flip flops, waving. "Duke! Duke! Join us!" He was sitting with a women I didn't recognize. Her hair was flecked gray and brown. She was impeccably dressed in a black cotton dress, with matching pocketbook and heels.

"Leah, Duke. Join us. Come, come. Let us eat together. Join us. Come. My treat. I want you to meet Miss Lynn, here. She's a follower of the Good Book like all of us," Father Salazar said, while also ordering a vodka tonic from a waiter, as soon as we sat down, and I noticed already two empty cocktail glasses on the table above his plate with crumbs from egg rolls. Miss Lynn was thin and nervous-looking. She wore her long, graying, brown hair up. There was something about her face that was attractive and lonely—her skin seemed too fair for sunshine.

Another waiter stepped up.

Father Salazar ordered for all of us: sizzling rice soup, beef steak with rice noodles, beef with snow peas, Sha-Sha Shrimp—"that's just for us, honey," he said to Leah, "don't you worry, don't you touch shrimp, I know"—followed by catfish fried rice, and fresh tilapia grilled with a spicy sauce.

While we waited for the food, we small-talked best we could. At first, neither Leah nor I flinched, even though we were sitting to dinner with Salazar's father and a woman we'd never seen before. But, Leah and I hadn't been raised the son of a rabbi and the daughter of a cantor without knowing a thing or two about discretion.

"You been here before?" asked Lynn, her voice unchallenging, putting her hands into her lap with a single, swift movement, as if she were in someone else's seat.

"Oh, yes," Leah said. "My family comes here every year on Christmas Day."

"Are you kidding?"

"No, ma'am," Leah said. "This whole place is filled with Jewish families on Christmas."

"On Christmas Day?" Lynn said.

Father Salazar laughed. "Tell her, honey. She's been missing out."

"It's really interesting," she said. "In the early twentieth century, in New York City, many Chinese people, Chinese families, and Jewish families ended up living in the same neighborhood, the Lower East Side. My relatives once lived there. Not like Duke's family. They've always been Southerners."

Leah loved telling this story, her entire body lit with connection to Jewish history. She'd done a report on Jews and Chinese food at school more than once.

"I just didn't realize there were so many Jews in Texas," said Miss Lynn.

I said, "Afraid so, ma'am."

"Don't joke, Duke," said Leah.

Miss Lynn said, "You know, there's just so much history."

"There were something like a million Jews," Leah went on, "a quarter of the city's population in New York City back then. Lot of the Chinese people in the Lower East Side actually came from California, and a lot of them went into the restaurant business. Assimilated Jews began eating out at Chinese restaurants. They were even attacked for it by rabbis because Chinese food isn't, by definition, kosher. Few Chinese dishes mix meat and dairy anyway. Besides, German restaurants and Italian restaurants in New York wouldn't accept Jewish families as patrons. Chinese restaurants didn't have Christian images, or anything like that, so it seemed less threatening to the Jews, even the assimilated Jews. I think that's the point. I don't know much about that. But, what Reverend Salazar is asking me to tell you is, for a Jewish person to eat at a Chinese restaurant was kind of exotic. But, also, it was okay. It was allowed."

Waiters swarmed the table delivering the dishes and, around

the table, hand to hand, we all shared the plates.

"Back to the story," I said. "Not customarily Jewish. Jews going to Chinese restaurants. But they could break free of kashrut. They could be eccentric. You know, they could be sophisticated."

"American," Leah said.

"These two kids, I'm telling you," Father Salazar said. "They're the highest of the high. Tell her honey. Where do Christmas meals come in?"

"Newark. Newark, New Jersey. That's where. This Chinese restaurant owner in Newark, during the Depression, brought chow mien to the Jewish Children's Home on Christmas Day. Then, on Christmas Eve and Christmas Day, in the years that followed, Jews in Newark kind of paid him back by going to his restaurant to eat. Over time, Jews went to Chinese restaurants to eat during Christmas every year. A tradition. Besides, it was the only thing open!"

"Immigration, convenience, hospitality," said Father Salazar. "Same with our Mexican restaurants today."

"Not the only Christmas tradition," I said. "Other than a nice Jewish boy like Jesus being born, I mean. In Europe, before World War Two, Jews chose Christmas Day as a day to stay at home and not study Torah. On Christmas Eve and Christmas Day, Jews would get attacked. Too dangerous for Jews to leave home those days. Some places even made it illegal for Jews to go out in public on Christmas Day. So, the rabbis created this fake holiday called Nittel Nacht. To protect Jews, rabbis said they were to stay home. Could've used some Chinese take-out."

"We all love Christmas now," Father Salazar said. He pushed the plates away, causing the white table cloth to stain from the brown sauce from the beef with snow peas, stacked up the empties, and waved me close.

"Merry Chow Mein," said Leah, and we all laughed.

"You ladies talk amongst yourselves," Father Salazar said abruptly, and he turned toward me and held my eyes. "Your friend Manolo, he comes to me two days ago. He says, 'Papi, I want to a new life. Nothing special. Just a new life.' I says, 'a new life? What kind of life? What's wrong with the life you got? You think you can stamp out the life you got? Don't believe your own dreams,' I say to him. 'This is why you want to go to the army?' You hear about this, Duke? Manolo in the United States military. Manny the Minuteman. Going to shine his shoes. Going to press his slacks. My son can't even shoot a sling shot at a squirrel from three feet out. 'At least choose a career you can do,' I say. I say to him, 'what's wrong with being a preacher?' Oh, Duke, I was not happy one bit with your friend, Manolo Antonio. Then, he says, 'If I'm a preacher, I'm going to take a vow of poverty.' 'Oh, my, my,' I say. 'This I got to see. Even when you're a fancy preacher, you're always poor in the eyes of Jesus. You learn nothing from your old Papi? Even when you're leaning over the pulpit in a thousand-dollar suit, I says to him, with a church of parishioners at your feet, you no longer are a man who has trained in the Good Book. You are no longer a man who has studied the lessons of Paul, who says, *We walk by faith, not by sight*. No. You're a man who is alone. You're a man who must know his own soul, his own spirit. Poverty or no poverty. Riches or no riches.' Duke, I know that you know. You come from God people. Your old man, he doesn't like me. I know that. It's okay. It's okay. I know that your old man is a good man. He's a God man. Gee-hyphen-Dee, as he would have it. *Baruch Ha'Shem*. Right? Right? See? Mexicans and Semites are one and the same. Look, Duke, I know, and your old man knows, and I know you know, you are alone when you're with your people, you are poorest when they need you most."

Father Salazar paused. He closed his eyes, his lips wet, and reached across his plate for the vodka tonic the waiter had put down in the meantime, and he drank it halfway. He shook the ice until it clinked, then set the glass on top of his empty plate, his eyes shut tight.

"But, you're not really alone," I said, countering.

He opened his eyes. "Not you, too, Duke."

"I mean, when I take a test at school, I'm alone. But, I'm in company with the knowledge. Same for the Good Book. Right? You got to be attentive to all the voices that have read the passage you're reading. Your life, your soul, is talking, or listening, to all those voices from all that time, far back to Eden."

"You fooled me. You're good. You fooled me. You're going to be some rabbi, Duke. Talk to your compañero. Talk to Manolo."

Leah was kicking my foot with hers, and her hand was on my thigh, squeezing firmly, but also in her sensual way—if that's what you'd call a girl of eighteen, raised on the north side of Meyerland—of being strong, present, languid. Lynn was watching Father Salazar order another round of vodka tonics.

Could I tell him? Could I come clean with Father Salazar, confess to the ex-*el sacerdote*—he who was not in the least embarrassed to be caught by his son's best friend on a tryst with Miss Lynn here, dining on egg rolls and pork fried rice—as I couldn't with my own father? It wasn't like I had come to China Gardens to call myself out, or to be the bag man to straighten out Salazar.

Father Salazar was talking again. "The life of the cloth is a life of eating and drinking experience. You swallow births and deaths and affairs and bankruptcies and confirmations and marriages and brain surgery and hip replacements. All that goes in your guts. You chew on everyone's suffering, everyone's pleasure. You got to get something for yourself from it, Duke. I know you know. You can never doubt it's worth your effort. Never. Never. Never. Am I right? Never. Never. I look at you and I see a handsome rabbi-to-come. And, you, young lady, what a beautiful young lady you are. You're going to make a beautiful, beautiful, beautiful rabbi's wife. Two of you are going to be a couple. I tell you. The two of you. A couple."

"Couple of what?" Leah said.

It was soft retorts like that when I was most taken with Leah, her reluctance to be interrogated.

"I can see you, Duke," Father Salazar went on. "I can see you. Not the slightest doubt that what you're going to do in your old man's footsteps is worthwhile. But, you'll walk your own path. Your father, he's a good man. He's a God man. Doesn't care for me. I can't take away what he's done for his people. He's seen them born. He's seen them die. He's seen them gentle. He's seen them rotten. I've been there. I've felt it. I've felt it. I've tried to teach Manolo. He's not getting the point. It's not hard. It's not difficult. It's straightforward. Am I right? No? What?"

"I suppose so," I said.

"You want to be a rabbi? Since when?" asked Lynn, as she pulled her pocket book into her lap and fiddled with the strap. She pulled out lipstick, then put it back in her purse without dabbing any on her mouth. "Honey, let's go," she said. "Let's get out of here. I got to get to back. We've been here too long. I told you I got to get back."

"This kid's a million bucks, Lynn. What a pretty girl," he said to Leah.

"Don't get married right away, honey," Lynn said. "You don't know where you'll find yourself. Far from this place." The waiters began clearing the table. "I'm from far away from here. Hate to say it, sugar, I learned my lesson the hard way."

"I won't. I'm going to college. I want to be a buyer for Saks Fifth Avenue. I want to live in New York. I'll come back. We have an understanding."

"Sugar, Lady Di has an understanding. The rest of us ladies," she nodded in my direction, "require a ring."

"Yeah, Duke!" said Leah, extending her arm.

"Left it out in the car," I said.

"That's what they all say, honey. Diana's ring, have you seen that? It's so gorgeous. Have you looked at that? Oh, my Lord. 12-carat sapphire. 14 diamonds. 18-karat white gold. Not going to get one of these from a ranch hand."

Father Salazar whistled. "Or a rabbi's son. Eh, Duke? Cost the Prince of Wales sixty K. Not sure your salary at Beth Tikkun is going to cover that? No? What?" Leah crossed her arms, mock despair. "That's all right, sweetie. Your man here is going to be a great rabbi. Hall of Famer. Duke, you're going to say, 'I'm Rabbi Jon Wain. For three thousand years a Wain has been a rabbi.' That's your wealth. It's right in here." He tapped his heart. "You're going to say, 'I'm going to lead you, my friends.' Like Daniel in the lion's den, it's going to work out all right. *Be not conformed to this world, but transformed, by the renewing of your mind that you may prove what is that good and acceptable and perfect will of God.* That's grace talk. Through grace, the great Lord has dealt to every man and every woman the measure of faith. Let that soak a minute, you're going to say to your people, going to say, 'swallow that down, friends, and drink a good glass of everlasting water with it. Everybody has the same measure of faith. The great Lord has given all y'all the same measure of faith.' This is what you'll say. Now, use it, you're going to say. You're going to say, 'I'm going to stay with you. I'm going to lead you. I'm going to stay with you for the births and the deaths.'"

"And the hip replacements," I said.

"Listen, Duke. Most people who get their hips replaced should have done ten years earlier," he said, reaching his arm and rubbing the back of my neck with his palm. "But you're going to be right there with them, holding their hands, seeing they're comfortable. *Baruch Ha'Shem.* That's what you're going to bring to your people. Tell her what it means, Duke." He stabbed his thumb in Lynn's direction.

"Blessed be the name of the Lord," I said, and stood, dropping my napkin, while Leah and Lynn excused themselves to go the Ladies.

"Blessed be the name of the Lord! Waiter. Check. You have a great future, Duke." He bowed his head, "Lord, praise Duke! Please, Lord. Praise his great name. Take him places, Lord, and his friends and companions. Amen. Amen. Amen."

Oh, he can bring it. I give him that.

"You're going to say, 'I'm Rabbi Jon Wain.' Still, you're going to be alone, Duke. That's the beauty of it." He downed the last of his vodka, sucking a cube of ice into his mouth and chewed it. "Rabbi. Jon. Wain. The Duke. At the O.K. Corral." He was laughing, and at the same time saluted one of the waiters.

"That's Wyatt Earp. Reverend Salazar? You okay?"

"Come on. No? What?"

"You want me to drive y'all home? Let me drive y'all."

"Am I okay? Come on, Duke. I know you've been doing the ganja all day long. Going to ruin this country, that marijuana. Are you in the game? I know what you lovebirds are up to. Suit up. That's bad for you, bad for the girl, bad for America. Stay in the game, Duke. Talk to Manolo Antonio. That's what's important here. What the hell is going on with him?"

"He's fine, Reverand Salazar. Really, he is. It's just, him and me, you know. We're just not sure going into the family line, and all, is what we should be doing. There's a big America out there. You know."

He leaned forward and shook his head and laughed. Wild, hiccupy laugh. Slapping both hands on the white table cloth with the stains from the beef with snow peas, then, in a slow primitive rhythm, he beat on the table like he was drumming the bongos. He looked exhausted—drunk and exhausted. Marriage, divorce, maybe more than one of each, the trial for fraud, contempt from his oldest son, desperate, or exasperated, to be someone, to have meaning in life. And, still, he could be tender. Give you his blessings.

"America. What? It's easy to be a preacher. Easy. Easy to be a rabbi. Oh, you suffer. But, they love you. Your people love you. It's easy. Easy as drinking chilled tea on a blistering hot day. Easy. Easy as strawberry ice cream on a sugar cone. I'm talking about luminous mysteries. I'm talking how through thick and thin God has been the light of our lives. The Lord Jesus has been the light of my life. In each mystery, in every prayer we offer, you cultivate a sense of awe and gratitude at the light that the Lord Jesus has cast into our lives, so that we can see in him our salvation and our hope. You hear what I'm saying, Duke. Heaven is fun. That's the only message. The human eye can see ten million colors. That's just a fraction of what you can see in Heaven. Michaelangelo is going to be giving art classes in Heaven. Heaven is fun. Your people got a version of the same thing, the same story. I don't have to tell you." He looked at Leah who had returned and was sitting down, setting her elbows on the table and her hands under chin in a gesture that said, *Let's get out of here, Duke.* "You're a pretty girl, and our own lovely Lynn here, from West Texas way. We pray in the name of the Father and of the Son and of the Holy Spirit. Amen. Amen. Amen."

"Amen," I said, along with Leah and Lynn, for whom, I could suddenly see, that all that West Texas wind and sun had freckled her nose and cheeks and outside her eyes.

Yes, I could see why people fell under his spell. People often said of him: Isn't he wonderful? It's a pleasure to see such a fine preacher. His suits are immaculate. He stands tall. He makes Jesus understandable with every single thing he says. You can learn any subject from him. That's what people said. The shopkeepers, bus drivers, the waiters, waitresses, telephone linemen, house cleaners, the corporate types exalted and yielded to him. That was what he craved. Was it vanity? Maybe. To see how he put people in a rapture when he talked to them, I could feel it. What a bizarre bird he was, Father Salazar, with that soft, tan skin inside the silky suit, the flip flops, the red veins coursing across his nose, his shoe-polish black head of hair, his short hands, like blunt mittens, and those brown, pointed, bloody eyes. He spoke of what mattered in life, and it took you by surprise, stirred you, troubled you. Perhaps he saw himself as doing good, perhaps uplifting whomever he spoke to, perhaps believed his own testimony, perhaps he was moved by his own talk. Who knew? What did it matter? But, to see how others loved him sometimes made his son afraid.

"I believe on Sunday, and you believe on Saturday. That's the spirit, and you got the spirit, Duke," he went on. "I believe in God, the Father Almighty. Creator of Heaven and earth. I believe in Jesus Christ, His only son, our Lord, who was conceived by the power of the Holy Spirit and born of the Virgin Mary. He suffered under Pontius Pilate, was crucified, died, and was buried. You don't have to be told any of this. I know. I know you know. My Lord descended into Hell. On the third day he rose again. He ascended into Heaven and is seated at the right hand of the Father, as if he was right here inside China Gardens. Right here! Seated underneath these pictures of white bridges and little Chinese ponds with goldfish. In Heaven, you can see five million types of gold. He will come again in glory to judge the living and the dead. I believe in the Holy Spirit, the communion of saints, the forgiveness of sins, the resurrection of the body, and life everlasting," he said, wiping his hands like he was wiping away dust. "See? It's just talking. Anywhere, anytime. Church. China Gardens. Beth Tikkun. Broadcast station. When you know how to do it, Duke, it's easy. Don't overthink it. You'll see. "

Oh, he can bring it.

"Talk to Manolo. Do it for me, please. Whither thou goest, he shall go. He trusts you."

I nodded.

"Atta baby. Atta baby. Look, Duke, if you two were bad kids, if you two were bad students, and nothing you did was right, and nobody cared about you, and if you were getting wrapped up in gangs, well, okay, okay, I'd say, go to jail. I'd say, get straightened out. Become an insurance man. Open a restaurant. That's not you fellas. No. I can see it," he said, pointing a finger at the stain from the beef with snow peas on the white table cloth. "You know who else can see it? Your old man can see it. He sees you. He's a good man, Duke. He's a good man. A God man," he said, nodding his head without stopping.

"I'll tell him you said so, Reverend Salazar," I said and watched him down the last drops of vodka in every glass still left on the table, one after the other, chewing the ice, without looking up.

"Your father tried to screw me one time. You know about that? He had the reputation. Recognition. He had the clergy of the entire city against me. Entire city of Houston. Fifth largest city in America. Against me. He had the public. In the end, there wasn't nothing to it. That's the truth. Don't believe all the stories. Okay? I'm not going to get into that now. Had too much to drink. Some other time." He clapped his hands lightly, then held me with his eyes. "I'm just a simple, cotton-picking country boy, who went to a one-room school house. You know that, Duke. I lost my people, Duke. Lost my recognition. I had to go into hiding. Had to preach into a tape recorder. Not just me. Lot of us men of God. We do what we have to. You know what that's like? I'd already given up my collar for love. You know that. I know you know. Lynn here knows all about that. Don't you, honey? I didn't want to be anybody's confessor no more, anyway. It wasn't for me. I loved Maria. I loved Manolo's mamá. I still love her. Don't tell her that. She hates to hear that. Okay? Duke, I love God. God is good. God is famous. I love God. Couldn't give up God. And, God hasn't given up on me. That's something you can tell that father of yours, the Grand Rabbi, our King that hath brought forth from his loins to our beautiful dinner tonight the one and only Duke. The Duke and the Duchess—you are a pretty girl, pretty girl. What a couple. Look, Duke, God hasn't given up on me. God isn't finished with me yet. Don't get me wrong, Duke. He's a good man. A God man. Your old man. A famous man. Not as famous as God. There's nothing more ridiculous than going around pretending to be a good man."

"Pretending not to be," I said.

We were the last table in the restaurant. Waiters were pulling up the table cloths all around us, wiping down the counters.

"You got to earn a living. I made money. Buckets of money. Lost it. Made it back. Lost it. Back. Lost it. Back. What did it get me? Tell me. My namesake, my first born son, wants to go to the army. Okay? Okay, enough. We must take the ladies home. Okay? Okay. Talk to my Manolo Antonio. You know what to say. Fix it, for me, your friend. That's a beautiful girl you got there. Come on, Lynn, baby. You're a peach, honey," he said to Leah, and took her hand with both of his, then stood, and we all joined hands. "Thank you for dinner, my young friends. Beautiful young lady. Pretty girl. Thank you for your grace and goodness. May God bless you. You deserve the blessings of God."

"I'VE GOT A STORY FOR YOU. Just for you, M'lady Caroline Cahill of Alpine, Texas," Salazar said, unfolding the slip of paper from his pocket.

He appeared cheerful, but I could see something else. The spirit, the distinct anxiety of his sense of himself appeared to have built up overnight, like a knot in his face. He could hide it from some, but I could see he was hauling this nameless weight, and all he could do was scrawl it out of himself onto paper.

"What's it called?" she said.

"Where'd your friends go?" I said.

Jim Bob and Cassie were nowhere to be seen since Caroline and I had strayed over to the red pickup.

"They left. They do that sometimes," she said.

We were sitting on the sand, but Salazar stood to read.

"I'll tell you the title at the end. Here's how it goes: A boy told his abuelo, 'I won't be seeing you again, not after today.' 'No, I guess you won't,' Abuelo said. Then Abuelo said, 'I once was a man fighting a mountain. Did you know that?' 'No, Abuelo,' said the boy, 'I never knew.' 'Oh, yes, the mountain had come to take revenge against me, breaking free from its range, free from all the other mountains. It rolled over the earth. *Vámonos*, called the mountain, and the birds shirked from the branches. *Vámonos, vámonos I am going to fall on you*, called the mountain. The mountain shook its trees and rocks.' The boy's abuelo stopped to catch his breath. Of course, the boy knew his abuelo was dying. But, the day was bright, and Abuelo wanted company. The boy thought he should feed the ducks in the pond. Abuelo continued, *Ought we not talk about this?* I shouted at the mountain. *Ought we not talk about this!* mocked the mountain. *What is this all about?* I called. But, before I could decide what steps to take, an avalanche from the mountain had rolled over my legs. *Now do you see?* said the mountain.' The boy's abuelo broke into a big smile. The boy smiled back. Soon, the boy walked out of the door. He felt like he could live forever. When he came to the ocean, he sat down on a bench and watched the swimmers. A seagull was waddling nearby. An airplane flew overhead, leaving a scent of smoke. The boy left the beach and crossed the bridge into town. A woman with a poodle stopped the boy and asked if he knew directions to Calle Visión. The boy pointed south, and walked on. He bumped into an old man carrying grocery sacks of fruit and vegetables for his family. When he got home, nobody was there. *There's nothing to do,* he thought. Then he heard a rumbling of rocks and trees outside his window."

I took the page from him, read it over, and handed it back. "That's good, mi hijo, really good. Disaster story," I said.

"You know it. I was thinking of that Texas City thing. Right? Seventy-four years ago. 9:12 a.m. The SS Grandcamp carrying ammonium nitrate exploded at the docks. Fifteen-foot tidal wave swept the dock. A second ship was ignited. Thousand buildings destroyed. Like, six-hundred people killed."

"Texas City Disaster."

"April 16, 1947."

"What's it called?" Caroline said. "Your story? What's the title of it?"

"It's called, The Mountain," Salazar said, looking at the paper.

"That's a sad story," Caroline said.

"I don't mean it to be sad," he said.

Caroline wasn't sure what to make of that. "My friends will be back soon," Caroline said, more or less to no one.

"Will they?" I said, and we watched Salazar sit with his legs stretched out together on the sand and re-read the story to himself, using a black pen to cross out words and add others. How could I tell either of them about China Gardens?

"How do you two know each other?" asked Caroline.

"Us? We were born seven days apart, in February, 1964," I said. "We got made under the same sky."

Salazar didn't look up. "The very same."

"And you're both sons of clergymen?"

"Heirs to the throne," I said.

"Keys to the kingdom," said Salazar.

Caroline motioned me closer. "I dreamed of you when I was sleeping."

I kissed her mouth.

Several boys walking by in wetsuits with surfboards whistled and jeered.

"I've embarrassed you, sorry," I said.

She looked at the surfers, put her arm around my neck, and she kissed me again. I wasn't sure if it was from defeat or defiance. More cheers from the surfers who were toeing the foam.

"Fuckers," she called at them. "You have someone else," she said to me. "Don't you? I'm sloppy seconds. I get it."

"I could help you," I said.

"I'm not nice," she said.

"Neither am I. Not always," I said.

"You're going to help me? What? Find my mom? She doesn't want me. I'm behind schedule already." Caroline pantomimed a toke and looked Salazar's way. "Let's party, Major Sergeant."

He saluted. "Ma'am!"

"Schedule?"

"Spark it up!" Salazar sang out. The two of them smiled joyfully.

Then, her faced turned stern. "Thanks for trying to save me. It's okay. I have you two figured out. You guys are on your own trip. You got what you wanted," she said.

She marched alone toward the pickup to rummage through her back pack.

Here, Mac returned in the black pickup, puttering to a stop on the beach, while stray church bells rose out of nowhere.

I watched Caroline Cahill thrust an arm into the back pack and pull out a patterned bikini, turn away, bend low near the truck, and quickly she tore off her tube top and replaced it, pulling a white halter over her head. It was that reminded me my own clothes were still damp. Silently, she resettled the things inside her bag. I was thinking what to do next. It was all I could do not to say, *Really, come home with me. Rabbi Gadol and Batya the Rock will help.* That's what I was thinking. *I'll help you.* What I said, when I walked over to where she was near the pickup, was something else. I said, "I know who the Man of God is, and I've met your mom. I'm pretty sure."

She lifted her face at me, and went back to tidying her things.

One by one she was pulling out her belongings and dropping them on the sand—makeup pouch, mints, lighter, a set of keys, hairbrush, earrings, tampons, bathing suits, panties, a pair of pliers, t-shirts, hooded sweatshirt, pillbox, lip gloss—tending to them and neatly stowing them deep in the bag. There was a wad of papers, like stationery. Were these the letters from her mom? The brochure from Our Lady of Charity? Were these her props, her act, to show no one could take advantage? Was Mrs. Cahill in Alpine, or Marathon, or Marfa, worried sick about her runaway daughter? And not Miss Lynn from far West Texas in a hurry to leave China Gardens? Caroline? Carolyn? Cathleen? Carmen? Crystal? Was it even to me she was talking the night before, tenderly telling her story in the dark? Was this always the hour she made that stern face? And, Jim Bob and Cassie? Were they missing? Coming back? Were they her friends? Or had she just caught a ride from them? Sitting in the back of their green pickup speeding down the Gulf Freeway?

She was bending over, wiping sand from her legs.

I said, "When did you leave Alpine? When did that happen?"

"Why does he call you, *Duke?*" She rolled her eyes, then closed them, and ran her hands through her hair to smooth out a tangle. How worn tired she was. Neither of us had slept much the night before. I'd hardly slept the night before that, even on the living room floor at Mamá Salazar's. Nor the night before that, when I'd broken up with Leah.

I was loaded and I was strung out.

"Because that's my name," I said, and it seemed to me, as I said, *Because that's my name,* I thought, for our different reasons, neither of us would likely tell another living soul about what had happened overnight, except if the story was yanked out of us.

She crossed her arms. "You think I made this up?"

"Alpine? I don't know. Maybe it's Westbury? Alief? What is it?" I said.

"Wherever it is," she said, "I don't miss it."

"I mean it. The Man of God. I know where he lives." I looked at Salazar talking to Mac. "I know him."

"Fuck you. You're a joke."

"We could take you there. You don't know what I know." I grabbed my knapsack and slung it over my shoulder.

"Oh, fuck. You really did just fall out of a boat. Didn't you? I'm not going to get crushed by a mountain. I got the story. Wow."

Even as she said these words, I realized fully how good she was. High and drunk as she was, she was good. She could bring it, all right. Right in front of me was something I'd never seen, a master who spooled out a portrait I couldn't have dreamed up if you gave me three thousand years with a fifty year head start. How could I? She invented her life while sitting in the back of a pickup truck in the middle of the night. No studious little black notebook. No desk pretentiously named Monk's Island. No silver Cross pen. No broadcast ministry. *When you know how to do it, Duke, it's easy.* Just the flatbed of Salazar's red pickup truck, thank you very much. Just any old reason to blurt it out for comfort's sake, ream after ream, her so-called confession. Total fabrication. Maybe she ran away and maybe she didn't.

Something must have happened. But, who can tell with a master like her? The heartbreaking nights under the Marfa stars, the wind and the desert. The uncertain dangers she portrayed, tiptoeing up to her old house, finding the letters. The tears even. The whole distorted burlesque. No Meyerland Jew had that talent. She was awe-inspiring. The staggering timing, par excellence. *I simply stared at the ink and rubbed my fingers on the paper, just as I'm touching you now.* Break out the Oreos, baby, because she destroyed, in one night, my buttoned-down conceptions, the very well-water of scriptural plausibility I'd drunk until I could drink no more in my father and grandfather and great-grandfather and great-great grandfathers' dim synagogues—the line of rabbis so long nobody can keep count. All I could do, at best, at best, was scrawl slanted lines interrupted by wiggles into my $1.99 notebook. All my knowledge added up to the three things: ancestry, posterity, and endurance. It was no use pretending I could ever match that. What was astonishing was how she seemed never to run out of whatever scene or character made her story click. Oversexed ranchers! Open-tomb clothespins! She made me see them, feel for them, feel sorry for her. It was a brilliant sham. It was as though she wasn't so much running away from her life, but giving voice to her true self. Her affinity for misfortune, accident, delusion, made it seem to me that the life I had lived was, for better or for worse, blessed. The war with my birthright was but a skirmish, the abnormalities less strange, or, worse, rooted. And yet, her story—her story to end all stories—had changed me, because it was a pure pleasure to hear it. To be confronted with life counter to the values and beliefs learned at home was to situate oneself at risk beyond what I ever imagined, twenty-four hours earlier, when I hauled my hungover body off Mamá Salazar's living room floor on the morning Nolan Ryan mowed down twenty-seven hitters in a row at the Astrodome. Meyerland was the place where I was forced to conform to someone else's image of who I should be, what I should be, the duty and obligation and the three Rs. For a time, while she spooled out her story, I forgot that self, only to have this maestro from Marfa reinvent it right back into my own skin. Was mine truly the face of someone suffering? The son of ordinary American life, growing up in safety in—Mac would insist I say it—bourgeois comfort? I knew sorrow as a trope and had worn it as makeup, make-believe, a disguise, and I called all that, bondage. It was here, finally, while she packed up her belongings and appeared ready to leave, I was looking right past Caroline Cahill, past the sand, the scrub grass and Seawall Boulevard, past the church bells tolling above the island, past the pelicans and black-masked seagulls, past the Gulf Freeway and Alameda Mall and Fiesta and Hobby Airport, past Gulfgate and the South Loop, all the way up Braeswood Boulevard. The following morning, Monday morning, I was expected at minyan prayers, sunrise, 7:15 a.m., at Beth Tikkun, in full regalia, looping my arm inside the leathery t'fillin and the soft white tallit around my neck and shoulders. No, the story that must be told to end all stories, the story that must be told to relinquish the past without lying awake in the dark and weeping for your troubles, the story that must transcend shepherds and strangers, as much as life and art, wasn't hers. It was mine.

"Your friend," Caroline said, pointing to the black pickup truck with Mac at the wheel.

Salazar was climbing into the cab. Mac passed him a joint. He took a swig from a bottle of beer.

"What's up?" I called.

"Mañana! Get the truck from you later! Do it, Duke! Don't be—" But the high winds blew the words back into his mouth. Salazar raised the Michelob bottle. They were laughing and blowing rings of smoke out of their mouths.

Nothing to that point in my life prepared me for what happened next, what he had yelled from the window of the black pickup as it began to roll its wheels onto the hard-packed sand. Nothing I'd been taught in the bickering household of Rabbi Gadol and Batya the Rock and the Wounded One, nothing underlying the airy, bubbly orderliness of my Jewish existence, nothing solemnly communicated to me of devotion to the Jewish ritual laws by the jowly men of Meyerland with their stubble and shtetl-pocked faces, their crinkled davening, their living and working and raising families, and nothing that animated my restlessness from the desert tents and desert tenets of scripture, nothing from the cul-de-sacs of that tree-dappled neighborhood, under which the Meyerland mothers wiped the noses of the Meyerland boys and girls. None of it prepared me for what Salazar said. But, what had he said? Was it, *Don't be frightened!* Was that it? The wind was fierce. I wasn't sure. He said, *Don't be frightened! Do it, Duke! Don't be frightened!* Meaning what? Or, had it been, not, *Don't be frightened,* but *Lighten up.*

Do it, Duke! Lighten up!

Let go. Capitulate. Have pity. Forebear.

How noble and heroic I felt.

Had I the presence of mind, I might have thought of what Whitman says: *If I worship one thing more than another it shall be the spread of my own body.*

Here, Mac's truck, with Salazar in the passenger's seat, bucked over the sand and tore off up the ramp onto Seawall Boulevard.

This was followed by Salazar's red pickup rattling and flapping in the other direction speeding away under the scorching sun. Caroline Cahill was steering with one hand, adjusting her hair with the other, and drifting side to side on the bench seat, gazing into the rearview mirror, exhaust billowing out of the tail pipe, mixing with the smell of the humid, salty air. The red pickup, like a released balloon, twisting down the beach, barely grazing the hard-packed sand, swerving onto Seawall Boulevard, and gone.

IT WASN'T BUT A FEW MINUTES after that I heard the car crash, like a horrifying boom against a metal drum.

From the top of the seawall, in the sunshine, I could see near to where Gaido's Restaurant sits, there was none of the usual carnival of activity: buskers, tourists, parents pushing strollers, teenagers on roller skates, children running noisily in bright bathing suits, beggars, dogs, crowds entering and leaving their dusty cars, people milling at the curb in a haze of exhaust fumes, the traffic of cars and pickups revving endlessly, and sand tornados whisking like shadows. There was only, across Seawall Boulevard, a yellow Volkswagen Beetle upended on the curb, smoke curling from under the hood where the engine was still running. Two men with black grocery aprons from a market that had yet to open were talking to the driver through the open window. I thought one was asking, Can you talk? Followed by instructions not to move. The yellow Volkswagon's radio was on. Sirens in the distance. Shopkeepers came onto the sidewalk with expressions of fright and curiosity.

A woman with a flower-patterned smock was walking from the wreckage. She had dodged a speeding, blue station wagon while crossing Seawall Boulevard. About seventy, with square dark sunglasses, rising on her toes, she said, "Did you see what happened?"

"No," I said. "You?"

"I heard brakes screech, then a horrible grinding," she said, with one palm over her mouth. "People over there said a pickup truck hit the Bug, then drove off. Didn't even stop to check on the driver. I hope they got the license plate."

"Did they say what color? The pickup?" I asked.

She shook her head.

I felt as though some magic trick were taking place. A ghoulish abracadabra. I thought, any second Salazar would come running. I'd feel him squeeze me by the arm, and tell me again about his amazing vision. Saying, I was making noises all night, waving my hands, and I understood everything. I have been transformed, he'd say, then look away, like he was starving, half-cocked. In his eyes was the look of a guy who thought he might be dead. Finished. Or, he'd have a look that made him seem like he felt something had died. Life, his eyes said, was too good for him. Too reputable, virtuous. I'd put my arm around him. He'd say, Pilgrims, Duke. What am I going do? Live like this? This secret, forever? Don't answer. It's okay, Duke. I'm okay. Let's just chill. Let's just hang tight. Just, hang loose for a second. I need a second. Sit with me, man. I'd try to soothe him. My arm around his shoulders, while he held back tears. Duke, I'm sorry, Duke. Help me out. Have mercy, Duke. Here, he's crying, at first softly. Then sobbing. Sobbing loudly, the tears covering his face, and his mouth grown distorted. Past coherence, past wit, past words, rationality, he can't stop sobbing. Jerking his head, his shoulders bowed, his face twisted, then covering his wet eyes with his fists. The origin of his tears from some briny, gaseous murk I could never imagine, as if from a deep, black, convulsive star. Nothing for me to do. He's sobbing with all his body, like he might go blind, so that into his mouth comes a cry, comes something he could no longer hide from himself, something deeper than suffering, and torn from him, a wail, and then he sings—

> *There is a fountain filled with blood,*
> *Drawn from Immanuel's veins,*
> *And sinners plunged beneath that flood*
> *Lose all their guilty stains,*
> *Lose all their guilty stains,*
> *Lose all their guilty stains,*
> *And sinners plunged beneath that flood*
> *Lose all their guilty stains.*

Helplessly, I said to the woman in the flowery smock, "Is there something we should do?"

"Girl seems okay," she said. "God only knows if they'll find that truck that did it."

I returned to the beach, utterly confused, and sat cross-legged in the spot Salazar and I had parked the red pickup the night before, the pickup underneath which Caroline Cahill had come barreling into my life and sent it swerving. If this spot had, for a time, been intended as the launch to who knows what future, that future was still far away, natural enough as it may be. Natural, but also, strange enough, bizarre, fantastic, extraordinary enough, astounding.

With my forefinger I drew a triangle in the cool, thick sand, deepening the trench with each pass, absentmindedly layering over it an upside down one, deepening the trench of that second triangle, then wiped the triangles away, clutched a fistful of sand, and sprinkled the grains over my boots.

The weed was gone, the spliffs, the beer.

The beach spanned into high waves, and miles ahead the water was rough all the way out to the contour of the horizon beneath an unbroken, blue sky but for a plume of a cloud.

After a time, I wondered what I should do. I had a ten and couple fives in my wallet. I no longer wanted to go home, so I stood and walked west along the beach until the tide forced me up the concrete stairs of the seawall onto the highway. I continued on. It was comfortable walking past the fishing piers and motels. A luxury, really, to walk, a wealth I would never have to give back. I thought of Leah, and wondered what she would think of me, out there atop the seawall, turning down my own life. Foolish, is what she'd have called it. Without scruples.

For an hour, I felt courageous. A weight had been lifted. I imagined finding odd jobs at gas stations or with a roadside work crew. One of the oil platforms. Who knows? I'd stay in a motel, eat dinner every night in the same fried fish joint. Red-checkered oil tablecloths. Paper food boats with wax basket liners. Have the same seat each time I came in. The table closest to the entrance. On the wall was a commemorative newspaper clipping under the headline *Best Fried Fish in Texas: 1972*. I'd be alone a lot. Plenty of time to write. I imagined Leah would come in and walk over to me. Out of the clear blue day, just stroll into the red-checkered fish joint, wearing terry cloth shorts and a t-shirt, and sit down at my table underneath a faded blue and white crawfish festival poster, with the block letters, *Crawfish Crawl*, on it. She'd be reluctant and hesitant. I would say to her, Salazar come back? Then, I imagined it over again. Imagined, one night, the owner of the joint noticed I wore the same thing every day. Advised me to go home. He could tell. Seen it all before. Imagined, at dawn, where I would be staying in the motel, I'd say morning prayers, and, come dusk, the evening ones.

Traffic was picking up, and I kept a thumb out, hitching for a ride, when a white pickup slowed and pulled over, a maroon Texas A&M sticker on the back bumper. White guy, handlebar mustache, straw cowboy hat with a green handkerchief instead of a buckle set, crisp blue jacket, and snap-button shirt with his name, Bill, stitched over his heart.

"Where to?" he asked, whistling to the radio.

Aerosmith, ZZ Top, I couldn't make it out.

"Freeport," I said.

He smiled. "I'm turning at the South Freeway. Hop in the back. You can get out at Surfside." When he spoke, the words had flown out of the tense corners of his mouth with a kind of reedy twang that made you think his tongue was braced up against his back molars and the opening in the back of his throat had shrunk. "Beer in the cooler. Help yourself." He gave me a glassy look, whistled with the radio, and said nothing more.

I climbed into the bed and could see his image in the review mirror, eyeing me. His jacket was lopsided, and his shirt was creased. His face, in the mirror, had a smudged expression, like he was unused to other people. He ran his fingers over his mustache, then turned his eyes toward the windshield, and we took off alongside the gulf past miles of beach houses on stilts.

The cargo bed was trashed. There was a wooden dog house on its side, the hinge on the door broken, and the lining torn. Near the gate, there was a steel, three-door, red toolkit, an empty, plastic Pepsi bottle rolling around, along with a propane cylinder. There were Bungee cords, what looked like a motorcycle headlight and muffler. Next to the toolbox was a yellow bucket of sand with the aluminum handle of a small landing net stabbed into it, the nylon mesh catching only the sunlight that stained the slats.

I placed a palm over my heart and felt it beating. Reached into the cooler. There were four gold cans of Coors floating in icy water with nearly a dozen crushed empties. I felt for one, opened it, and knocked on the window with my wet knuckles. "Muchas gracias!"

Whistling Bill waved with his thumb and pinky.

It might have been noon when we rumbled west alongside Jamaica Beach, and I tried to think about what had happened and what I should do about it. Again, I thought of Leah, and wondered what it would be like to disappear for a time, weeks, longer, and then come home, late in the year, December. I might walk up to her house at night, after dark, after her parents had gone to sleep, and gently tap on her window, the one I had snuck into many times. Seeing her look out at the night, at my face behind the window glass, I would remind myself that this was a special bliss for her and me. I would see the light coming from under the closed door to the hallway to her parents' room, and see her jump from the bed to check behind the door, peer into the hallway, like she always did, before unlatching the lock to the window. I'd enter the room and close the window and stand and look at her for a long time. Her hair would be tied back, and lanky, and graceful. We would sit on the bed, and again I would look at her, without speaking, then look longer still, and I would not know if I had made the right decision.

Whistling Bill rapped on the dusty window. "You all right back there?"

"Yep!" I shouted. "Fine. Fine indeed."

He shouted, nasally drawl. "Nolan Ryan acquitted himself well last night!"

"Yeah, now! He was incendiary!"

"Hitters couldn't find their asses. Eh? Just fidgeted in the box. Couldn't have happened to a better man. I went to Alvin High School same as Ryan did. Before my time, about five years."

"No way!" I shouted, and turned to see him flash a thumb's up in the rearview.

A few miles from the turnoff, near Drum Bay, he pulled the pickup onto a beach access road, got out, and threw the empties into a metal garbage can. They made a clacking rattle. I climbed out, too, and stood on the asphalt, then crouched, feeling nauseous. High winds. Smell of salty air.

"I just need a minute," Whistling Bill said. He grabbed an unopened beer from the cooler, snapped off the tab, and stood drinking, then lowered the can and got his breath, before turning to look at the water and drink again. I walked behind him to the top of the dune. The grass blades were ratty and taut, and the loose sand swirled in the wind in furrows, stopping, again sifting. Miles up the road toward the causeway where the highway curves were petroleum plants and the glow of refinery fires, and I was thinking that this whole atmosphere was a holy music, the notes flying up around my body like the red-beaked gulls floating overhead in big circles. Far across the breakers, almost out of view, was a solitary swimmer doing the crawl, bobbing in his wet suit like a seal, parallel to the shore line, with paddles in his palms, wearing swimmer's goggles. From time to time, he paused and treaded water, lifting the goggles to his slick, bald forehead. Then, he resumed swimming, splashing his feet and lifting his elbows high and slapping his arms down, over and over, kicking hard.

It was no longer necessary to dream. My mind was devoid of reverie. If a chimera entered, it would settle in my thoughts with no more substance than a wisp of smoke. All that would remain was the verb of my existence, and the air, full of wind and sea salt, would be easy to breathe.

We stood listening to the waves in silence. No traffic coming or going on the highway. I looked at Whistling Bill in the wind, while he looked at the dry grass where it flayed, then at the big waves splashing in rows. Shreds of tire tracks on the beach, a dozen or more automobiles parked far apart on the sand, everything bright.

"I just came from a funeral," he said.

"I'm sorry," I said.

"My uncle. My daddy's only brother. Yeah. My daddy died three years back. Heart attack."

"Was it in town?"

"Broadway Cemetery."

I knew the place. Rabbi Gadol led an annual Holocaust memorial service there behind a wrought-iron gate that marked the Jewish section for the Hebrew Benevolent Society, and I would go with him to make a little money setting up the folding chairs in the grass next to the low, red brick wall.

"He was a wonderful soul," Bill drawled. "I loved being around him. Made me feel complete. He truly cared about me, and it showed every time I saw him. I wish we could have spent extra time together. I wish I could just sit on the beach out there and speak to him for a while. I could really use that, just as much as anyone else. Uncle Dan loved this stretch of the beach. Texas is a hard country. He lost everything." He straightened his crisp blue jacket and snap-button shirt, hitched up the waist of his baggy pants, then took off his straw cowboy hat and stepped forward toward the pounding waves, his black hair thin as thread. "Like to wait here awhile," he said and stood near the dune grass that leaned away from the wind. He stared down at his boots, while pressing his free hand into a pocket, his face caved and drawn, the handlebar mustache grayer than I'd first thought, his skin paper thin. It was bright and humid and windy. In the distance, a seagull bawled. He stood with his cowboy hat in one hand. "Where you from, kid?" he said, with a look off along the highway, behind us, where the traffic was now moving fast.

"Meyerland," I said. "If you'd like, you know, I can say a prayer with you. If you'd want. You know? For your uncle? If you'd like that."

He shook his head, and I thought about what a man like

Whistling Bill might need, in this moment, while standing at the end of the beach access road a few miles from the turnoff to the South Freeway—so soon after Uncle Dan was buried in Broadway Cemetery, nearby the Jewish section of the Benevolent Hebrew Society. Must have been in the very hour Salazar and Mac jumped into the black pickup and bucked over the sand and tore off up the ramp onto Seawall Boulevard and Caroline Cahill stole the red pickup and rattled and flapped in the other direction, and somebody rammed into the yellow Volkswagen.

Whistling Bill stood watching the vanishing waves his uncle loved. I thought: he was no longer a nephew, no longer a son. We serve time, I wanted to say to him. *Z'mahn*, I'd say. Means, invitation. Same root. *Z'mahn*. Meaning, we are invited into time. *Man is like a breath*, I wanted to say. Psalms. Fourteen. Something. Salazar would know. *His days are like a passing shadow*, that one. Whether the tide is high or low, I thought to say, we ride the waves of time. No, too corny. C'mon. That's something Rabbi Gadol would've cooked up a thousand years ago and repeated ten times a week. Time, I wanted to say, it's our structure. That's all. Over weeks, over years, over our lives. We serve time. We mark it. It invites us to pass through it. That's what our lives are, that which we pass through. But, unlike everything else, time goes in one direction, I thought I could say. Or, was all that just *ru'chah, ru'chah, ru'chah* seeded into me? Because wasn't time always being lost beyond the surface of things? Wasn't concentrating intently on the fine details the best anyone could try? Meditational concentration? On any object? Any perception. Real? Hallucinatory? Time as the sensory qualities? Time as associations a mind makes? The conceptual significances? Time as watching the vanishing waves Uncle Dan loved, before everything moves, breathes, vibrates, breaks, falls away? But, I said nothing, sure only that I was entering the blazing heat of the day and watching the buoyant surface of the water and the wild ripples that seemed to carve the letters of my own name, like some future recollection of letters of my own name lost to time.

He turned and faced me, his face terribly sad. "What's your name?"

"Jon Wain."

"The Duke, huh? Okay. Let's go. God help Uncle Dan. That's all the prayer I got, kid." He threw his empty Coors into the metal garbage can with a clank, and walked along the truck bed, running his large hand along the edge, and peered inside, as if to review a secret. "Look, I can take you up to Houston, if you'd like."

Alongside us, the water flattened like open country. Salt wind blowing in our hair. Beyond the flats, a tanker appeared stuck on the horizon, like a tack. Beyond that, the vast ocean, unheard and unseen.

We set off down the highway.

In the back of the pickup truck, I was leaning against the cab to stay out of the wind. The clouds were awakening in the blue sky. I fished from my pocket what was left of the quaaludes the singer had given to me in cellophane, and dropped them on my tongue.

Immediately, the high kicked in.

It was impossible to close my eyes, impossible to conceive of the things I might now do, impossible to choose among them all.

The wind from the highway went straight through me. Now and again, I was scared, wondering if this search were fruitless, and I questioned why I had left the beach. Was it naive of me? All this was a long time ago. I think of this whole episode with a great deal of loneliness.

From the truck, I watched the waves build and fall. The next hump of waves taking shape.

I remembered that, a few years earlier, when I was in junior high school, my father would bring me down this way on Sundays in the fall, after summer crowds and the heat had tapered, while he attended a meeting of East Texas rabbis at B'Nai Israel on Avenue O, the synagogue that, before World War I, took in ten-thousand Jewish immigrants—fleeing persecution in Eastern

Europe. B'Nai Israel's rabbi met the ships at the Galveston docks, some nights housing them inside the synagogue's sanctuary. Ragged Eastern European Jews—Jews who had been forbidden to own property so had clustered in shtetls and villages and urban quarters and had taken up trades as glaziers and goldsmiths, glassblowers, cabinet makers, watchmakers, jewelers, bookbinders, peddlers, grocers, and dressmakers, furriers, haberdashers, tailors, and tanners—gathered with their dead-tired wives and loud children and stacks of rickety suitcases, swapping stories of the lives struck from them, their memories torn like doors from their hinges, windows they once looked out of in dusty foyers now missing their glass, boarded over, the floors unswept, littered.

In the afternoon, my father let me swim and goof off in the waves and drift, like a jelly fish, far out with the tide, far from our pair of beach towels, styrofoam cooler packed with cans of Root Beer and Schlitz, and the blue umbrella he stabbed into the sand next to the car parked on the beach. I'd drift and drift, beyond the plunging waves, and then I'd have to trudge up the shore, barefoot, to find him, sitting alone on a sandy towel next to the styrofoam cooler, his face puckered up at the sun. Sometimes, my father and I would throw a soggy tennis ball in and out of the water to each other, a monkishly simple game, where I stood in the shallows, with the waves battering into my body, and he, the Grand Rabbi—standing barefoot on the wet sand in his clean, rolled-up, khaki trousers and white-buttoned shirt and yarmulke, with the foamy water splashing at his ankles—threw a high one and I would try to make a spectacular, slow-motion, aqueous dive to catch the ball in my bare hand, belly-flopping onto the salty water. Submerged, I'd triumphantly thrust the caught tennis ball high above the waves into the air to show that I'd caught it. Watching, Rabbi Gadol limbered his body, rotated his waist, with his elbows bent at his sides, squatting and dropping his rump down, hopping up, squatting, hopping again, twisting his waist, rotating his neck, but this time his hands, one on top of the other, might be on the back of his thick gray head of hair and press against his yarmulke, then he dropped to his knees and stomach and did a half dozen push ups, turning his cheek to the side so not to get grains of sand in his mouth and nostrils, then he might add jumping jacks, or march in a circle, his back arched, stomach lifted, swinging his arms, wiggling his feet above the loose sand, striding, like some nomadic man wandering the desert, searching for water, foraging for food, for shelter, his brown camel clumping behind him with a tent strapped to its back, as if, on the beach along the Gulf of Mexico, Rabbi Gadol might be thinking, "Oh, House of Jacob, come let us walk with a light of the Lord," and never did I think of him with more awe as on those days playing catch with a soggy tennis ball on the beach. He appeared, striding in circles in the sand with his trousers rolled above his ankles, invincible, the way he looked with his white tallit wrapped loosely about his shoulders when he carried the Torah around the gloomy sanctuary of Beth Tikkun in a procession of *L'Cha Adonai*, for the congregants to pledge their obedience to the greatness, the power, the glory, the victory, and the majesty of the good Lord, by kissing and touching the Torah scroll with the tassels of their silky tallit or with the black binding of their prayer books, accepting the gift of God's word composed in slanted lines interrupted by wiggles, and the congregants swelling toward my father and swelling back, every one of them in suit jackets or skirts and high heels, aisle after aisle in the gloomy sanctuary, swelling to him and swelling back, kissing the white fringes of their silky tallit and their black prayer books and touching the goatskin of the Torah, pulling the books close tight to their ribcages. Rabbi Gadol limbering on the beach, twisting and rotating and squatting, hopping up, as if to say that life isn't enchanted or clairvoyant, not magical, not spiritualistic or wizardly. No, it was discipline, it was slow motion, practice, and working hard, studying diligently. Would it not be life if it wasn't bringing your mind and body into balance with the good

Lord? Would it not be life if it wasn't drilling into your heart a flexible capacity to love the good Lord, and training and training and training your mind to study the word of the good Lord so that, finally, last of all, above all, second to none, studying Torah matters to you? Only then, will your life begin and, maybe, you'll come to something, and something will come of that?

On those Sundays, we ate a late lunch on the sand while resting on our beach towels: peanut butter and jelly, Fritos, marshmallow pies, plus he allowed me foamy sips from his silver can of Schlitz. I kept a lazy eye on the horizon, the sun dipping, winter coming on. Sweaty, humid, autumn days at Galveston beach with the aroma everywhere, not of sunblock, but cocoa butter oil and lemons squeezed into girls' hair and windy bonfires and BBQ grills and exhaust from the cars driving on and off the beach. Always there were roller skaters and girls in bikini tops and terry cloth shorts, and shirtless men, venders selling hot dogs and snow cones and caramel corn. Come dusk—if I was still swimming or wandering the beach, looking for shells, barefoot, skinny as a twig—my father would stand near our station of half-buried, sand-dotted towels, held in place by the styrofoam cooler and the blue umbrella, and then he'd tongue-stab his bottom lip to whistle me to come back. He had a high, piercing whistle. It was impossible not to hear it even among the beach din and traffic revving on the road. Like sending an uncoded message in naval blurts, and I could hear it, all right, and knew well to heed the summons. Woe to him who offered the weak excuse that he hadn't heard the call.

About the Author

DAVID BIESPIEL is the author of six collections of poetry and four books of nonfiction, including, most recently, the memoir *A Place of Exodus: Home, Memory, and Texas*. A contributor to the *The New Yorker, New Republic,* and *Slate,* he is a recipient of Lannan, NEA, and Stegner fellowships, two Oregon Book Awards, (poetry and nonfiction), the Pacific Northwest Booksellers Award, and he has been a finalist for the National Book Critics Circle Balakian Award. The founder of the Attic Institute of Arts and Letters, he has taught at Stanford University, University of Maryland, and Wake Forest University, in addition to other colleges and universities and, currently, he is Poet-in-Residence at Oregon State University.